MW01658036

THE BRONX RIOT [illegible] NARCOTICS DETECTIVE KILLS AN UNARMED MAINTENANCE MAN. IS IT JUST ANOTHER EXAMPLE OF POLICE BRUTALITY AGAINST MINORITIES, OR IS IT PART OF A BIGGER SCHEME?

Celeste Santiago, an aggressive, successful, and ambitious Assistant District Attorney, sees the shooting as a chance to launch her campaign to become the next Bronx County D A. Meanwhile, a trial attorney, famous for garnering multi-million dollar verdicts, represents the deceased's widow in the lawsuit against Kevin Knowles and NYPD.

A Bronx Bust is a story of cops and lawyers, judges and perps. Their worlds collide around the criminal trial and the wrongful death case. It is a tale of brutality and vengeance. The backroom deals and alliances formed on the street end with a twist that no one will see coming.

Praise for A Bronx Bust

"Uriel Gribetz knows the rough side of the law. His portraits of New York crime and its players deliver vivid, high-tension drama. Recommended."—***John C. Boland, Publisher of Perfect Crime***

A Bronx Bust by Uriel E. Gribetz is a tenacious crime thriller and police procedural that unfolds, as the title tells us, on the streets and courts of New York's famous borough, the Bronx. After a police shooting, we follow Sam Free, a retired homicide detective and sometime private detective helping his ex-partner, Frank Cortez, search for the murderer of Frank's nephew. It was Frank Cortez, Sam's former partner, also retired, who threw Sam under the bus years before, but they need each other to solve one last case, and possibly find some form of closure. The result is bittersweet; the reader learns deep and delicious secrets, but the sorrow of human suffering lingers in the reader's mind long after closing *A Bronx Bust*.

This is a gripping story, written with humor and detail; Gribetz delights with sleight-of-hand mastery, keeping everything moving nicely in this well-constructed crime novel. With deft dialogue, crisp plotting, and a likable central figure make this an exuberant and involving read. Highly recommended.—***Geoffrey Gatza, poet, author and editor of BlazeVox***

Excerpt

Sam approached the stiff. He was a young guy with wire rim glasses. The lenses had been shot out, and where his eyes were there were just holes with flesh, tissue, and blood exposed. His position looked staged, like someone had propped him up against the chimney as if to make it seem as though he were looking at something. Part of the stiff's face had been eaten away by the rats, exposing crooked buck teeth. The shooter had left the shattered lenses of his wire rims in place.

"Jesus, Mary, and Joseph." Frank let the flashlight float up and down the length of the stiff. His voice was cracking. "That's Nooney. I'm pretty sure. That's why they called him Nooney, on account of his buck teeth." Frank aimed the light behind Nooney's left ear where there was a splotchy red birthmark that looked like an image from a Rorschach test. "Oh my God, that's him. I remember since he was a little kid, he had that mark behind his ear. We used to tease him and say someone spilled paint on him, and it couldn't be washed off."

"Small caliber." Sam leaned over and studied the blown-out eyeballs. "I think it was a .22. I don't see any exit wounds." Whoever did this was sending a message. It was as if Nooney was watching something and then had his eyeballs blown for seeing what he saw. The shooter must have purposely used small bullets that didn't penetrate bone, and they traveled around the skull and tore up his brain.

A Bronx Bust

Uriel E. Gribetz

Moonshine Cove Publishing,
LLC

Abbeville, South Carolina
U.S.A.

First Moonshine Cove edition
February 2021

ISBN: 9781952439032

Library of Congress LCCN: 2020901257
© Copyright 2021 by Uriel E. Gribetz

This book is a work of fiction. Names, characters, places and incidents are products of the author's imagination or are used fictitiously. Any resemblance to actual events, locales or persons, living or dead, is entirely coincidental.

All rights reserved. No part of this book may be reproduced in whole or in part without written permission from the publisher except by reviewers who may quote brief excerpts in connection with a review in a newspaper, magazine or electronic publication; nor may any part of this book be reproduced, stored in a retrieval system or transmitted in any form or by any means electronic, mechanical, photocopying, recording or any other means, without written permission from the publisher.

Cover images public domain; cover and interior design by Moonshine Cove staff

For Laura, Joshua and Klara, Always

About the Author

For more than 30 years Uriel Gribetz worked as a public defender, defending the rights of the indigent accused of any crime. *A Bronx Bust,* like many of his stories, emanates from Gribetz's experiences in the criminal justice system, in the world of perps, prosecutors, judges and cops. He also grew up in the Bronx and he feels the pulse of the borough infused within.

A Bronx Bust is the third and final novel of the Bronx Crime Trilogy. *Taconic Murda,* the first novel of the series, was published by Moonshine Cove in 2014, and *Hunts Point,* the second novel, was published by Perfect Crime in 2017.

urielegribetzbooks.com

Chapter One

In the primer-colored, dented, police-department-issued Nova, Kevin Knowles found a parking spot on the north side of Webster Avenue. It was parallel to the barren expanse of the Metro North tracks that ran from midtown Manhattan to Westchester and points north.

The other cars parked on the avenue had a coating of snow on them. Would the lookouts notice him? Was he being paranoid? Maybe, but he wanted to make sure the knuckleheads didn't make him. He had parked across the street at an angle to the location so that it was difficult to spot him.

He pushed the seat all the way back and pulled the flat rim of his Yankees' lid down. It looked like he was sleeping. He had a clear, unobstructed view of building number 1275.

Kevin watched Ray Santos, the manager of 1275, double park the cherry-red late-model Mercedes. Ray inspected his reflection in the rear-view mirror and began smoothing down his mustache and the small patch of hair below his lower lip.

"Look at this little douche." Kevin spoke to himself. "He thinks he's God's gift." He pushed the rim of the baseball cap up.

* * *

In idle, the Mercedes' diesel engine emitted a knocking sound. Ray left it running, locked it, and entered the building's courtyard. Inside the building a group of teenagers gathered in the lobby and waited for the elevator.

"*Gallo*!" they shouted in unison when they saw Ray.

Ray ghetto-strutted, with a hitch in his step like a gangster, toward the group, and they surrounded him.

"Don't youse gotta be in school?" He raised one eyebrow while lowering the other, giving them the look the Rock was famous for, as he searched their faces.

"You crazy, *Gallo,*" one of the girls in the group yelled as the elevator came, and they departed. Their shouts and laughter echoed through the shaft as the car rose.

"Crazy fucking kids." Ray shook his head as he murmured to himself.

Ray turned and headed down the hallway. He rang the super's bell. It was the apartment closest to the elevator. There was no response. Ray pressed it again and then put his ear against the door. He balled his hand into a fist and knocked. This time he heard some mumbling from inside the apartment.

"Jose, you needs to shovel and throw some salt on the sidewalk. Somebody is going to bust their ass. It's gonna be a lawsuit." Ray stood on his tiptoes and shouted at the peephole. "I dunno why we pay you motherfucker." He walked back over to the elevator and pressed the button.

The elevator arrived and, once inside, Ray's cell phone ringtone filled the confines of the car. It was a salsa mixture of maracas, trumpets, and congas. It sounded like the dance music that reverberated in the Latin clubs, that featured the rotating and glittering disco balls of another era. Ray snatched the nickel-plated cell phone from the black case attached to his belt like a holster.

He looked at the screen, and when he saw the caller ID he scowled. "*Dime.* Hold on, you breaking up. The reception is shit. I'll check you later."

He put the phone back in its holster and smoothed out the shoulders on his leather trench coat. It was too large for his small frame and hung from him like a cape.

On the sixth and top floor, Ray exited and began his first-of-the-month routine. He would knock on each apartment, and if there was no answer, he would slip a small yellow envelope underneath the door.

"Que?" 6L asked.

"*Gallo,*" Ray answered.

Senora Borbon in a house coat and cloth slippers counted out the cash with gnarled arthritic fingers. Ray wrote a receipt from a spiral pad he kept in his back pocket. It looked like the kind that newspaper reporters favored.

When he was finished with the sixth floor, Ray took the stairs to the fifth. In the stairwell the ringtone from his cell phone began again. The Latin music echoed off the walls. It followed Ray almost like the tune that followed the Good Humor truck, as it cruised from block to block.

"Jesus!" Ray paused on the landing between the floors. "*Dime.* I'm busy, I tole' you. I'll check you later. It's not that, Mommy. Lemme finish. . ." He studied the screen and then spoke to it. "First you call me then you hang up on me. I don't understand women."

He was trying to put it back in the case on his hip when the phone rang again. He fumbled with it and then nearly dropped it. *"Dios Mijo."* He saw the caller ID again, disconnected, and turned off the phone.

At apartment 5K Ray banged furiously. "McCullough!" He stood on his tiptoes and hopped to see through the peephole. "I know you're in there. I'm tell'in you the boss is getting his lawyer to evict your ass. Three months you owe." He stepped back, then pointed and gestured at the door to 5K. "Deadbeat motherfucker! The Marshalls are gonna throw your shit all over the street."

Ray went floor to floor until he reached the first, and there he reached for his cell and turned it back on.

* * *

Kevin checked his wristwatch. It was time. Ray Santos should be done collecting the rent. Now he didn't care who spotted him. He crossed the northbound lanes of traffic on Webster on foot. He waited in the middle of the street for traffic to clear on the southbound side and watched the kid in the brown bubble North Face who stood at the corner where the "no parking" sign had been sheared off, and all that was left was a spear of rusty metal sticking up out of the sidewalk.

The kid put two index fingers in his mouth and emitted a shrill whistle, like at a ball game after the home team hit a home run. Kevin knew that whistle warned the pitchers to clear the block. There was a bodega with its iron gates shuttered on the side of 1275. Kevin tried to avoid looking at it, but it drew him to it like a bad memory that wouldn't fade. It was a physical reaction to that spot where his life had changed forever. He had to catch his breath when the images of what had happened there reoccurred.

When Kevin reached the other side of Webster, the kid who gave the warning disappeared up a side street.

"Five O," someone yelled from one of the windows that overlooked the courtyard.

"Loco," another voice shouted from another window.

Kevin looked up, but he didn't see anyone at any of the windows. He couldn't place which floors the voices came from. He walked quickly to the vestibule for cover. Out there, in the pathway to the building's entrance, he was too vulnerable to someone who might throw a brick or some other projectile from above. It was referred to as a "doming" when someone got smashed in the head.

He hoped that the lock on the door that led to the lobby was still broken. Kevin pushed on it, and it gave way and opened into the lobby.

There was Ray in the vestibule, leaving the building. As he approached Kevin, the ringtone from Ray's cell filled the air.

"Motherfucker." Ray reached into his waistband for the phone.

Kevin drew his Glock and assumed a flat-footed shooting stance. Ray froze. Kevin drew a bead on Ray's chest.

The muzzle flashed as the bullet passed through Ray's clavicle and lodged into the wall.

There was a moment of silence before the shell casing made a jingle sound, almost like the sound spare change makes, as it landed on the marble-tiled floor.

Ray turned and tried to run, but instead he stumbled down the hall. He stopped at the door to 1F. He raised his hand to knock at the door and then reached for the door knob. It was like the messages from his brain to his limb were skewered or short-circuited. He collapsed against the door.

Kevin approached with the weapon in his right hand.

Ray reached toward Kevin with the cell phone in hand.

"Drop it!" Kevin yelled, and fired twice more.

The bulb of the camera, like a black eye in the ceiling of the lobby, watched it all.

Chapter Two
Sam Free

This just in. There has been another police shooting of an unarmed civilian in the Bronx.

Sam Free had on the all-news station on the car radio.

The names of the police officer and the deceased have not been released.

He was following a Hassid, who drove a late-model Lincoln, from Monsey. Feldman, an old-time lawyer Sam knew from the Bronx, who threw him a bone from time to time, had given him this gig. The Hassid's wife wanted a Get. If she caught her husband in the act it was grounds for divorce.

Sam had seen the red Hyundai behind him as he followed the Hassid around Monsey. He tried to slow down so that it would pass him, but instead of passing him the red car slowed down as well. Who was this fuck face that was tailing him? Wasn't this some shit?

They were crossing the Tappan Zee Bridge. It was a floating bridge that was a favorite for jumpers. The currents in the Hudson always made it difficult to find the body.

A new one was being built right alongside it. In the headlights of Sam's minivan, its blue girders towered above the cranes that were perched on the barges above the water, like steel statutes. Traffic slowed at the toll. Sam looked in his rear-view mirror.

"Why are you following me, motherfucker?" With his beefy paws Sam grabbed the steering wheel. Maybe he should go on the offensive and give the driver of the red Hyundai a good going over before the piece of shit knew what was coming? The best defense is a good offense. With the tire iron Sam kept under his seat, he could walk back there and make him sorry.

There wasn't enough time for Sam to get out of his car and do some damage. He'd lose the Hassid. The three cars ahead of the Hassid's Lincoln passed through the toll. Now it was the Lincoln's turn.

He had to catch up to the Lincoln.

The Thruway to the Bronx was empty. Sam shut his lights. He looked in his mirror to see where the Hyundai was. The son of a bitch had turned off his headlights too. In the darkness Sam could barely make out the silhouette of the Hyundai.

Asshole! Did someone hire the douche? He hadn't had any beefs with anyone recently. He stared down at the camera on the front passenger seat. It was times like this that he wished he still had his pistol. Maybe he should bag the surveillance of the Hassid? Better safe than sorry. This red Hyundai was giving him the jitters. Fuck it. He needed the money that Feldman was going to pay him.

Protests are planned throughout the city. They may close the Brooklyn Bridge. Sit-ins are expected at the Bronx Hall of Justice and City Hall.

Last reports were that an undercover officer shot an unarmed super at a building where drug activity was suspected.

Crowds have gathered in the area of the shooting around Webster Avenue and Fordham Road. There are no reports of violence. Everything seems peaceful for now.

The Hassid exited the highway at the Van Cortlandt Park exit in the Bronx. Sam stopped because the Lincoln slowed to a crawl and he didn't want to be noticed. He looked for the Hyundai and didn't see it. Did he get off the exit? The Hassid seemed to be trolling as he passed the empty park benches. There were no street lights in this part of the park. Where the cross-country track wound around the soccer fields it was pitch black and flat. When Sam looked out onto it, it gave him the illusion that there was an abyss that dropped off the edge. The Lincoln came to a stop.

Had the Hassid made him? Sam drove past and caught the image of the man's bearded, spectacled face.

Then the Lincoln took off and passed Sam, who was now in front of the Lincoln. Sam waited until there was some distance between them. In his teens, in the dark confines of this park, he and his friends would climb the fence behind the handball courts and sneak into the pool. At two o'clock in the morning on a humid August night the pool would be packed with a crowd of trespassing teenagers, and the air felt so thick he could touch it. That was in 1977, when the Son of Sam drove past this park to hunt and shoot long brown-haired teenagers necking in cars.

Where was this man going? Why would he leave his nice house in the suburbs to drive around the Bronx at night? What was he looking for that he didn't have at home?

He followed the Lincoln as it crossed the Bronx from west to east. They reached the Two train El, and the Hassid drove under it to the city line at Mount Vernon.

That was where the Lincoln pulled over and a group of women gathered around it. Sam made a U-turn. From the south side of the street, hidden behind the steel girders of the El, he had a perfect view.

The hookers leaned against the Lincoln. Sam focused the camera with the infrared lens on the group. They reminded Sam of a school of fish gathered around bait. He snapped away until one of the girls teetering on high heels walked over to the passenger side, slid in, and the Hassid sped away.

That should do it. Now the wife could get her Get. He pulled into traffic, and at the next red light the Hyundai appeared behind him. He was inches from Sam's bumper. Sam reached for the tire iron, jumped out of his car, and rushed toward the Hyundai.

"Do you got a fuckin' problem?" He stood by the driver's window and was about to rear back with the tire iron so that he could bust it out.

The window rolled down. "Sammy, baby." It was Frank Cortez, his old partner.

"For fuck's sake, Frank!" Sam lowered the tire iron. "You scared the shit outa me."

"Gotcha." Frank's smile revealed a missing front tooth. He lost it playing fullback at Clinton High School.

"I almost caved your skull in."

"If you tried, I would have put two in your chest." Frank's snub nose .38 lay on the passenger seat.

"You wouldn't have capped your old partner?" Sam wasn't sure. He and Frank had a rocky past. They were partners on the job, and it didn't end well.

They pulled their vehicles over to the side of White Plains Road. The El was silent. There were no other cars on the street. It was early morning, still dark out, between the time that the bars closed and before those who started the early shift were on their way. Sam sat in Frank's car.

"Look it." Sam gestured at the used car lot on the other side of the street. It was surrounded by a fence topped with barbed wire.

"That's right. Leo Ramsoon."

"That piece of shit."

"No doubt." Frank nodded. His hair was thinning on top.

"That was the case that unraveled my life. It was a free-fall shitstorm after that."

Seeing Frank and being at this location brought it all back. Ramsoon was a piece of shit Rasta drug dealer who murdered his ex-wife because she knew too much about his operation, and wasted her son and her new boyfriend because they were there.

"The Job really fucked you over." Frank shook his head in agreement.

"You've really got some fuckin' nerve saying that to me when you could've spoken up and saved me. All you had to do was say what you saw."

ADA Celeste Santiago, who was trying the case, wanted Sam to testify that he found the murder weapon in Ramsoon's apartment. Sam and Frank had really found it in a dumpster. Sam refused to lie. Frank suddenly got amnesia and wouldn't back him up. The jury walked Ramsoon and Sam's name turned to shit. It turned out that Ramsoon's murdered ex was Santiago's best friend when they were little kids. Talk about a shit storm.

"So, what's up, Frank? Why are you bothering me?" Sam knew Frank for most of his life. They went to Clinton High School together. They had been teamed up in Narcotics, and then they got their gold shields and became partners in homicide.

The used car lot was lit up, and the prices on the windshields had little messages like "brand new" or "low mileage." Back in the day, Ramsoon owned this lot and used it as a front from where he sold weight.

"What are you tailing the rabbi for?"

"I dunno, Frank. It pays the bills. Maybe his wife don't like him screwing street hookers and then coming home to her?"

"You can't blame her."

"For God's sake, Frank, what do you want from me?" Frank's midsection had a paunch. Back when he was on the job, Frank worked out religiously. He was short and thick as a brick shithouse with no fat. "Last I heard you were retired, living the high life in Boca or Tampa or someplace."

"My sister's kid disappeared." Frank blurted it out. His eyes were moist and he bit his lip.

Sam remembered Frank didn't have kids of his own. "Is your sister still in jail?"

"Yeah, she and her husband got pinched by the Feds. They're both doing twenty-year bids for selling guns and kilos."

"Yeah, I remember." Sam was the only one who Frank talked to about his sister. He didn't want anybody on the job to know.

Chapter Three
Celeste Santiago

Celeste Santiago lingered on the bowl, toilet paper in hand. The Ambien she had taken at two a.m. had forced her into a helpless, dark, unnatural, and comatose fugue state. It reached the point that she wasn't even sure if she was awake or dreaming. From the bathroom window she had a view of Riverside Park and the ice on the Hudson River, but only in the winter. That's really what the realtor meant when she first showed Celeste the apartment and claimed it had a view of the river. River views from the toilet, but only in the winter. That was because once the trees grew leaves in the spring and summer, there was no view.

Fuck. Celeste couldn't remember walking to the bathroom from her bedroom. Where was Kurt? Then she remembered that piece of shit didn't live here anymore.

She stood and looked at her skinny legs in the bathroom mirror.

Was she in this state because asshole Kurt Schneiderman had moved out and was now living in Brooklyn? Once the governor had appointed him to the Court of Claims and he had been transferred to Kings County, he had moved out and sublet a studio in Park Slope, so he could walk to court. After three years of living together it was the perfect escape from any commitment. She squinted at the mirror with a mean and hateful look meant for Kurt. They had been hot and heavy when Kurt was Deputy Chief of Narcotics in the Bronx District Attorney's Office and Celeste was one of his minions, but once he got appointed to the bench things cooled down.

She could smell the coffee from the automatic drip in the kitchen. Celeste didn't remember making coffee last night. She needed to stop taking all these pills. This breakup had hit her hard. What was worse was that everybody in the office and in the court knew about it. Her doctor had wanted to put her on Prozac, but she didn't want any more drugs. She wanted Kurt to come back, but that wasn't happening.

From the kitchen Celeste took her coffee to the bedroom and sat with her knees pulled to her chest. On the TV a correspondent from one of the morning news shows stood in Rockefeller Center, shoulders hunched against the cold, barely able to contain his shivering as he struggled to stand there and hold the microphone against the gusts of wind. She decided she wasn't going to work today.

Across the screen came the announcement that there was breaking news.

This just in. There has been another shooting of an unarmed civilian by a police officer, this time in the Bronx. We have a reporter on the way to the scene.

Celeste saw the strange-looking cell phone on the nightstand next to the bed. Shit. It was the one given to the assistant district attorney on homicide duty. None of the other assistant district attorneys in the office were going to want to take her shift. She wasn't very popular with her coworkers. She didn't try to be. She wasn't a team player.

Celeste decided that she would stay home unless they called her. The news didn't say whether the cop shooting victim died. Otherwise, it should be quiet. People tended to kill each other less in the winter. Tempers flared more in the heat. In the summer more people were out and about. In the winter it was less likely that somebody would blow a gasket and, in an angry rage, kill someone.

The cell phone on the nightstand vibrated. Oh fuck, she had jinxed herself. "ADA Santiago," Celeste answered.

"Is this ADA Santiago?" The woman from dispatch asked.

"Isn't that what I just said?"

"Oh, I didn't recognize your voice. You sound like you had a rough night?"

"No. Just a little under the weather. What is it?" Celeste was bitchy. That was why no one in the office liked her.

"Cop shot at 1275 Webster."

"What?"

"A cop shot somebody," The woman corrected herself.

"Oh." Celeste sucked her teeth. She remembered that ADAs on homicide duty were also required to attend any cop shooting that occurred on their shift. "Did he die?"

"I dunno."

"Did they give you any details about the shooting?"

"No, just that it was a cop that shot someone."

"Thanks for the detailed info." Celeste rolled her eyes to herself. She hung up. Did it matter if the perp or the victim died? A murder was just an assault where the victim died.

Either way it was going to be a nightmare.

Celeste made the shower as hot as possible without scalding herself. At least she didn't have to do homicide duty on the weekends like the newer ADAs in the office.

She brushed her teeth and remembered the worst scene she had ever visited. It had been an old lady dead inside her apartment on Burnside for two weeks in the dead of winter with the heat blasting. She gagged on the toothbrush. Was it the memory of that stiff's stench or the after-effects of the Ambien wearing off that was the cause of her nausea? The stench from the stiff had gotten into her coat, and even the dry cleaner couldn't get it out.

In the lobby, Celeste waited for the car service that the District Attorney's Office sent. Through the doors she watched a little kid on the street nearly ripped from her mother's grasp by a gust. Against the wind, the two of them looked like they were walking in mud as they made their way to Broadway.

* * *

After he dropped her off, the cabbie pulled off quickly. Probably afraid of being robbed. 1275 Webster was like the multitude of other six-story buildings that dotted the Bronx like mushrooms. A lot like the building Celeste grew up in over by Mount Eden.

She stepped into the zoo of cops and flashed her DA badge to the uniform at the entrance to the courtyard blocked by yellow crime scene tape. He pulled up the tape so that she could step under it.

"Stop killing us," someone shouted from the crowd. Their collective breaths formed a cloud in the arctic air.

As she made her way to the body, Celeste almost hop-scotched over pieces of bloodstained gauze

"Hey, kid, what're you doin'?" Desante always asked her the same thing. He wore an outdated gold-colored cashmere overcoat, silk scarf, and shiny Italian loafers with little gold buckles. With his hand under Celeste's elbow he guided her gently toward the stiff. The body was lodged against the door to apartment 1F.

"What you got?" Celeste didn't like older men, but Desante was easy on the eyes in a Dean Martin sort of way. He looked like he frequented the tanning parlor.

"Not so kosher." He moved his right hand back and forth like a rudder.

"How so?"

With his hand still on her elbow, Desante led her back to the front of the lobby by the vestibule. "The vic takes one here. You see where we found the shell, and the rest of the bullet lodges their in the wall. It was a through and through." He pointed to where it was marked by a marker and a crime scene cop was taking pictures. "Then our vic runs and ends up here, where we have two kill shots at close range. The two shell casings were recovered wedged under this hallway radiator."

They had walked back to the corpse, and Desante reached and pulled back the sheet. The stiff's eyes were still open in a look of terror. It was as if he knew his ticket was about to be punched. "Ridiculous. Short guys don't look good in trench coats or double-breasted suits. Look at this. He is almost wrapped in the leather like a shroud."

Celeste smelled the gunpowder. The Latin music ringtone from the cell phone the deceased clenched was never-ending. "Pretty popular fellow."

"You think?" Desante's teeth were bleached. "Look at the pattern to the spatter. You could see he was shot at close range. I'll bet there's gunpowder residue on the vic's coat."

Celeste bent over the body to where her head and Desante's were almost touching. She could smell his cologne. She saw the tiny red droplets, like drizzle against the lapel of the trench coat, close to the black soaking hole through the leather into his chest.

"Hey," Desante called to one of the crime scene guys. "Did you get this?" They began snapping pictures. "Don't forget to dig that slug out the wall."

"Who's the cop?"

"Kevin Knowles."

"From Narcotics?"

"That's him."

"I know him. He's a real cowboy. The dealers call him Loco. Did anyone talk to him?"

"He went to the ER to get checked out for shock. The bus took him away before I got here. I'm sure the union rep has gotten to him by now and probably told him not to say anything until he gets a lawyer."

"I wouldn't expect anything less." Celeste said.

"Do these cameras work?"

"I dunno."

"Is someone working on seeing if they work and then getting a copy of the recording?"

"They're working on it."

"Who's the deceased?"

"His name is Ray Santos. He's a local knucklehead supposedly gone straight." Desante used his fingers as quotation marks on the words "gone straight." "He manages the building.

"Maybe he was hustling to supplement his income?"

Desante shrugged. "His old lady is over there." Desante gestured with his head. "Why don't you go talk to her?"

"Oh great," Celeste muttered. She turned in the direction that Desante was looking. The tiny woman in an azure-colored bubble parka was standing by herself in the corner of the lobby watching the commotion. She wasn't the hysterical mess Celeste might expect. Maybe it was just shock? It hadn't sunk in yet. Celeste had seen that reaction with relatives of the deceased at murder scenes. At first they were numb with disbelief and then the grief set in. Maybe it was that death wasn't that uncommon in the hood? Life could be cheap in the South Bronx.

Celeste walked over to her. The vic's wife noticed Celeste approaching, and she gave Celeste a once-over in a hard way. She started at Celeste's heels and let her eyes travel up until their eyes met, and then she squinted as if to ask *"What the hell are you doing in my neighborhood?"* It was like Celeste was the new kid on the block and the vic's wife wanted to show her that she wasn't soft.

"Ms. Santos, I'm sorry for your loss. I'm Assistant District Attorney Celeste Santiago."

"Millie." She had one long braid tucked inside her North Face.

"Excuse me?" Celeste asked.

"Call me Millie. You don't need to go with that Ms. Santos. Just Millie, okay?" A tissue appeared in her hand. She dabbed at the tears in her eyes and blew her nose.

"Okay." Celeste understood. Keep it real.

"Are you gonna stay with this case or is it gonna go to another ADA?" Millie watched the medical examiner wheel her husband away in the stretcher. She didn't look at Celeste. Millie could have been talking to herself.

"This is my case." Celeste didn't know why she said that. Just because she was the ADA on homicide duty who responded didn't mean she was going to stay with it.

Millie pointed at Celeste. "The cop will walk for what he did. Please, lady, you know there ain't gonna be no justice. So don't be acting all official like you're all over it and something is gonna be done. Because you know and I know that ain't gonna happen."

Celeste was flustered. "Ms. Santos, give me your number. I want to pass it on to our victim assistance bureau in case you need any help."

With the back of her hand she waved Celeste off, as if to dismiss the whole idea. "I don't need no stupid victim assistance bullshit. I told you to call me Millie. My phone isn't working. I'll call you. You got a card?"

Celeste saw that Desante was making his way to the vestibule. She gave Millie her card. "I'll be in touch."

Celeste caught up to him. When Desante opened the door, the temperature seemed like it had dropped even more. It was the deep chill, New York winter kind of frost that went into her bones.

Desante watched her flinch. "You don't got enough meat on those bones, that's why the cold goes right through you." He held the door for her. The crowd was larger and louder now.

"Speak for yourself."

The crowd was shouting "Hands up, don't shoot." It was a good thing it was so cold or there would have been more people.

A young black reporter she had seen on the news shoved a microphone in her face. He looked at the badge around her neck. "You're with the Bronx DA's Office. Is it true that a Narcotics detective shot an unarmed employee of the building?"

"The District Attorney's Office is going to do a full and thorough investigation of the matter."

"Are you going to convene a grand jury?"

"Yes." She knew she shouldn't have said that. It slipped out before she could stop herself. That was for the district attorney himself to decide. Simonetti was going to be pissed. She turned and walked away with Desante.

Desante moved close to her, shielding her. "You should let me take you for a meal. You look like you could use one, Flaca."

Celeste felt her nose freeze. She reminded herself that she didn't like older men. At first she let Desante get close to her because she didn't mind the way his cologne smelled, but then she could smell garlic on his breath. It was a turnoff. He would have to take care of that.

Maybe it would help her to rebound from Schneiderman? He would probably be nicer to her than a man her age. Maybe she would be more appreciated.

Desante's unmarked car was parked right in front. When he turned the key, the heat blasted.

"Do you think it was justified?" She could feel the heat making her face rosy. She pulled down the visor and fixed herself in the mirror. With a rubber band from her purse she put her thick mane of red hair in a ponytail and dabbed some lip gloss on her lips. She hated her freckles. Always had.

Desante waited for the uniforms, setting up the wood horses as barricades, to get out of the way. He watched her from the corner of his eye. "Questionable at best. I think Kevin Knowles fucked up."

"Any witnesses?" She studied Desante. He looked like he was ready to pack it in. Retire. If he put what he thought about this shooting in his DD5, his name would be crap.

"Not sure. They're doing a canvass."

"What about the people in the apartment where the vic was lying? Did anyone look out of the peephole? Was anyone home when it happened?"

"Not sure. We're checking it out. You know how that goes. It's tough to get these people to talk to cops. It's all about that 'snitches

David Gold came in a short time later. Like he had been caught in the act of committing a felony, he shuffled his Florsheims, hunched his shoulders, and arched his eyebrows when he saw Sam.

No, asshole, I'm not here to see you, Sam wanted to tell Gold. Gold was like a bad rash that Sam couldn't get rid of. They had a long history. After Sam had gotten pinched, Gold had gotten Sam out of a big jam, but his relationship with Gold had soured in the last case that they had worked on together. That was when Sam had found out Gold was not beyond selling out his client to get a piece of the action. Son of a bitch, piece of shit douche bag Gold turned out to be.

"That reporter from the *Post* keeps calling about the Kevin Knowles case." Sheila had ignored Gold when he came in, and now, as she spoke, she didn't look up from the computer, like she was talking to herself.

"Tell him I'm not here." Gold turned and went into his office.

"Look at him." Sheila rolled her eyes. She used black pencil eyeliner to fill in the gaps of her eyebrows. "He gets one press case and now he's a fuckin' prima donna. Ain't he fuckin' famous? Just like Clarence Darrow?" Her laugh was throaty and hoarse, like she had just chewed on a piece of sandpaper.

She put on her earphones and began to type. "Go on in," Sheila shouted above the volume. She liked to make Sam stew on the couch for a bit and listen to her bullshit, hoping to get a rise out of him.

The familiar potpourri odor of Feldman's pipe tobacco grew stronger when Sam approached Feldman's office. He knocked on the door and a muffled voice responded. Sam opened it. The long fluorescent tubes of light buzzed from the ceiling of the cheap peanut-butter-colored Formica-paneled office.

The old man looked up from a small DVD screen that sat on the desk blotter. The rest of its surface was covered by mounds of paper piled like columns around the perimeter of the desk. With ancient, watery eyes he peered through Sam.

Sam didn't like being studied, and he didn't like being closed in. The dark walls with no windows brought on his claustrophobia, and he could feel himself perspire. This shouldn't take long. He took a deep breath and sat across from Feldman on the opposite side of the huge desk. It felt like a cave. He met the old man's gaze. Polar rings blurred the separation between Feldman's iris and cornea.

"I got some good stuff for the wife to get her Get." Feldman wasn't amused by his play on words. Sam handed him the surveillance photos of the Hassid and the hookers. The skin on Feldman's arms was scaly and liver-spotted. The ancient ink smudge of numbers from Auschwitz was tattooed above his wrist. The old man looked away from the screen, went through the photos, nodded, and then, with a flick of the wrist, threw them on top of one of the paper piles.

"Look at this." Feldman motioned for Sam to come around to his side of the desk. Sam leaned over the old man, who smelled of mothballs, tobacco, and pee. Feldman pressed play.

The frozen images on the screen came to life. A man exited a double-parked Mercedes. Sam recognized the street as Webster Avenue. He was a little man, barely taller than the car. With one hand he preened himself in the windshield and with the other he pressed his cell phone against his ear.

The video was like a silent movie. It reminded him of watching the funnies without sound on the TV, the size of a small fridge ensconced in wood paneling, on Sundays at his grandparents' house. Why did they always turn down the sound? He never understood how his grandparents could watch TV that way.

The little man in the video wore a long leather trench coat. In the stick-figure-like quality of the footage, it looked like a robe a monk would wear. The little man entered the vestibule of the building with the number 1275 on the entrance.

Feldman breathed through his nose. "Here it is," he said. With his German accent the sound of "s" sounded like "z."

A tall man came into the picture and followed the little man into the building. The footage was grainy and blurred his features. There was something about the man's long, quick strides that was familiar. He wore his hair in a ponytail.

"Is that Kevin Knowles?" Sam asked.

"Wait."

In the next shot, the footage was from a camera inside the lobby of the building. The lighting was poor. The little man in the trench coat approached Kevin. He reached for his waistband. Kevin pulled a pistol out from under the armpit of his jacket. There was a muzzle flash and the little man stumbled backward down the hall until he collapsed against the door to an apartment. Kevin stood above him, pistol in hand. There were two more muzzle flashes.

"You know the tall one?"

"He looks like Kevin Knowles. We used to work together."

Feldman nodded. It was as if Sam was confirming something he already knew.

In the next frame Kevin stood over the stiff. He opened his jacket and pulled his gold badge out so that it hung off the chain on his chest. He spoke into his Kell, which was hidden under his shirt sleeve. The collar of the trench coat covered the little man's face. He lay on his side, turned away from the gunfire, pressed against the apartment's door. Underneath him a blood pool spread away from the welcome mat. Kevin leaned over and searched inside the collar of the coat for a pulse.

Cops filled the lobby. EMTs rushed over and cut away his coat and clothes. An official-looking cop came in the picture. He wore the white shirt with the bars of a captain. He was flanked by other uniforms. Kevin reached into his waistband and gave him his weapon.

Someone had thrown a sheet over the stiff. Others were stretching yellow tape across the width of the hallway around the body. Some of the crime scene guys Sam recognized from his time on the job.

The flashes from the cameras were like more muzzle blasts. With NYPD emblazoned in white letters on the back of his windbreaker, another cop approached the captain with an evidence bag, and the captain dropped Kevin's burner inside it.

How did Feldman get his hands on this so quick? Sam had just heard about the shooting on the news. Anything that happened in the Bronx seemed to flow through this room.

A duo of heavyset female EMTs approached Kevin. They unfolded their stretcher and guided him onto it. Just as he was about to sit down, Kevin collapsed into the arms of the one who had a tattoo of Chinese letters on her neck. It looked like he was going to fall. They struggled with his big, lanky body and pushed him onto the gurney. Was he playing it up for the cameras that were taping his every move?

Two cops as big as defensive linemen dwarfed the captain and the EMTs. Their giant girth and height seemed to block out some of the lighting in the hallway.

"You got to be fucking kidding me." Sam shook his head and closed his eyes as if he weren't seeing what he was seeing. When they worked in Narcotics together, these two gorillas, McBride and Ryan, were the dirtiest cops he knew. Since then he'd had a few nasty run-ins with these two very dangerous apes.

"What?" Feldman pronounced "w" like "v," so it sounded like "Vhat?"

"Nothing."

The next frame of the video switched back to the exterior of the building as a skinny woman in stiletto heels and black tights departed a cab. She looked like she was clubbing in Manhattan. A group of protestors held up signs that said "Our lives matter" and "Don't shoot." Behind the police barricades they raised their hands and pumped their signs up and down. There were TV trucks and reporters.

Sam put his face real close to the screen.

"That's her." The same ADA that had turned his life to crap. "How did she catch this case?" His nose almost touched the screen.

Feldman paused it on the skinny female. "As soon as she sniffs the press around a case she puts her nose in it so she can get her name in the papers. She'll be district attorney one day. Mark my words."

"Please don't say that." Celeste Santiago hated Sam's guts so badly that she almost had him locked up for ten years.

These were not people Sam wanted anything to do with. They were bad news all around.

Santiago spoke to a detective. His gold shield stuck out of the breast pocket of his shark tooth blazer. He was dark, with jet black hair greased back and gray at the temples, and he wore leather loafers and cuff links. He looked more like a croupier than a cop.

"Who's that?" Sam didn't recognize him.

"That's Detective Desante."

Santiago and Desante smiled at each other like they were on a date.

In the next frame, the shot followed Celeste Santiago into the lobby as she was walking over to a tiny woman bundled up in a North Face, with a long braid hanging to her waist.

"That's our client, Milagros Santos."

Why was Feldman using the word "our?" She sure as shit wasn't Sam's client. It worried Sam that Feldman was already including him in this when he hadn't agreed to anything.

"She's the wife of the deceased, Ray Santos. She retained us to bring a wrongful death suit against the city."

The smart thing for Sam to do would be to take his check from Feldman for the work on the Hassid and leave. But who was he kidding? He wasn't going to turn work down from anyone. Even if it meant dealing with those horrors from the past. Sam was desperate. Unless of course he wanted to end up in the poor house. Iris wasn't living with him anymore, and she wasn't helping him pay the bills. He needed cabbage from somewhere. It was a matter of survival.

"How did you get this video so fast?" Sam walked back around to the other side of the desk and stood across from Feldman. There was nowhere else to sit as all the other chairs were piled high with papers and files. It was probably by design.

Under his hooded eyelids, Feldman gave Sam a dull look. Everyone worked for Feldman. Even the 911 operators were in on the action. If a call came in for an accident, Feldman would get notified, and one of his runners would be at the scene signing up the case. Feldman would then farm the case out to different trial attorneys throughout the city for a one-third piece of the recovery. Juries in the Bronx loved to award baskets of money to injured plaintiffs. It was a way that the poor could give back to the big corporations. Payback was a bitch.

"What about Gold?"

"What about him?" Of course, it was no wonder that Feldman had the tape before anyone else.

"How is it that Gold can defend Kevin Knowles?"

"How do you know that Gold is defending Knowles?" Feldman ripped the check he wrote to Sam out of the binder and handed it to him.

Again, it occurred to Sam the smart thing to do would be to take his check and leave.

Anyone that wanted a piece of the action took part in Feldman's scheme. The worse the accident, the more injured the party they referred was, the bigger the finder's fee they received. It wasn't rocket science, just the basic value of life and limb.

"I heard Gold and Sheila talking when I came in." Sam stared down at the check. Five hundred dollars for a night's work wasn't bad. How much did those hookers that waited on the Hassid make on a good night?

"So, you worked with Knowles in Narcotics?"

"How did you know that?"

"I thought you mentioned it."

"I said I worked with him, but I didn't say I worked with him in Narcotics. I guess you also probably know that I worked with him in the Sheriff's Office when I lived upstate in Maplewood." Kevin lived in Maplewood too.

"Do you know him well?"

"He's a fucking worm."

"Here." The old man handed Sam a business card for Bankman and Associates on Lexington Avenue. "Go see the lawyer I sent this case to. His name is Bankman. Maybe he'll want you to go up there to Maplewood and see what you come up with. New?" Feldman used the word "new" indiscriminately, putting it in a sentence where it made no sense.

Feldman began to fidget with his pipe. He ignored Sam. It was his way of letting Sam know they were done.

"Isn't Gold defending Kevin a conflict when you're in the same office representing the widow in the lawsuit against Kevin and the city?" He had been in enough trouble for a lifetime. He didn't need to risk going to jail again over some shady shit so that Feldman and some other lawyer could get richer.

Sheila knocked and opened the door. "Someone is here to see you," she said to Sam.

"Me?"

"Yeah, you. He says his name is Frank something."

Sam didn't move. He wanted to hear what Feldman's response was.

"Conflict schmonflict. Who gives a fuck? New? Since when did you become a lawyer?" Feldman waved him off. "It's not a conflict, genius, because Bankman's office is representing the widow in the wrongful death lawsuit. I'm not involved. Bankman is not connected to my office in any fashion. New? I've got a lot of work to do. Go see Bankman and keep me in the loop."

Feldman wasn't involved but he wanted Sam to keep him in the loop. If Sam didn't need the money . . .Yeah, yeah, he sounded like a broken record.

Frank Cortez sat on the brown couch in the waiting area.

"Do you know this man? Who is he? I don't need to be bothered, I've got a lot of work to do." Sheila looked from Sam to Frank.

"He's nobody." Sam stood over Frank.

"Oh, that's not very nice." When Sheila shook her finger at Sam, the ample flesh on her arms rippled. She smiled to herself. She loved drama.

"Yeah, Sam. She's right, that's not very nice. Maybe you forgot I was your partner for a very long time? Don't that count for something?"

"You're kidding me, right?" He stared down at Frank and balled his fists, not because he wanted to fight with him, but because it brought back bad memories that made him mad as fuck. "You really got big ones to talk about us being partners and act like I owe you something. Frank, why don't you just fuck off already?" Frank must really be desperate for his help. He had to know that he was going to be abused because of what he had done by not stepping up for Sam way back when. And he must have known from all those years when they were partners together that Sam was not the forgetting type.

Sheila couldn't hold it in anymore. She laughed and then coughed and gagged. She took a tissue from the box on her desk and spit into it like she had eaten a rotten fruit. "Son of a bitch Feldman is killing me with that smoke from his goddam pipe." She looked from Sam to Frank and then gave them a second once-over. Their drama was irresistible. "So, what's this? You two teaming up again? Like *Miami Vice*. Crockett and Tubbs? Dream team assholes." She shook her head at the screen. "A bunch of ridiculous morons," she muttered under her breath. She placed the earphones back into her ears and began typing again.

Frank stood and took a step forward toward her desk to say something.

She looked at him for an instant. It was the disinterested look of a tabby. "Fuck off." She waved him off with the back of her hand covered with rings. Even her thumb had a ruby on it.

"What the fuck did you just say to me?"

"Come on, Frank. She's an old lady." Sam stood between Sheila and Frank. Frank had a short fuse as well. It didn't take much to push his buttons. A lot of the cops who had spent years on the job had bad tempers. Was it an occupational hazard from seeing the horrible acts people were capable of doing?

"Who the fuck does she think she is?" Sam was walking with him out of the storefront, and Frank turned as if to go back in. Frank hated being disrespected. "I don't give a shit if she's an old bag. No one talks to me like that."

"Yeah. Yeah." They stood facing each other. Across the street the line to get into Family Court stretched around the block. "How did you find me?"

"When I ran into you last night you said you were watching the rabbi for Feldman, so I figured you'd be here."

"I never told you that I was doing surveillance for Feldman."

"Well, maybe I figured it out."

"What the fuck are you following me for, Frank?"

"I need you to take a ride with me."

"I'm tired. I haven't been to bed yet."

Another group with signs that said "Our lives matter" passed. Someone from the crowd waiting to go through the magnetometer shouted, "The police are killing us! When is it going to stop?"

"Please, Sam, I need your help."

"What the fuck for? You hung my ass out to dry, partner. I shouldn't give you the time of day."

"I'm sorry. I admit it. I was watching out for my own ass. All that time we spent together watching each other's backs, locking up the bad guys, don't it count for anything?" Frank followed Sam. "Here's my car. Just come with me for a quick ride over to Davidson. I heard that Nooney, my nephew, hung out over there in the abandoned buildings."

"Frank, what good am I going to do? Did you forget I'm a convicted felon, and I can't even carry."

He was desperate. Sam started to feel bad for him, and then he got angry at himself for feeling that way. The prick had thrown him under the bus after more than twenty years of being partners.

Frank stood in front of his red Hyundai. "You can't deny me this, what I'm asking you to do."

"Fuck I can."

"Sam, just go with me this one time, and I'm outa your hair forever."

Brothers in blue through good and bad. Never let your fellow cops down. They brainwashed them with that bullshit in the academy.

"Oh, what the fuck. After this I don't want to see your face."

"No problemo." Frank held his hands up, palms facing Sam.

He rode shotgun as Frank drove north on the Grand Concourse.

"Like old times."

"Douche bag." Sam couldn't believe that Frank had somehow convinced him to go with him.

Frank laughed.

"Ain't that incredible about Kevin?"

"The kid was always fucking loco. The dealers even called him that. It don't surprise me in the least that he would bury some unarmed super. Face it, we all knew the kid wasn't wrapped too tight to begin with." Frank laughed. "Remember when he first came to the squad and the Louie Dobbs found out he was a track star in high school. He told Kevin that his job was to run down any perps who tried to get away. Sam, you remember that time this one kid was running away down the Concourse." Frank let go of the steering wheel and mimicked the motion of a sprinter with his arms. "Kevin caught up to the unlucky bastard and with his radio he came across the back of the kid's head." Frank made a swinging motion with his arm. "POW! The kid flew in the air. He was airborne for a good ten feet, remember that. That was crazy. They called Kevin 'wheels' after that."

"That was a long time ago, Frank, and I don't care or remember any of that. Whatever," Sam said. "I told you, I'm bone-tired. Let's go and do whatever it is you can't do alone." Sam made like he was going to spit, and he stopped and gave his old partner that look that showed his contempt for Frank at not being able to take care of his own business. It felt good to break Frank's balls.

"You don't remember those days on the squad?"

"Really, Frank, are we gonna insist that we reminisce about the good old times? What I remember is how you guys were getting rich off the dealers." Sam snorted and laughed to himself, like it was a private joke.

"Fuck you, Sam, and your holier-than-thou bullshit. It turned out you weren't as honest as you made yourself out to be."

"You want to go there? Because I'll get out of this car and you can find your nephew by your fucking self."

Frank didn't say anything.

"For years I looked the other way when you, McBride, Ryan, Kevin, and Dobbs robbed the drug dealers blind." Sam pointed his finger in Frank's face.

Frank didn't say a word because he needed Sam. Sam knew it.

"You got nothing to say about that, do you? It's exactly what I thought about you."

Frank stared straight ahead.

* * *

They turned left on Fordham Road and passed where Alexander's once was.

"His grandmother told me that he would stay on Davidson. Over here." Frank parked the car. He reached across Sam and from the glove compartment removed a long flashlight.

It was a section of abandoned one-family homes boarded up after a fire. Down the block, the city's urban renewal project had built a series of neat one-family cinder-block homes. The plan was to do the same with these.

"Nice," Sam said as he stepped out of the car and surveyed the twelve-foot dense wire fence topped with shiny barbs. "No trespassing" and "Keep out" signs were attached to it.

"Now you see why I wanted you to go with me to this crap hole?"

"Christ, Frank, what was the kid doing hanging around here?" Sam followed Frank across the street.

They walked the perimeter of the fence. They tried to look through it but couldn't see anything.

"Can't see shit." Sam smelled the acrid odor of burnt plastic. It gave him a headache. The whole scene gave him anxiety. He didn't owe Frank anything. Why had he let Frank convince him to go with him?

Toward the rear of the lot they found a hole in the wire big enough to squeeze through, and on the other side of the fence was a lot covered with broken glass, garbage, clothes, and mattresses. It had become a dumping ground before the city had fenced it up. There were pieces of stoves, washing machines, air conditioners, toilets, and sinks dumped there.

"Nooney." Frank cupped his hand over his mouth.

Some of the boards blocking the entrance to one of the houses had been pulled off. Frank shined his flashlight into the interior. "One thing good about the cold is that in this weather the garbage don't stink as bad." A few rats scurried away.

"Nooney, are you in here?"

Even though it was freezing, the unmistakable smell still greeted them as they approached another house with a wraparound porch that had collapsed into the cellar below. Frank put the sleeve of his windbreaker over his mouth and nose.

"Fuck." Sam found a glove in his pocket and used that as a mask. The feeling that he was about to heave came and went.

They both knew what the smell was.

The windows were all boarded up. In the house they found an opening to the basement. Sam followed Frank. They had to step down into a cellar with a dirt floor.

Frank shined the flashlight around. The light caught the stiff. He was sitting against the base of a red brick chimney. Frank's breathing was short. "Mother of God!"

All those years of seeing bodies on the job desensitized Sam. He heard Frank in the background repeating himself. "Oh my God."

Sam approached the stiff. He was a young guy with wire rim glasses. The lenses had been shot out, and where his eyes were there were just holes with flesh, tissue, and blood exposed. His position looked staged, like someone had propped him up against the chimney as if to make it seem as though he were looking at something. Part of the stiff's face had been eaten away by the rats, exposing crooked buck teeth. The shooter had left the shattered lenses of his wire rims in place.

"Jesus, Mary and Joseph." Frank let the flashlight float up and down the length of the stiff. His voice was cracking. "That's Nooney. I'm pretty sure. That's why they called him Nooney, on account of his buck teeth." Frank aimed the light behind Nooney's left ear where there was a splotchy red birthmark that looked like an image from a Rorschach test. "Oh my God, that's him. I remember since he was a little kid, he had that mark behind his ear. We used to tease him and say someone spilled paint on him, and it couldn't be washed off."

"Small caliber." Sam leaned over and studied the blown-out eyeballs. "I think it was a .22. I don't see any exit wounds." Whoever did this was sending a message. It was as if Nooney was watching something and then had his eyeballs blown for seeing what he saw. The shooter must have purposely used small bullets that didn't penetrate bone, and they traveled around the skull and tore up his brain.

"Poor kid." Frank held back a sob and shined the flashlight on the dirt floor. It was littered with empty crack vials and garbage. "I don't see any shell casings. The perp was careful and cleaned up after himself or they were lost in the mess."

"Maybe a Beretta?" This wasn't random. It was personal. "Frank, shine the light here. What does he have in his hand?"

"That's a stem." Frank shined the light on Nooney's right hand clutching a glass cylinder. "Live by the pipe, die by the pipe." Frank's voice was broken. "I got to get out of here."

"Let's call it in." Sam followed Frank out of the cellar. His back was stiff from bending over the body. With both his hands on his hips, he leaned backwards and stretched.

Frank called 911. They waited in front of the fence.

"Fucking cold." Sam turned to Frank, who stared away.

"His name was Walter Rios." It seemed as though Frank spoke to stay warm. "Who am I kidding? I haven't seen him in years. Maybe if I had taken some time and given the kid some guidance he wouldn't have ended up like this. The problem was nobody cared about him. He was a burden that my sister left for all of us to take care of. What am I going to tell my mother?"

Frank stared off into the distance, down the block and away from there.

"Jeez, Sam, what chance did a kid like that have? My fucked-up sister and her loser husband locked up. Not even his real father." Frank shook his head and looked up as if to find a reason as to why this could happen. "I can't tell his grandmother. My mother. She's too old to handle it. I think she would drop dead if she found out her grandson perished."

"You have to tell your sister, his mom."

Frank didn't seem hear. "I want to find the motherfucker who did this."

"I'm sorry, Frank." Sam patted his old partner on the shoulder.

The RMP stopped right in front of them on the street. Sam recognized the two cops. "Look, it's Benitez and Ramos that caught it." He hoped seeing some familiar faces from their days on the job would ease some of the horror for Frank.

Ramos rode shotgun on the side of the RMP that was closest to the fence. He stepped out of the patrol car and onto the curb. "It's Sammy and Frankie."

"This is like a blast from the past." Benitez parked the cruiser and joined them. "Did you guys call in the body?"

"It's my nephew." Frank looked down at the rubble-strewn ground.

"Oh my God, Frank, I'm so sorry." Benitez approached Frank.

"It's okay. It's okay." Frank walked toward the space in the fence through which they had gained access to the burnt-out buildings.

"I'll show you guys." Sam didn't want Frank to have to see his dead nephew again. Frank stood back as Sam led them to the place where the body was.

"Jeez. Poor Frank." Ramos had the same long flashlight that Frank had used.

"It looks like he's been there a while." After the three of them came back out from underneath the porch, Benitez studied the crowd that began to form outside the fence. Word had spread that they had found a body. Half these people probably knew Nooney.

"He was missing. That's why Frank came up from Florida to look for him." He shouldn't have given Frank a hard time. Now he felt bad about it.

Ramos spoke into his radio as another patrol pulled up. Benitez and Ramos walked over to the other uniforms.

Benitez took Frank's cell number.

"Let's go." Frank walked toward the crowd. His Hyundai was parked behind them.

"Frank, don't you think we should wait for Homicide?"

"For what?" Frank faced Sam in the middle of the street. They both knew that the cops were just going through the motions on this one. It was another crackhead found dead. On the hierarchy of cases, this one fell to the bottom of the heap. Nobody gave a shit, and it didn't matter that the deceased was Frank's nephew.

"One more stop?"

How could he say no after what Frank had just been through? "I'm bone-tired, Frank."

Through the windshield, Frank waved at the crowd to move so that he could pull away. He drove south on the Concourse. "It's on your way to your car. Come on, Sam."

"Where we going, Frank?"

"Remember Stumpy?"

"Stumpy?" When they were cops, he was their snitch. "Come on, Frank. You don't even know if he's around." It was a wild goose chase that Sam wanted no part of. He wanted to get home to bed. The gnawing guilt about not helping Frank out got to him. Even though Frank had been a prick to him back then, the poor guy's nephew had both his eyes blown out.

"So what's the harm? Let's give it a shot. You never know? Right? Right, Sam?" Frank took his eyes off the road. The light was red up ahead and they were speeding toward the rear end of another car.

Frank slammed on the brakes, and they squealed.

"Frank, please look where you're going."

When they reached 161, Frank made the left toward Yankee Stadium. There on the benches in front of McDonalds was Stumpy, their old C.I., at his usual spot. Unbelievable. It had been years since Sam had seen Stumpy, and here he was back at his old spot. Did some things never change?

"What I tell you?" Frank double parked.

"Detective Frank and Detective Sam, what's going on?" Stumpy's big eyes were wide with fear. The left sleeve on his sweat jacket was empty because his left arm below the elbow was missing.

Sam stood behind Frank. There was a rough-looking fellow with a beard standing with Stumpy. He wore an enormous parka that could have concealed an arsenal. Who knew. It was the guns that scared Sam. Why was Stumpy so nervous? Sam hoped that they hadn't come upon something. The other guy talking to Stumpy had his hands in his pockets. He turned and walked into the McDonalds.

"Why so nervous, Stump? We ain't cops no more." Frank patted Stumpy's good arm.

"Must be force of habit." Stumpy had a deep baritone voice. He sounded like Barry White.

"You look good, Stump."

"I finally got a kidney." When Stumpy smiled, his gold grill gleamed. "No more of that fucking dialysis."

"Did you know Nooney?"

"Huh?"

Stumpy had a tic or a tell. Whenever he was about to lie, he always asked "Huh?"

"The kid they found over by Davidson."

"Not really."

Frank stepped back, cocked his head to one side. He looked at Stumpy sideways. "Is it not really or no?"

"That kid was Frank's nephew."

"Huh?"

Frank clenched his fists. They were as thick as a brick layer's hands. The big knuckle on his right hand was broken. It wouldn't have been a big deal for Frank to stomp him. Sam had seen Frank stomp many people over the many years they had been partners. It was something Sam got used to after all those years on the job with Frank as his partner. It was when Frank got impatient that he took his pound of flesh from the source of it.

"I didn't really know him," Stumpy stammered.

"What the fuck does that mean?" Frank was up on the balls of his feet. His frozen breath blew in Stumpy's face.

"The only thing I know about Nooney was that he was the godson of Ray Santos, the super that was killed by the cop over by Webster. It's a bad coincidence was all I meant. That's all I know, Frank. I swear to God." Stumpy began to walk away toward the entrance to the McDonalds.

"Don't fucking walk away from me." Frank stood in his path. He stood real close to Stumpy. He was smaller than Stumpy, but Stumpy looked away and took a step back. Toughness and the ability to back it up ruled these streets.

"Relax, Frank." Sam stood between them. Frank was very emotional. Who could blame him?

Sam turned his back to Frank, and he warned Stumpy, "If you know what's good for you, you'd better not be holding out on Frank. Because given these circumstances, if Frank were to find out that you held out important info about his nephew's murder, there's no telling where his temper would take him once he found out it was you."

Stumpy shook his head in agreement and stared down at Sam's feet. "Okay. Okay." He was weighing his options. He knew after all these years of being Frank and Sam's snitch how dangerous this could be for his well-being if Frank lost his temper. "All's I know is that Nooney used to chill with this big white boy."

"Oh yeah? What's the white boy's name? I hope you're not making up some bullshit to get rid of us."

"I swear to God. I think his name is Sean."

"Oh yeah, and where does this Sean live?"

"That building on the corner of Marion and Bedford Park. It's red brick with a red awning."

"You better not be lying to us."

"I ain't lying." Stumpy turned and went into the McDonalds.

"What was Stumpy so nervous about?" Sam turned to Frank. He hoped this would be the last he saw of Frank. That Frank would try to hunt this white kid Sean down and leave Sam alone.

"I dunno. It ain't like we have any juice. We're not even on the job. Why would he be worried about us?"

"Maybe it has to do with Knowles shooting that super, and now Nooney's death has him spooked?"

"Who knows? It could be a million different things. Maybe Stumpy's got his own beef that he's afraid?"

They got back into Frank's car, and Frank drove Sam to where he had parked his car. When they reached his car, Frank stopped and looked at Sam.

"The thing about all of this that made me swallow my pride and reach out to you for help"—Frank cleared his throat—"was when I started looking for Nooney and it came back to me from one of the crackheads that Nooney hung out with that Nooney was Ray's godson. When I heard that, I got worried, and that was when I decided to look you up and ask for your help, and it turned out that I was right to be worried." Frank looked away and his eyes grew watery.

Sam put a hand on his shoulder. "Good luck with everything, Frank, and I'm sorry for your loss."

* * *

Sam drove slowly across the Bronx to his apartment. His reflexes were shot from not having slept.

When he opened the door to the apartment, he thought he heard Iris. Sam called out her name as he walked through the apartment. She wasn't there.

In the kitchen, he opened a can of tuna and placed two pieces of white bread in the toaster. Since Iris had been staying with her folks, Sam had been living on a diet of tuna sandwiches. He was down to two hundred and ten on his six-foot-two frame. He hadn't weighed that little since he was in high school. When he looked in the mirror, he could see he was losing his gut.

At the kitchen table he could hear the noise of buses and traffic on 231st below. He took a few bites of the sandwich. It was dry and needed mayonnaise. He felt himself begin to nod out. He was too tired to eat, especially this crap. He put the uneaten food in the fridge, went toward the bedroom, and thought how nice it would be if he was wrong and Iris was there in bed waiting for him. The image of Kevin chasing that perp and smashing him in the head with his radio passed through Sam's mind's eye. It was weird that that was the last image he saw before he fell into a deep slumber.

Chapter Five
Celeste Santiago

"Levin wants to see you," the new receptionist with the purple streaks in her hair told Celeste Santiago.

"Any other messages?" Celeste was lost in thought about Desante. He obviously liked her, but did she want to go out with an older man? Celeste was forty-two in a couple of weeks. Maybe that was the way to go? Older men were more desperate. Did that mean they would be nicer and more appreciative?

"Huh?" She'd never been with a guy over fifty. Since Schneiderman left she had been lonely. Was she becoming desperate. "Did you just say something?"

"Levin." The girl pointed with nails that were painted with encrypted psychedelic designs and curled in length at the edges. Obviously, she wasn't hired for her typing skills.

Celeste looked into his office. Levin's back was to her. He was watching the protestors fill the plaza of the courthouse and spread out onto 161st. She knocked. "No justice," someone shouted over a bullhorn. "No peace," the crowd responded. She knocked again.

"Howard?"

"Oh, Celeste." He motioned her to the couch and the seats around a coffee table in the center of the room. "This is a tremendous mess with the cop shooting. What's going on with it?"

"There are problems." When Levin had interviewed her for the ADA position out of law school, he had a full head of hair. Now he had taken to dying the little gray hair left on his head to shoe-polish brown, which he combed turban-like to cover as much of his bald pate as possible. The trimmed salt-and-pepper beard helped his appearance, but the dye job was awful.

"I heard." Levin squinted his eyes and pressed his lips together, as if he had tasted something that was too tart. "Write up a memo and pass it on to whoever gets assigned."

"Simonetti is pissed that I spoke to the press. So now he's going to punish me by taking the case away from me. Is that why he told you to talk to me?" Levin was Simonetti's hatchet man. Old man Simonetti rarely left his office, and when he did it was to attend some political function. Running the DA's office was left to Levin.

"That's not it and you know it. The proper procedure is that the ADA who catches the case on homicide duty doesn't stay with the case. It gets reassigned."

"Well I want to stay with it, so fuck your proper procedure bullshit, Howard." Levin continued to squint at her. He and Schneiderman were friends. Did they still stay in touch? Since the breakup Celeste thought that Levin avoided her. Did he feel bad for her? What secrets had Schneiderman told him about her? That was why she shouldn't have dated a coworker.

"I'll give you another homicide."

"I don't want another homicide, Howard." She stood. Celeste could talk to him like that because Levin and Simonetti needed her. In this thankless job, where the juries in the Bronx hated the cops and the office's conviction rate plummeted to an all-time low, she was the one bright spot in the office. She had ten convictions in a row because the juries loved her. She was one of them. Celeste came from the South Bronx. At least something in her life was going right.

Most of the senior people in the office had left. They got their experience and went to better paying jobs in private law firms, but she stayed, and now she wasn't going to take no for an answer.

At trial Celeste came out swinging. Even if she thought the defendant might be innocent, she didn't care, because in her mind he may not have done that crime, but he was probably guilty of committing some other crime he hadn't been pinched for. It was the law of averages catching up with the perp.

"Don't you think there's a problem with you going after Kevin Knowles?" Levin looked up at her.

Was this why they didn't want her to take the case. Sure, back in the day she had been thick as thieves with the cops from Narcotics, and now she was turning on them and going after one of their own.

"I always thought you loved the Narcotics crew. Don't they have the highest arrest and conviction rate of any narcotics team in the city?"

Celeste went to the window and looked down at the crowd. This could be the case that she needed to propel her, to get her noticed by the hotshots in the Democratic Party. The demographics had changed, and now the political bosses were nominating Hispanics and Blacks. Maybe they were ready for a Hispanic woman to be DA of the Bronx. Could this be her ticket? Simonetti and Levin were on their way out, and they knew it.

The speaker was a well-dressed black man in a cashmere overcoat, and he was working the crowd into a frenzy. They pumped their signs and fists in the air.

"It's not right and you know it." She turned from the window to Levin. His shoulders were hunched. "They're a bunch of cowboys. All of them. Kevin Knowles along with McBride and Ryan. They think they can do whatever they want as long as they're getting drugs off the street. How many times are the perps they arrest charged with resisting arrest? How many times do the perps they arrest end up at Lincoln or Jacobi with broken noses or broken jaws? How many complaints of excessive force have they had filed against them with the Civilian Review Board?"

"You know Gold is representing Kevin Knowles?" Levin looked down at the carpet. It was a losing battle. He was running out of excuses.

"So what? Because we dated years ago, you think I have a problem with Gold representing him?" She snickered. "I'll kick his ass."

Levin shrugged. He was tired of doing Simonetti's dirty work. "Simonetti thinks you want his job."

"I want justice for the poor bastard that Knowles shot for no good reason." She sat across from Levin and crossed her long legs. "Howard, I need something to keep me occupied. Since Kurt left me, I've been in a funk. I need something to work on to get me out of this rut I'm in." She choked and sniffled, and acted like she was pushing back the tears. She put on the act hoping to convince Levin.

"Be careful what you wish for." He clasped his hands together. "Don't say I didn't warn you. Do whatever you want. You want the case? Take it. Take it to the grand jury. See where it goes, but mark my words—at the end of the day, with all the grief, tsouris, and aggravation you're going to get, it's not going to be worth it."

He threw his hands up in the air and left her sitting by herself in his office.

Chapter Six
Sam Free

In the morning when Sam Free left his building, he saw Frank double parked. It was one of a string of days and weeks where the cold was unrelenting and stubborn. It hung on, and the temperature refused to budge above the freezing mark. Spring was supposed to be around the corner. Not so fast with this cold.

He hoped Frank hadn't seen him. Who was he fooling? A man of Sam's size just didn't fade into the woodwork. Maybe Frank's attention was diverted, and he didn't see Sam leave his building? On his way to the El and the IRT Number One Subway to midtown, Sam hunched his shoulders and bowed his head away from the fucking icy wind that came off the East River and blew through the streets. He breathed in through his nose and his nostrils froze.

Frank put the Hyundai in reverse and pulled alongside Sam. He opened the passenger side window and shouted, "You need a ride?"

Sam ignored him and continued walking against the sting of the wind that cut through his coat and clothes to his skin.

"Come on, Sam. You'll freeze your ass off."

The frost made his eyes tear. He turned away from Frank, and another gust came at him with a fury that made it hard for him to walk against it. Again, Sam was forced to turn away from it, and he faced the passenger door of Frank's car from the sidewalk. His fair features, which had turned red from the cold, now looked purple, particularly his nose. "What the fuck, Frank?" He was so cold that his lips and mouth had trouble forming the words. "Are you stalking me?" he shouted above the wind, and then shoved his hands into his pockets.

He needed to get rid of Frank and get to his appointment with Bankman in midtown. He had tried to be a nice guy, but now Frank was imposing and cramping his style. The gig with Bankman on the Santos wrongful death case could turn into a cash cow. He didn't need Frank to put the kibosh on it.

"Just go with me to find this kid that hung out with Nooney. I'll take you wherever you want to go. I'll be your driver. Please, Sam, I know I got no right to ask." Frank continued to follow him in the Hyundai.

Damn right that he had no right to ask. Frank must be desperate to almost get on his hands and knees and beg for help. For Christ's sake, he was willing to be his chauffeur.

He wasn't looking forward to freezing his ass off on the El's platform waiting for the Number One train. Then he would have to endure the rush hour ride to Manhattan, squeezed like a sardine with the working stiffs. He hated riding the subway when it was so crowded that he had to squeeze so close to the other passengers that he could smell what his neighbor had for breakfast.

"Come on, Sam. My nephew got both his eyes blown out. I need to find the bastard that did that to him."

Frank was getting as much mileage as he could out of that one. "What do you need me for, Frank? Find the kid yourself. What do I got to hold your hand for? You can take care of yourself."

"I just do." The cold air was filling the car and Frank was shivering sitting there in shirtsleeves.

"What the fuck?" Sam said to himself as got into the front passenger seat. He couldn't believe that he was getting into the car with Frank again.

Frank took the Deegan to the Willis Avenue Bridge, and from there he got the FDR south. It was jampacked.

Sam switched the radio from the Latin station to the all-news one.

They rode in silence the rest of the way. Sam didn't want to engage him for fear that they were going to get into an accident. It was why he tried to never let Frank drive when they were on the job. Frank got off the FDR at 42nd Street and headed west.

Traffic was at a standstill.

"I'll get out here." Sam got out before Frank could respond.

It was faster to walk, and he didn't have to worry about Frank's driving.

In the elevator going up to Bankman's office, Sam recognized the chubby guy struggling under the weight of a trial bag. He couldn't place where he knew him from.

"Hey, Sam." The tail of his white shirt hung out. His breathing was labored.

"Matt?" Matt Prey had been a court officer in the Bronx. From court officer he became a clerk, and then he went to law school at night.

"What are you doing here?" Matt had rosy, chubby, whisker-free cheeks.

"Seeing a lawyer." From his days on the job Sam got to know some of the court officers and clerks. "Is his name Bankman?"

"How'd you know?" Sam remembered they called Matt "doughboy." He always had an issue with the weight, but now he had really let himself go to shit. The buttons of his dress shirt stretched under the pressure of his gut. It was probably the pressure from being a lawyer that caused him to stuff his face compulsively.

"I work for him." They reached the 28th floor. "Come in. Bankman told me he hired a PI for the Santos case. He didn't tell me it was you." He led Sam into the office.

Frank was right, this was big time. They walked through the mahogany-paneled waiting room.

There was a black girl, a Spanish girl, and a white girl sitting at separate desks in front of their respective computer screens.

Everything seemed so neat. There seemed to be not one file or piece of paper or magazine in the waiting room or on any of the secretaries' desks that was out of place.

They passed the vast, cavernous conference room with a large table in dark wood. Then there was a huge office; it had to be half a city block. Sam guessed it to be Bankman's. It smelled like money. In the hallway covering the walls were laminated newspaper articles of Bankman's monstrous verdicts. One was for a sixty million dollar award covered by the *Post.* Sam lingered and skimmed the article. It was for a brain damaged baby born with cerebral palsy. On and on, the walls were plastered with a dizzying amount of multi-million-dollar verdicts Bankman garnered in trial victories.

Sam followed Prey to a windowless back office.

"Bankman should be here soon." On his desk was a bulging accordion file labeled "Milagros Santos v. The City of New York." He left his door open slightly so that he could hear when Bankman came in.

"What's this Bankman fellow like?" Sam tried to keep his voice down.

"You mean what's he like to work for?" Matt rose from his desk and looked into Bankman's office next door. He put his index finger and middle finger together and pointed them at his temple and made a circle shape. "He's a little zooey."

"Zooey how?"

"Did you notice the office? That everything is in perfect order, no dust and everything is polished to perfection? That's Bankman. I think he's got obsessive compulsive disorder. He goes nuts if he finds dust. In his office, under his desk, he has Windex and Pledge. Every morning he wipes everything down. If he finds something misfiled, he has a shit fit."

"How long you been here?"

"Ten years and I don't know anything about him. I know he's orthodox. He leaves early on Friday. He went to Yeshiva. Did you notice every doorway has a mezuzah?"

"It's not what I look for."

"He's a religious fanatic," Prey whispered. "You wouldn't know it because he hides it. I don't know how old his kids are, what his wife looks like, where he lives. I've never seen the guy in ten years without a shirt and tie."

Outside, the small talk between the secretaries stopped. It was like a presence had entered the office.

"He's here." Matt mouthed the words.

Bankman entered. Sam remembered where he had heard that name before. Years ago, Bankman had an ad on cable TV for his law firm. It always came on during the Yankee games. It was Bankman on the screen telling the viewer that "he could bank on Bankman." The multi-million-dollar verdicts were listed on the screen.

"You must be Sam Free." Bankman's hand was soft, small, and moist. "Donald Bankman." He wore black-rimmed glasses over eyes that were small, beady, and black. "Come into my office."

It had a wall of windows that made it feel like they were in a tree house suspended in a sea of skyscrapers.

Bankman seemed to squeeze his butt cheeks together as he walked. His slight body was compact with tension so that he looked like he was marching all the time. Interspersed across the length of the office, Persian rugs juxtaposed against the gleaming and perfect wood floor.

Sam looked out the window. Below he could see the people, small and indistinct like bugs in a rush.

Bankman sat behind his mammoth antique desk. There were photos of Bankman with the big four of Clinton, Obama, Cuomo, and de Blasio displayed on the engraved built-in shelf behind the desk.

"This Milagros case is tricky. The city is going to try to get this dismissed. Our lawsuit is based on our claim that Kevin Knowles was unfit or unstable. The city argues there is no proof of any of that." Bankman's gold tie bar was so taut around his neck that pieces of loose, splotchy skin from his chicken neck spilled over his collar.

"That's where you come in. We need you to dig up evidence on Kevin Knowles to show that the city knew or should have known that he was not suited to be a police officer, but they kept him on the job anyway."

"I used to work with Kevin in Narcotics, and then I worked with him for a while when I lived in Maplewood."

Bankman ran his index finger along the edge of the desk. His fingernails were polished clear and manicured to the quick. "Go back up there. Fish around and see if you can find some dirt on Knowles. Matt lives up there. See what the two of you can come up with."

He opened the drawer to the desk and took out a gleaming leather satchel that contained his checkbook.

"Here," he said as he wrote out a check and handed it to Sam.

It was for one thousand dollars.

"I'll pay that a day, and I'll pay for as many days as you think can be helpful to the case."

Sam liked the sound of that.

"Just so we understand ourselves. You work for me and not for Feldman. My office is not connected to Feldman's in any way. I know you were worried about a conflict. Don't, because there is none."

"Okay." Sam looked at the check again.

As if on cue, Matt appeared at the door.

"Don't put anything in writing until you speak with Matt first. Come back in five days and I'll pay you for that. Keep me posted." He walked over to the large fish tank that spanned the wall.

Bankman examined the glass on the fish tank and saw a spot. He walked over to his desk and removed a bottle of Windex and a paper towel from the draw. He bent down on his hands and knees and sprayed the glass and wiped it furiously with the paper towel. Afterwards, he stood and examined the glass to make sure he had gotten all of it. Matt and Sam watched him. Matt turned to Sam and arched his eyebrows, as if to say, *"What did I just tell you?"*

Sam followed Matt from the office. "I didn't know you moved to Maplewood."

"What a shitstorm we walked into with this. We just bought the house, and the whole town found out about the lawsuit. They think I'm suing Kevin, and everyone hates us."

They stood in the hallway between the two offices. Bankman closed his door.

"That can't be fun." When he lived in Maplewood, it was all cops and firemen and civil servants. It was Trump country. Only sixty miles from New York City, but it might as well have been another planet with a town filled with conservatives and right-to-lifers.

"Please, Sam, I hope you can come up with something on Kevin." Matt's features flushed and he clasped his stubby hands together like he was praying to Sam. "Bankman is all over me on this. If this case gets dismissed, it's going to be my ass."

"Nice of you to put the pressure on me." He felt certain that Matt was playing head games so they could get the most bang for the bucks they were paying him.

Matt shook his head. "I didn't mean it like that. It's just venting, Sam, that's all it is."

"Sure, no problem."

Matt was walking him out of the office. He turned to Sam and made sure Bankman's door was closed. He talked softly in Sam's ear. "Bankman just won another sixty-one-million-dollar verdict in the Bronx for a kid who became paraplegic after he jumped into a pool and hit his head on the bottom. He got a twenty-million-dollar fee, but he wants more. He's never satisfied."

“I guess that’s what it takes.” This Bankman seemed to be dripping in money.

When they reached the secretary’s station, Matt Prey turned abruptly. “Just do the best you can and I’m sure I’ll see you around.”

Sam waited for the elevators to take him to the lobby. No doubt they hired him because he knew Kevin and had lived in Maplewood. They were probably hoping that Kevin would see him as a friend, and this might make it easier to get the goods on Kevin.

He breathed a sigh of relief. In five days he would make five thousand dollars. He could pay his bills, eat something worth eating, and maybe put a little of it in the bank.

Chapter Seven
Sam Free

The first thing Sam saw when he left the lobby of Bankman's building was Frank's red Hyundai parked at the curb in front of the building. Nobody bothered Frank, even though he was parked on 34th Street in a no-parking tow-away zone, because he still looked like a cop on the job.

The wind had died down, and it wasn't as cold. Sam had forgotten that he had to do this with Frank, and he was pissed off. He did not want to go to the Bronx to try to find some crackhead. Reluctantly, he got into the car. "So, let's go."

Frank pulled away.

"After this, I don't want you bothering me anymore, Frank."

"I swear to God, Sam. After this, I promise I won't bother you anymore." He turned toward Sam and barely stopped again in time to avoid rear-ending another car.

"Oh my God." Sam used both his hands to brace himself against the dashboard for the crash that he thought was about to happen. "What the fuck? Please! You're not going to be happy until you kill me or kill somebody."

Christ. He wanted to get this over with. He switched the radio from the Latin station to the all-news station.

This just in. The grand jury of Bronx County has indicted Kevin Knowles, the police officer accused of shooting the unarmed super in a building in the Bronx, on manslaughter in the first degree.

"Kevin's screwed if he goes to trial with this in the Bronx. The people in the Bronx hate the cops. They'll convict his ass in ten minutes." Frank shook his head in agreement with himself. He had the same cauliflower ears he had since high school.

Sam wondered if Celeste Santiago was the DA who indicted the case.

There wasn't much traffic, and they got to the Bronx fast.

"Where's the building?"

"It's right here." Frank parked the car.

"That's it."

It was the red brick building on the corner of Bainbridge and Bedford Park with the red canopy that had the rips in it.

The stringent odor of ammonia cleared his nostrils as he followed Frank into the lobby. A stout man in overalls with a huge beer gut mopped the black and white tiled hallway.

His stomach was like a pouch on a kangaroo. He looked up as they entered.

"You remember me from the other day?" Frank asked.

"No."

"I came by looking for Sean Ferris. You told me his mom lives on the third floor, and she wasn't home. You remember now?"

The super leaned against the mop. "You cops?" He spoke broken English with an Eastern European accent. He was probably Albanian. They bought up a lot of buildings in the Bronx and hired their own.

"Used to be," Sam said. Frank hadn't told him that he had scouted out the building previously.

"I knew it. I can tell always. I was a cop in my country before I came here."

"Is the old lady home?" Frank smiled.

He didn't give a shit what the man with the mop did in his country before he came here. He could have been prime minister for all Frank cared.

"Who?"

"Sean's mom. Mrs. Ferris. Who else?" Frank lost the smile. He was getting impatient.

Sam wasn't sure if it was a language thing or the guy was just dense.

"I think she is. She lives in 3C."

It was a walkup. The marble stairs were spotless. Frank was winded when they reached the third floor. It was a small hallway in the shape of a triangle with three freshly painted black doors leading to each of the apartments.

"Frank, you're out of shape, man."

"Don't remind me. Since I moved to Florida, I stopped working out. Sure, my wife has me doing water aerobics, but that's for old farts and it don't help. Look at this fucking gut. Can you believe it?' Frank grabbed his stomach and banged on 3C.

"You're almost the size of the super. Did you see his gut? For fuck's sake, he could hide another body in there."

Sam continued, "You're fucking shameful. You should take a chapter from my book." He patted his stomach. "Since my wife moved out, I have been losing weight like mad, because I stopped eating. Have a little self-respect, man."

"Go fuck yourself."

An old lady dressed in a black coat and carrying a patent leather purse with gold snaps opened the door of 3C. She wore Uggs.

"Did we catch you going out?" Frank asked her.

She looked at the two of them. Mrs. Ferris was real proper-looking, like a Margaret Thatcher lookalike. Her brain was working overtime. She was trying to decide if she should shut the door and go back in and wait for the two goons to leave. Instead, she turned away from them furtively, shielding herself as she reached into her coat pocket with the faux fur collar for her keys and locked the door, and then, with her head down, she walked toward the stairs.

"Is Sean home?" Sam stood in front of her. He wanted to get this over with and get on with his day.

"I'm very busy." She spoke in a brogue, and continued to look down at the tiled floor. This neighborhood had been all Irish back in the day. Then there was the mass exodus to Yonkers and points north for the suburbs and good schools. What remained were these old timers. Stragglers who were too used to the Bronx and found the suburbs, where they needed to drive to get anywhere, not their cup of tea.

Mrs. Ferris looked up at Sam and Frank. There was no room for her to pass in the narrow hall.

"We're just here to see Sean."

She looked at them askance, as if she recognized them, and put her hand to her mouth and gasped. "You're the ones that locked him up, and then you come round asking for him? What are you bothering a poor old lady for? Is it to get your kicks?"

"We're not the cops, ma'am."

"Well, you could have fooled me." Mrs. Ferris paused to catch her breath. She fanned at her own face with her hand.

"Are you okay?"

"Fine. Just a touch of high blood pressure is all. Now, if you don't mind, I must be on my way to court for Sean right now. He is to see the judge today."

"What was he arrested for?' Sam thought that she was playing them with the defenseless old lady bit.

"How should I know? He called me and said he was in jail, and they're taking him to court today. He wanted me to post bail for him, but I don't have that kind of money, but I did promise him that I would be there." She seemed to look to them as if to say, "What choice do I have?" This was the hand I was dealt.

It probably wasn't the first time that Sean had been pinched.

"How 'bout we take you to court? We're going that way anyway," Frank said.

Sam couldn't believe Frank just made that offer. "I'm not going that way. Why don't you take her yourself? I got things to do." No way was he going to the Bronx Courthouse.

"Give me a break, Sam? Please. I told you, do this one thing for me and I'll be out of your hair. I won't bother you anymore."

What could he do? Throw a shit fit in front of the old lady? If he could just do this and not have to see Frank after today, it would be worth it, but that wasn't likely. Frank was like a headache Sam couldn't shake.

Mrs. Ferris followed them haltingly down the stairway.

"Do you need a hand?" Sam saw it was going to take forever for her to get down these three flights. At that age, if she slipped and broke a hip, she was a goner.

"I'm quite fine." She gripped the railing like she was descending into a precipice. With her other hand she carried the purse like a football, tightly against her side.

* * *

Frank drove up the hill on Bedford Park to catch the Concourse to the courthouse. He hit a large pothole dead on.

"Goodness gracious!" Mrs. Ferris squealed in the back seat as she flew in the air.

Sam turned just in time to see her airborne with legs spread, showing her pantyhose that reached to her thighs. "Are you okay?"

She ended up on her side with her face pushed into the seatback. "Fine, fine." Mrs. Ferris struggled to right herself and face forward, which she did, and her features turned crimson with the effort, and then she pulled her coat around herself and clung to her purse. She fanned herself with her free hand. "Oh dear."

"So sorry, lady, the suspension and springs in the back are shot." Frank surveyed her in the rear-view mirror and then shot a glance at Sam, arching an eyebrow.

"Slow down," Sam told him with clenched teeth.

When they arrived at the courthouse, Frank reached across Sam, opened the glove compartment, and removed an NYPD placard and placed it in the window. "I hope it still works."

They parked in front, the area restricted to law enforcement. "You hope it still works. Genius, they are going to see that it's the wrong year."

"You can't tell it's expired unless you look real close." It was the same color as the placard in the windshield of the car they parked next to, just a different year.

Sam helped Mrs. Ferris out of the back seat. He held her underneath the elbow.

She shook his arm off, brushed her coat off, and adjusted her hair.

Mrs. Ferris walked between Sam and Frank, and they entered the courthouse and waited on the line to pass through the manometers.

She checked the board in the lobby where the court's calendars were posted. She pointed to Sean's name with a stubby fingernail covered with chipped red nail polish. "His case is in Part 73 on the fifth floor."

* * *

The courtroom was packed. On the back wall, there was a clock with no hands. A young attorney with a bunch of files with "Legal Aid" written on them followed them into the courtroom.

Sam watched the young attorney try to enter the well through the waist-high swinging door.

"Not now, we're taking a verdict." The court officer who ran the bridge blocked his path.

"I got so many cases on today. You sure I can't get back there to see my clients while you guys take the verdict?" The legal aid's suit looked like he had slept in it.

"Is that like multi-tasking?" the court officer said. He had a shaved head and a gray Fu Manchu.

"Yeah, exactly."

"For Christ's sake!" The bridge man's pate had a sheen of sweat. "Counselor, how many times do I have to say it? Not right now, they're bringing down the defendant who's on trial." He shook his head and rolled his eyes in disbelief. "Like I told all your colleagues about a hundred times already, we'll call the calendar after we take the verdict, and then you can go back there and talk to your clients."

Sam and Frank followed Mrs. Ferris to the second row by the large window that overlooked the Grand Concourse below. Sam had to squeeze in next to her. She smelled like Ponds cold cream.

The court officer came from the door to the right of the bench with the defendant on trial. They led him to the table where his lawyer sat. Wearing gold wire rim glasses, he puffed out his chest and sat straight and confident as the court officers removed his cuffs. He mouthed words to some spectators and pulled his chair closer to his attorney. The ADA sat alone at counsel table.

"Quiet!" shouted the bridge man. "Come to order." The judge entered.

It was Fitzmorris. He was old when Sam started on the job. Now, thirty years later, he was hunched over with a cane, and he could barely make it from the robbing room and up the three steps that led to the bench.

The clerk in the bolo tie handed him a piece of yellow legal-size paper.

"We have a note from the jury." The judge's voice was clear and loud. "Court's exhibit one. We have reached a verdict." He paused and held the paper. His clerk approached and whispered something to him.

Just then, about fifteen extra court officers entered the courtroom and stood in the aisle. Five other court officers in the well formed a wall around the defendant and his lawyer. The rest stood blocking the entrance to the well.

That was never a good sign. Court officers always knew the verdict before it was read.

"Bring the jury in."

Another court officer knocked on the door to the left of the bench. "Jury entering."

They were not looking at the defendant. That was another bad sign.

"Mr. Foreman, has the jury reached a verdict?" Fitzmorris asked the old black man in the green button-down sweater who sat in the first seat of the box.

"We have, Your Honor."

"What is the verdict as to the one and only count in the indictment murder in the second degree?"

"Guilty."

Sam could hear the air let out of the courtroom like a beach ball with a leak.

The defendant put his forehead on the table.

"Oh my God, Lord Jesus!" From the back of the courtroom, a heavyset woman in a black woolen hat stood in the aisle and shrieked.

"He got what he deserves." someone from the other side of the courtroom shouted. Shouts of joy filled that area.

"Shut the fuck up."

It was the deceased's family against the defendant's. Some of the court officers stood in the aisle between them. Who knew what was going to happen if those two groups met outside the courthouse?

The weeping lady in the black woolen hat sank into her seat. She was too overcome to stand.

"Oh dear," Mrs. Ferris mumbled under her breath.

Sam didn't need this drama. He blamed Frank for bringing him here. After today, he had to get rid of Frank.

"We would like the jury polled," the defense attorney told the judge.

The defendant sat up.

It was terrible to see this. It wasn't like Sam was getting paid to be here.

"Poll the jury," the judge told the clerk.

"Your verdict must be unanimous. When I call your number and ask if your verdict as to this defendant is guilty, you must answer 'guilty' if that, in fact, is your verdict. Juror number one, is that your verdict?" the clerk asked.

"Guilty." They said it twelve times.

Afterwards, the jurors were led back to their room by the court officer.

This wasn't shit you see on TV. This was real blood and guts where people's lives were torn apart. As a cop, he had seen enough depravity for a lifetime; he didn't want to see any more.

"The defendant is remanded for sentence."

Handcuffed, with a court officer on each arm, the defendant bent over and his glasses fell. The clerk picked them up.

The judge sat there, not moving, and for a few minutes, it was completely quiet, like a moment of silence for the passing of this young perp, who was not going to see freedom until he was an old man, if he lived through the violence of his prison life.

Then, just like that, it was over, and the clerk taped the sign-in sheet to the stand on the rail for the attorneys to print their names, the names of their clients, and the number of the case on the court's calendar.

"Do you still got your ID and your badge?" Frank asked.

"Yeah, but it's expired. Why?"

"I want to talk to Sean in the pens." Frank stood. "Let's get back there before it gets too crowded."

"They're not going to let us in with expired IDs."

Frank waived him off. "They never look at the IDs. Just show him your old badge with your ID. We look like cops, that's what matters."

"No, Frank, we look like retired cops." Sam followed Frank into the well through the waist-high swinging doors. He might as well see this through.

Sure enough, they flashed their IDs and old badges at the court officer, and he nodded and didn't look at the IDs but looked at their badges instead. Fuckin' Frank was always right about shit like this.

They entered the door to the right of the judge's bench. The same door the defendant who was on trial came out of.

Sam remembered coming back here when he was on the job to interview perps or witnesses. Sometimes the witnesses in one case were perps in another. It was a dark stairwell crowded with handcuffed defendants waiting to be called into the courtroom with their lawyers. They squeezed past the bodies to the top of the stairs. There another corrections officer waved them through.

Back in the day, he was gung-ho about locking up the bad guys. It was his and Frank's mission to clean the streets of the riffraff.

Sam followed Frank past open holding cells filled with defendants sleeping on benches and on the floor waiting for their name to be called.

They passed an open area where inmates who had just come off the elevator waited, chained together.

Each morning, a caravan of blue school buses with wire mesh windows took them from Rikers, the Barge, or the Bronx House of Detention to the garage in the courthouse's basement, where they were packed into elevators and brought up here to the pens.

"Who do you need?" A CO at a desk sat with blue index cards that had all the information about the prisoner. Each time an inmate was brought to court the court officer filled in the next date the inmate had to be back on the back of the blue card. An inmate who had been back and forth to court many times had a worn-out blue card, whereas the newer bodies' blue cards were fresh.

"Sean Ferris," Frank said.

He looked through his index cards and stopped at the name. "Sign the book."

Sam looked over Frank's shoulder to see what name Frank might make up to sign in as. Frank's entry was illegible gibberish. That made sense. No one was going to be able to decipher it, and so no one could claim that he made up a name. Sam did the same.

"Ferris, Sean!"

"Yo," someone answered from the cells.

The CO pointed down the narrow hallway to the interview booths. Bars separated them from the side the defendant would enter from.

What the fuck was he doing here with Frank, acting like cops, showing expired IDs to talk to a prisoner? How many laws had they broken? If they got caught, there was no telling what a mess it was going to be. They had reached the point of no return now, and there was no going back.

Sean stepped through a door on the perp's side of the booth.

Plexiglas filled the open space between the bars.

Sean hunched over and surveyed them with empty blue eyes. "Who are you?"

"We're looking for Nooney."

"I don't know no Nooney." Sean's black hair was cut in a buzz. His hairline began at his eyebrows. He had a thick Adam's apple, with a scar that ran the length of his chin up his cheek to his earlobe.

"Yes, you do." Frank stood up from his stool.

"No, I don't."

"Asshole, I'm Nooney's uncle."

"Oh. I thought youse were cops."

"We know you hung out with Nooney."

"I ain't seen Nooney since before I been locked up."

"What for?"

"Huh?"

"What're you pinched for?"

"Strangulation."

"What?"

"Yeah. Strangulation is a crime. Ain't that some shit? Next thing you know, punching someone in the face will be a separate crime from assault." Sean shook his head in agreement with himself.

"This one's a real genius," Frank said under his breath. "Who'd you strangle?"

"My girlfriend."

"Did you kill her?"

"God forbid." Sean crossed himself. "It was just a misunderstanding that got out of hand is all."

"I'll bet."

"Were you in the courtroom when that kid got convicted?"

They ignored the question.

"I heard he had an airtight alibi." Sean leaned forward and grabbed the bars like he was sharing important information.

"Alibi defense is always tough. It doesn't work most of the time." Sam grimaced and shook his head. "Most idiots think, I'll just have someone say I wasn't there and that will get me off."

"Do you remember the last time you saw Nooney?"

Sean put his hands together. Resting his elbows on the counter, he rocked back and forth. "The last time I seen Nooney. The last time I seen Nooney. . ." A light seemed to go on inside his crackhead brain. "The last time I seen Nooney he was real burned up about something." Sean paused again.

"Burned up about what?"

"Afraid, kinda. He said... He said, if anything happens to him, I should look at his phone." Sean smiled like a little boy delighted with himself that he had remembered.

"Well, did you look at his phone?"

"No. I forgot about it."

"Do you know where his phone is?"

"Did something happen to Nooney?"

"He got shot."

"Oh shit. Is he okay?"

"No, he ain't." Frank held back a sob.

"Do you know where Nooney's phone is?" Sam was afraid that Frank's emotions about losing his nephew were going to get the best of him, and that Frank would break down.

"He gave it to me to hold. It's in the pocket of my hoodie in my room. Oh my God, oh my God . . ." Sean's Adam's apple was going up and down, and he was rocking and saying it over and over again. He began to blubber. It had begun to sink in that Nooney was dead.

"CO." Sam felt bad for Sean. He needed to get out of there.

When they returned to the courtroom, Sam had to knock on the door to the courtroom for the court officer to let him in. It took a while, and the feeling of being locked behind the door with all the perps made him anxious. Sam knew firsthand what it was like to be actually locked up. He never wanted to go through that again.

Mrs. Ferris was still in the spot by the window.

Sean was brought down, and he stood next to the legal aid, whose suit pants were so long they bunched up around his ankles and dragged onto the floor. He stood there next to Sean and shuffled through all those files until he found Sean's.

Sean towered over the legal aid. With his hands cuffed, he hunched his shoulders so that he wouldn't appear so huge and menacing. He was still sobbing from learning of Nooney's demise.

Up at the bench, the skinny legal aid and the tiny brunette assistant district attorney whispered with the judge. They turned and surveyed Sean. They must have felt sorry for him because he was crying.

In court, everything seemed to move in slow motion. Sam was wasting his time here. He needed to get going if he was going to start earning that money from Bankman.

Sean blew a kiss at his mother and mouthed, "I love you, Mom."

Mrs. Ferris let out a sob and reached into her purse for a tissue. Here we go. This scene in the court between mother and son went on every time he got pinched, which seemed to be a pretty regular event.

Finally, they brought Sean back to the pens. Sam held the door for Mrs. Ferris, and they followed her out of the courtroom.

"We can give you a ride back."

"I could take a cab." Mrs. Ferris' eyes were red from weeping.

"Sean told us that he had my nephew's phone in his room." Frank led her gently by the elbow toward the elevator bank.

"Yes?" She didn't understand what Frank was telling her. She looked into his face, and her eyes were glazed and unfocused.

"You know, my nephew was murdered." Frank was trying to snap her out of it.

"Oh dear."

"Did you know Nooney?"

"Nooney?" It sounded funny the way she said it in her accent. Like a character from a *Monty Python* movie. "Nooney?" she said it twice.

"There might be something on that cell phone that could help us find his killer. Can we get it from Sean's room, and we'll be out of your hair?"

"Sean told you this?"

"Yeah, just now when we went to see him in the pens."

Sam wasn't so sure that she was going to let them back in her apartment, but she followed them back to the car.

* * *

The ammonia smell was gone from the lobby. Mrs. Ferris had to rest on the landing between the floors in her walkup.

"Too old for these bloody steps," she mumbled, and fumbled inside her purse for her keys.

When she turned the key and the lock opened, she hesitated.

"They shot my nephew's eyes out," Frank said. "There could be something in that phone that would help find the animal that did it."

She sighed and opened the door, and let Sam and Frank enter. "Sean's room is the second door on the left."

There was a rosary with a small wooden cross that hung from the coat rack in the foyer.

In Sean's room, an AC/DC poster hung on one wall. On the opposite wall was a Jimmy Hendrix poster. Above the bed, Jennifer Lopez in a bikini had a smoky stare. "The girlfriend must have loved that one."

Frank went through the clothes in the closet, feeling the pockets of the hoodies and the jackets that hung from the hangers.

On the other wall there was a window that overlooked the alley below. Sam stepped around a lava lamp next to Sean's box spring. There was probably a crack pipe hidden under his mattress.

"I think this is it." Frank showed him a cell phone with a crack in its screen. He put it in his pocket.

They came out of Sean's bedroom, and the three of them stood in the foyer.

"Ever since he's been a little boy," Mrs. Ferris broke the awkward silence. "Ever since he was a little one, there was always something not right about Sean."

She walked toward the door. "You know, he's my daughter's kid."

It stuck. Mrs. Ferris struggled to open it.

He and Frank stepped into the hall. Funny how Nooney and Sean were both raised by grandmothers. That must suck for the grandparents. You're old and you brought up your kids, and now you've got to bring up your grandkids. Poor lady had to go to court in the South Bronx for her grandson. Why have kids if you can't take care of them? Sam thought about his kids, Tamara and Justin. When was the last time he had talked to either one of them? Did they talk to Iris more than they talked to him? Justin never came home from college, and Tamara lived with one of her professors in the East Village. Just now, he missed them only the way a parent can miss their children. He should call them. They should call him.

"How are we going to figure out the password to open it?" Frank studied the cell phone in his hand as they descended the steps.

"I hope you're going to give me a ride back."

"Of course. I'll take you right now." Frank tried to punch in different numbers and letters.

"What about his birth year? Try that?" He was never going to find the code. It was like a needle in a haystack.

"Nooney was twenty-three or twenty-four."

"Try 1993." That was Justin's birth year.

"That's it."

The phone came to life. It was cued to start playing a video. They stood in the lobby of Mrs. Ferris' building. Sam looked over Frank's shoulder.

On the small, cracked screen, a large man with folds of skin on the back of his neck held a two-by-four. He swung the plank from behind his head and smashed it against a figure, who was balled up like a fetus on the cement floor. There was another large man who was kicking the balled-up figure on the floor. The screams from the figure on the floor were piercing and primal, like the sound an animal would make if its paw was caught in the steel jaws of a trap, its limb slowly being severed by the pressure. It made the hair on the back of his neck stand up.

"Holy shit." Frank grimaced and clenched his teeth, almost like he didn't want to look but couldn't turn away.

When the board in the man's hand broke from the force of the blows, he used the piece of wood with the sharp, splintered end as a spear to stab at the figure on the floor. The figure rolled and twisted his body each time he tried to poke him with it.

"Where are your pig buddies now?" one of the men asked.

The video through the cracked lens was grainy. He couldn't make out any features of the men. The figure was wearing a bubble parka, which probably helped cushion the blows, and he covered his face.

The men paused. He could hear they were winded. The man with the stick bent over, his hands on his knees, trying to catch his breath. After a few moments he was able to stand straight again, and he grabbed one of the legs of the victim and pointed to the other man to take the other leg.

They dragged the body down the hall. The shoes were pulled off. They ripped the pants, parka, and flannel shirt off. The two men kneeled over their victim and wrapped his hands and feet in duct tape. There was an old Persian rug spread out on the floor.

"Oh no." Sam watched as they dragged him onto it and rolled him up in it. Who was videotaping this? This was sick.

They carried the rug with the body in it down the hall, through a hole punched into the wall, and outside. The video panned to the trail of blood on the basement floor.

The video recorded them on the street. He thought he recognized the location, but it could be anywhere in the Bronx.

"Play it back."

"It's hard to take."

"Pause it when you get to the street." Over Frank's shoulder, the light in the lobby was good, but he still couldn't make out what street it was. The top half of the sign on the corner was cut off.

"Why were they beating the shit out of him?" Frank asked.

"You can't see any of their faces."

"Do you recognize the location?"

They studied the snippet of the video that was paused. It had that brief view of the street.

"I can't tell. It looks familiar, but I can't tell."

"Looks like a murder."

"Pig buddies. What were they talking about?"

"Was he a cop?"

"It's hard to tell."

"Why would Nooney have this video on his phone? Did he record this?"

"I'm going to try to enhance it." Frank started the car. "You want me to drop you at your crib?"

"Yeah, and email me a copy of the video."

Chapter Eight
Sam Free

He was so full of hope when they first moved up county to the 'burbs. The memories flooded his mind's eye as he drove up the Taconic Parkway to Maplewood. It had been five years since he had been back.

It was going to be a fresh start for Sam, Iris, and Justin. When Justin had gotten beaten up at school, he and Iris had decided that they needed to get him out of that high school and away from the Bronx. Things were bad on the job, and the Maplewood Sherriff's Office had offered him an investigator position. It was a sweet gig. He thought there was no crime up here.

The apartment buildings faded as he went further north in the minivan.

Then the bottom fell out. He got pinched and brought back to the Bronx. Sam pushed those memories away. He was ashamed of them. That was all in the past. Now things seemed to be getting better. At least he had some money coming in.

He crossed over the bridge, and silver specks dotted the green water in the Croton Reservoir. The minivan's engine strained to get up the hill past the Yorktown exit. When was he going to be able to afford a newer car? The next exit was Route 6 and Maplewood.

Iris had hated it up here. Happy wife, happy life. Miserable wife, shitty life.

Who knew what would have happened if he and Iris had let Justin tough it out in the Bronx? It wouldn't have been good. Justin wasn't that kind of kid. Sam would've fought all of those punks to the death.

What a mess he had made of things. It was all in an effort to make things better, but no good deed goes unpunished.

Oh, fuck it. No sense in being a Monday morning quarterback with how things would've worked out if this or that had happened.

Kevin Knowles was going to wonder why Sam was all of a sudden coming up here and snooping around. He wasn't going to get the time of day. That was for certain. The thousand dollars a day was a lifeline he couldn't give up. Fuck it. If Bankman wanted him to poke around up here, that's what he would do, but it was going to be a big waste of time.

Kevin must have returned to Bronx Narcotics. There was no real action up here. Kevin loved to chase and lock up the bad guys.

Back in the day, the only way to get the gold detective shield was to go through Narcotics. The buys and busts were dangerous work. Kevin was good undercover. With his pockmarked, thin face, Kevin looked like a stoner from upstate coming to the Bronx to score.

On the GPS, Kevin's development was a couple of lefts on the winding country roads off Route 6. Sam had been to Kevin's house a couple of times.

He was a couple of years older than Kevin. When Kevin was first transferred to Narcotics, Dobbsy was the lieutenant running the squad. Kevin was like a puppy dog. He did whatever Dobbsy wanted, and Dobbsy was as crooked as they come.

Brian Dobbs took them all under his wing. They were his goons—McBride, Ryan, Frank Cortez, Sam, and Kevin. They all followed Dobbsy's lead and stole the drugs and money from the dealers. Dobbsy taught them all his secrets of the street. They learned how not to get caught, and they never did.

Sam didn't dip into the dealers' cookie jar like the others. He didn't steal back then. Of course, later on he lifted a bag of cash from a wise guy named Tommy Gulagi, and that was his undoing.

He remembered the blue split level on the cul-de-sac. A gray Explorer was pulling out of the long driveway. He recognized the driver as Sue, Kevin's wife. Sam got out of the minivan and waited for her by the mailbox. As she approached, he waved.

Sue rolled down the window. "Sam, what are you doing up here?" She had worry lines around her mouth.

"Not too much."

"Kevin isn't home." Her eyes were puffy and bloodshot.

"Mom, who's that?" There was a little boy about seven or eight sitting next to her.

"That's Daddy's friend. His name is Sam. You remember Charlie?" The little boy's nose was running, and he wiped it with the back of his hand and then cleaned his hand against his jacket.

"Hi Charlie." He remembered that Iris used to have that same kind of look about her in the morning after she'd taken her cocktail of Xanax and Lunesta, the night before, and washed it down with a big juice glass of merlot. What was it about living in the suburbs that made these women need to sedate themselves? Funny thing about it was that when Sam and Iris returned to the Bronx, Iris stopped the self-medication.

"I forgot my bookbag."

"Oh jeez." She rolled her big blues. "You'd forget your head if it wasn't attached to you."

Sam laughed. He remembered Sue from high school. She went to the all-girls Catholic school. The name escaped him. Those girls were a wild bunch. They were always very loud, screaming, shouting, and trying to create as much chaos as they could. When the weather got warm, he would run into them cutting school at Orchard Beach. There was crazy Kathy, who lived over by Ehrings on Broadway, and there was Sheila, who was from Bailey. The three of them used to roll up their green plaid Catholic school skirts to minis and drink beer and smoke joints on the empty lifeguard stands overlooking the Long Island Sound.

"I'm sorry, Mom. I thought I put it in the car."

"It's all right, Charlie. We'll go back and get it." Sue put the Explorer in reverse and paused there.

"Don't you have a little girl too?" He wanted to keep her talking.

"Erica." She grinned. "She takes the bus."

"How's Kevin doing?"

"He's doing good. He's in therapy."

"Therapy?" Kevin didn't seem the type. Unless the department was making him go.

"You didn't know?" She wrinkled her nose and squinted at him.

"Of course, I heard, it's been all over the news." Sue's hands fidgeted on the wheel, like she was playing notes on a keyboard. She looked like she had let the cat out of the bag. "I'm sure it's eating him up."

"It's hard on all of us."

There was a pause in the conversation. Was she talking about something else other than the shooting?

"I gotta go, Sam."

Before she met Kevin, they liked each other. He wondered why he and Sue never went out. "How's your mom doing?"

"She's good."

"Does she still live over by Woodlawn?" They lived across from the cemetery. He remembered Big Bill, her dad.

For forty years, Big Bill Nolan worked for the MTA driving the Number One bus from 231st Street over to the Concourse downtown to Yankee Stadium and back again. Sam never had to pay when Big Bill was driving.

Once, a punk with a shaved head was slapping his girlfriend around at the bus stop on Kingsbridge. Bill got off the bus to break it up, and the thug punched Bill in the face, knocking off his glasses. Big Bill carried a flat lead Billy Jack in the pocket of his MTA jacket. He slapped the kid across his face with it. The kid was left there holding pieces of his face and teeth in his hands. Bill picked up his glasses and drove away.

Almost six months to the day after his last run on the Number One, when he retired, Bill dropped dead in his sleep.

Chapter Nine
Kevin Knowles

When he neared the end of his run, Kevin liked to slow his pace to preserve the high he felt as the endorphins rushed through his bloodstream. Today he had to cut it short because of his appointment with his therapist. He checked his wristwatch. He had enough time to circle the lake before he headed home.

It was warm, and he jogged in and out of the patches of fog. It was too bad that he couldn't just blow off this session, but they wouldn't let him back on the job until she cleared him again to return. Until that happened, Marion, his shrink, was his best friend.

Even though it was warm out, on the lake the ice fishermen huddling over their lines resembled statues in the mist. Jeez, they could easily fall through with all the melting that had gone on these last few days. They must know how thick the ice was. Maybe they measured it.

The woods on the other side of the road that bordered the lake were gray. The forest was empty without leaves, and he could see far into the brush.

A van slowed down and passed him. Always the cop, Kevin studied it. It looked like that old piece of shit van that Sam Free drove.

He hadn't thought of Sam Free in a while. Kevin quickened his pace to get a better look at the vehicle, but it took off.

Maybe Celeste Santiago sent some cops up here to do surveillance on him. After all those years that they had worked together, now she was going to stab him in the back and try to throw him in jail.

He needed not to think about that skinny bitch Santiago. It would ruin his run.

Jogging always cleared his mind. It helped to get him out of the house and away from Sue and the kids.

Instead of slowing down, he ran faster just to see if he still had that kick. His breathing grew labored and his legs felt heavy. He could see that he didn't have it anymore. Sure, his body felt in tune, but he couldn't shift into that extra gear that once allowed him to run four-minute miles. Those days were long gone. He was only a fraction of the runner he once was. At one point they thought he could challenge the Kenyans in the Olympics.

Maybe he would just blow off his session today? No, that was not a good idea. It was such a pain to get down to her office. He called it "therapist row" on the west side at Ninety-Third and Riverside Drive. How many shrinks were located in those few square blocks in the area of West End Avenue. All the talking made Kevin uncomfortable. Marion, the shrink lady, wanted him to get in touch with his feelings. He hated that mushy shit.

Kevin was in touch with his feelings, but not the ones he discussed with Marion. She didn't know anything about him. He made her think she did, but she didn't have a clue who he really was, what he had done, and what he was capable of. If Marion knew, she would make sure that they never let him back on the street again. Kevin wasn't worried about Marion. She had cleared him the first time to go back, and he would convince her that everything was fine.

Kevin figured out that Marion liked him to talk about Charlie and Erica. At first, he was curious as to why she brought up his kids in their sessions. When he went to the bathroom and looked at the photos, he realized that she lived here, that this was her apartment too, and there were no pictures of kids. She didn't have kids of her own, and that was why she liked for him to talk about his own kids. He could see her eyes light up when he did. Almost like she was living through his kids. He tried to use this to his advantage.

He wanted to tell Marion that she couldn't know certain things until she had kids of her own. She would never understand that your kids see you differently from everyone else. He would never tell her this, because he wanted to keep her on his good side. She wasn't bad, just a nice older lady who had no idea what made him tick.

Although he had to admit that the whole therapy thing was not entirely useless, because it did help his marriage. Talking about his relationship with Sue made him understand certain things that he wouldn't have otherwise.

Cops don't keep regular hours because the bad guys don't. He would get home late, and Sue and the kids would already be asleep. It was like that for weeks and months when he was working on a big case. A cop's life was hard to reconcile with a civilian. And his affair with Sylvia also didn't help his marriage.

Oh, sweet Sylvia. He met her when he busted her dimwitted shit-for-brains brother Herman. He was a crackhead who was pitching for some Dominican crew.

Narcotics had taken down the whole block, and as they were loading up all the douche bags into the van to transport them to Central Booking, Sylvia came down the block. She ran straight to him with her long black hair, dark eyes like coal, and her twenty-five-year-old body that never had any kids.

"Let him go, Loco. Can't you see he's slow on account some kids jumped him and piped him? Look at his head, can't you see he's got a metal plate up there?"

She was right. Herman did have a wicked scar where they put the metal plate in his head.

They hooked up for a while. She liked to smoke weed before. There was a tattoo with an arrow through a heart over her left breast.

She called him whenever Herman got busted, and he made sure that Herman got a desk appearance ticket and didn't have to go through the system and be in lockup for at least twenty-four hours before he saw a judge. Kevin was Herman's insurance policy on the street.

At least all this time off from the job gave him some time to get back into the running. He finished his lap around the lake and headed home. This time of day, the roads were empty. He reached the entrance to his development, and he was tempted to pass it and continue. He wanted to keep running and not look back.

He wasn't sure if Sue knew about Sylvia. He and Sue had been together for so long, she knew what he was going to say before he said it himself. He was that way with her too. Who knew? Maybe she did know, but she denied it to herself.

Kevin still loved Sue. They had a lot of good times when they first met.

Marion, the shrink, wanted Sue to come to the sessions. Kevin put his foot down on that. He didn't want Sue coming because she would know that Kevin was just feeding Marion a line so that she would clear him to return, even though the department wasn't going to let him back on the street while the manslaughter charges were pending. He had to beat that case to stay on the job.

At the shrink's suggestion, he and Sue even had a date. Sue's sister came up from the Bronx, and they went to the movies and dinner.

He was Mr. Dad. He picked up Erica from the bus stop, went to those stupid fucking PTA meetings and the ballet recitals. He was bored out of his mind. He even coached basketball and baseball. He had to lay it on thick with the therapist so she could clear him again. The last therapy session went so well that Marion the shrink told him she was going to release him from therapy in two weeks.

What he needed to do was take care of his business and do some digging to get to the bottom of it all. That was why he itched to get back to work with the crew on the streets. He had gotten some justice, but there was more work to do.

Except for Dobbsy, who lived in town, not one of the guys from their squad checked in on him—not Frank, not McBride or Ryan, not even Sam. He and Dobbsy coached the local boys in basketball and baseball. Dobbsy retired from Narcotics after he got run over by UPS truck. It happened when Dobbsy was chasing a pitcher on East Tremont. Afterwards, Dobbsy lay in the street, his left leg inert like a puppet's, attached at a weird angle like it wasn't part of his body.

Fucking Dobbsy was the only person he knew who could turn a mishap into a fortune.

He received three-quarter-pay pension from the department on account of his accident and a seven-figure settlement from UPS. With the settlement, he bought a bunch of buildings and just sat back and collected rent.

Kevin walked the last block to his house. That he could go to jail behind all of this scared the shit out of him. He hired Gold because everyone said how good he was. Gold needed to move his case out of the Bronx. A Bronx jury was never going to give him a fair trial.

Kevin punched in the code to open the garage door.

He was hopeful it would all work out in the end and that this was just a bump in the road along the way. After all, hadn't he made it this far.

Chapter Ten
Brian Dobbs

Junior missed the bus and Dobbs drove him to school. Along the route, mothers lingered at their mailboxes in the unusually mild winter morning. He noticed a woman with thick red hair and pendulous, braless breasts in a T-shirt and gray sweats that said "Pink" on her ample, shapely butt. She smoked a cigarette like it was her last, puffing on it with all her might and blowing clouds of smoke while she laughed with the other women. They were stuck in the house all winter and horny as rabbits. Randy bitches. He smiled to himself.

"How 'bout we stop at Ralph's and get a bacon, egg, and cheese?" Junior was his spitting image at age eight.

"You'll be late for school."

"We don't do anything first period except take attendance and hear announcements. Come on, Dad! I love the bacon, egg, and cheese they make at Ralph's. Please!"

"Okay. I could use some coffee. But we have to go quick, Bri." It was good that Brian had an appetite. His leg felt better today. It was always worse in the cold winter months, where it hurt most right where the pins that held the bone together connected.

The nice weather made Dobbs think about baseball. "When do catchers and pitchers report?"

Consumed with texting, Junior ignored Dobbsy.

"It's got to be soon." Brian Dobbs answered his own question. He remembered when he was on the job in the Bronx, the sign on top of Yankee Stadium announced the start of spring training.

Chapter Eleven
Sam Free

Sam had to whiz bad. He found a parking spot right in front of Ralph's. He had taken the road from the lake into town. He pulled into a spot in front of Ralph's. He wasn't going to make it back to the Bronx if he didn't stop to take a leak. He was a regular at Ralph's when he lived up here. Besides the pizzeria and the diner on Route 6, Ralph's, the luncheonette right next to the Sheriff's Office and across Main Street from the American Legion hall, was the only place in Maplewood to eat.

When he entered the greasy spoon, the hunchback cashier lady surveyed him. Sam remembered her. The place smelled like bacon, coffee, and pancakes. Sam remembered that the hunchback lady also doubled as the transcriber for proceedings on Thursday nights when the town court was held in the American Legion hall. Ralph was behind the counter pouring coffee for those sitting there. Ralph, who looked like Mr. Rogers and wore the same sweater, doubled as the town judge. Maplewood was only sixty miles from New York, but it was another universe. Up here, there was no requirement that the judge be a lawyer. It was scary for those who got pinched up here, especially if you were black or brown. Civil rights for those accused of crimes didn't exist in these parts.

In the dining area in front of the window that looked onto Main Street, Sheriff Leland Crawford and his two young deputies sat. They were big and beefy. Crawford's back stiffened when Sam looked over at him. Not a good sign. Crawford mumbled something to them, and they turned and looked at Sam. They continued talking and smiling and laughing as they looked at him. He didn't like this vibe he was getting. It felt like they were thinking of kicking the shit out of him. The bad blood that he had left behind was still there.

He needed to take a piss and get the hell out of here before the rednecks decided to act out what they were thinking.

"Hi," the waitress said. She rocked from side to side as she limped toward him from behind the counter, dragging her right leg behind. She had puffy bumps of flesh under her white pantyhose.

"Regular coffee to go," he told her, and went to the men's room in the back. He turned to look at Crawford and the deputies, still snickering and eyeballing him. He wanted to make sure that the two of them didn't follow him to the men's room. Sure, he could take care of himself, but he didn't want to get into a brawl with these two mammoths. They were a lot younger than he was.

Crawford hadn't changed a bit. He had that same Teddy Roosevelt Rough Riders look, with the trademark mustache. The waitress brought Crawford's table their breakfast, and thankfully their attention was diverted.

Brian Dobbs was at the counter when he returned. Dobbsy turned to him and smiled. "Sammy, my brother." They hugged.

Dobbsy's straight blond hair was now almost white. He had slack skin that hung off his face like a bulldog.

He surveyed Sam with beady blue eyes that missed nothing.

Sam gave the waitress some bills, took his coffee, and headed for the door. The deputies were hunched over their eggs, flapjacks, home fries, sausage, and toast. Shit. Dobbs followed him out.

"Come 'ere, come 'ere." Dobbs motioned for Sam to follow him to a brand-new Cadillac SUV. "Check this out." He opened the driver's door and handed an egg sandwich wrapped in tin foil to a little boy in the passenger seat. The car still had that new-car smell.

The little boy had Dobbsy's beady blue eyes. He took a large bite, chewed with his mouth open, and surveyed Sam. "You remember Junior?" He reached in and ruffled his hair. The little boy pulled away. "Be careful not to get anything on the seat, Bri."

He turned back to Sam and stood between Sam and the minivan. "I heard you got jammed up bad. You okay?"

"That was a while ago. I'm good."

"That's good, Sammy."

"How you doing, Brian?" Sam saw that Dobbs wanted Sam to ask him that.

"I'm doing real good. You remember when that UPS truck hit me. I think you were still with Narcotics when it happened. I got a two-million-dollar settlement."

"No shit." People always lied when they said how much they got out of their lawsuits, just like they lied about getting laid.

"I had three surgeries, and I still got hardware in my leg. Almost lost my fucking leg." He looked down at the leg subconsciously. "So what brings you up here?"

"I stopped by to see Kevin."

"About what?"

Sam didn't answer. "I got to go, Brian." He stepped around him and walked toward the van.

"Don't tell me you're working for that scum bag Matt Prey and that bloodsucker Bankman. Jeez, ain't Kevin been through enough?"

Sam turned. What was he talking about? Sam wanted to ask him. What had Kevin been through? It had to be something else? It wasn't just the shooting. He got that from talking to Sue and now to Dobbs.

"Dad!" the little boy yelled. "I'm gonna be late for school. We got to go, Dad!"

"People don't understand us. On the job–what we saw, what we been through. We'd be criminals if we weren't cops." He guffawed and slapped Sam playfully on the shoulder. This was the same bullshit line Dobbs fed them when they were on the squad. He brainwashed them with this line of crap so they would buy into his belief that it was their right as cops to enjoy the spoils of the streets.

After all, they were the ones who risked their lives to rid the world of scum.

"Say it ain't so, Sammy. Don't be so serious. I'm just kidding. But the rules for cops like you and me are different. You don't want to admit it, but it's true. Being a cop is more like . . ."

"A religion than a job," Sam finished the sentence for Dobbs, his former lieutenant. "I got to get going, Brian."

"Yeah, good to see you, Sammy. Don't forget what we talked about."

"Dad, we got to go!"

"One second, Junior." Dobbs paused. "We're all in this together to the end. We all have each other's backs to the very end."

He watched Dobbsy limp into the driver's seat and pull away, and still he could feel Crawford's and his crew's eyes on him from inside Ralph's.

In the minivan, on the way to the Parkway, he sipped his coffee and remembered all the buy-and-bust meetings where they would plan which locations to send the undercover in with Photostatted money, and then the backup team would recover the pre-recorded buy money from the seller with the matching stash. Most of the time the undercover who went in to buy the drugs was Kevin Knowles. After they busted all the players, they would resell the stash and split the money. He always told himself that he didn't share in the profits, and that made it okay. He just looked the other way when the others did it. It didn't matter. He was just as guilty as them.

Chapter Twelve
Brian Dobbs

"Got your lunch money?" Dobbsy and Junior inched along in the long traffic queue of school buses and other parents whose kids missed the bus to get to the school's drop-off spot. It was a madhouse of kids. Some of them had stripped to T-shirts in the warm sunshine of the January thaw. It was a short break from the bleak winter.

Dobbs thought again of baseball. "I think the baseball team is gonna be better than last year." He was the commissioner of the Little League and got to pick the best kids.

"Well, our basketball team sucks." Little Brian was watching the action in the parking lot ahead. "Do we have to have Charlie Knowles on our team again?"

"You know his dad, Kevin, is my friend. When I was a cop, we worked together."

"The kid's a weirdo, Dad. Couldn't we take one of the other dads to coach with you?"

"I don't want to talk about it. Charlie is gonna be on the team. Stop your whining. I'm not gonna kick Charlie off the team 'cause you don't like him." They reached the drop-off point.

The little boy mumbled something under his breath, slid off the seat, slammed the door, and joined the group of kids entering the school.

Dobbs followed the line of vehicles as they exited the school grounds. Junior was spoiled because he was an only child. He and Debby should have had another kid. It was too late for all of that.

For one thing, Dobbs, with his bum leg, was too old to be chasing a baby. And besides, Debby wasn't that into kids. Of course, she loved little Brian. Doesn't every mom love her kids? It was just that as soon as Brian was two, she shipped him off to daycare. She told him that "she needed her life back."

He stopped at the light at the intersection of the school road and Route 6. He opened the console between the two front seats and searched for the small airport bottle of Jack Daniels he stashed there. It wasn't there. Debby had gotten rid of it. She was always searching for his stash of booze and then pouring it out.

Oh fuck, he could really use a taste. He opened the compartment in the ceiling of the Cadillac. It was used to hold sunglasses. There it was, like a breath of fresh air; she hadn't found the tiny bottle of Jim Beam he had hidden up there.

He emptied it in one gulp and used the back of his hand to wipe his mouth. It took the edge off. He needed a few more drinks, but that was all he had. He'd have to stop at the liquor store one town over, because if he bought his booze in Maplewood some loose-lipped fuck would get word of it and then it would be all over town. Debby was all over him to go to AA. She thought that he was a raving alcoholic because he had a few drinks to deaden the pain in his bum leg.

He wished that she would just let him drink. After all, he wasn't hurting anybody.

Dobbs' cell phone was vibrating in the breast pocket of his work shirt. He needed to get to Brewster and make sure the boiler was fixed in the multi-family he owned there. Then he had to go to the Bronx to make sure the leak in the ceiling was fixed in the building he owned on Bruckner. On and on, his list of tasks was never-ending. Unfortunately, Dobbs discovered that being a landlord wasn't just about collecting rent; there was a lot of bullshit to go along with it.

He didn't want to go home to Debby either. Her latest project was redoing the kitchen, and the house was filled with brochures of different tiles, cabinets, kitchen fixtures, and God knows what else. If she smelled liquor on his breath, she would have a shit fit.

Even in this warm span, from a distance, the fishermen on the lake still looked frozen onto their stools. What was the point of freezing your ass off waiting for a bite. That couldn't be fun. He hoped the ice had gotten too thin.

Chapter Thirteen
Sam Free

"I'm getting nowhere up there," Sam said. He watched Matt Prey bite into a foot-long chicken parm wedge with urgency. His cramped office smelled like a pizzeria. "They're suspicious, and why wouldn't they be? I haven't lived there in years. And now Kevin is in trouble, and I show up." It was stupid for them to send him up there, but why did he give a shit? It was a day's pay.

Matt nodded knowingly between bites. He looked flushed. The back of his neck was red, and where the hair met the collar of his shirt, there was sweat. There were large half-moons under his pits.

"You okay, Matt?"

Matt took a long swig from the liter of Coke. A loud ensuing belch followed. "Sorry." He punched himself in the chest. "Yeah, Sam, I'm a little stressed. I can't wait until this case is finished." He looked around the blotter for something and then found it. "Here." Prey handed him a check in the amount of five thousand dollars. "Bankman wants you to take Millie Santos to Poughkeepsie to attend the pre-trial proceeding. It looks good to have the bereft widow show up to court. That will cover you for five more days."

"Why Poughkeepsie?" Sam studied the check. This was turning into a sweet gig.

"They're moving the trial," he said as he placed the uneaten end of the hero on the wax paper. He dabbed at his mouth with the corner of the napkin he had tucked in his collar. "Gold made a motion to Fitzmorris, asking to move the trial upstate because he claimed that Kevin Knowles couldn't possibly get a fair trial in the Bronx." Matt inspected his white shirt to make sure that he wasn't wearing any of the hero. "Not that I give a shit," Matt added.

"No shit. Why, just because Bronx jurors hate cops?" Sam had experienced firsthand how the people of the Bronx despised the cops and vice versa. The relationship between the community and the police force was a shit fest.

Matt laughed. "Especially tall, skinny white cops like Kevin." He looked down at the papers scattered across the desk. "I saw him the other day at the gas station."

"Kevin?"

"He's not a psycho or anything, is he?"

"No, I don't think so." Kevin was no more of a psycho than any other NYPD cop might be, after working on the streets of the South Bronx for all these years and seeing the awful things he saw. Speaking from his own experience, seeing the horrible things people did to one another, changed Sam for the worse. "It's the city you're really suing. All cops get sued. It was an accident." If that's all it was, but after talking to Sue and Dobbsy, he couldn't shake the feeling that there was something else going on with Kevin.

"Fitzmorris was only too happy to wash his hands of all this mess. In the wink of an eye, he granted Gold's motion to change venue and send the case upstate."

"Can he do that?"

"You bet your ass, if he makes a finding that Kevin Knowles can't receive a fair trial in the Bronx, and he did. Lucky me. Not only do I live in the same town as the cop I'm suing, but his criminal trial is only a few towns away." He looked up at the ceiling with a why-me expression.

"You don't have anything to worry about with Kevin."

"Okay. I hope you're right." Matt didn't seem convinced. He changed the subject. "You should've seen Celeste Santiago and Gold go at it in the courtroom. She was going nuts, and Gold was talking a mile a minute about how Kevin is being denied his constitutional rights, blah, blah, blah."

"Is Celeste Santiago really going to try this case in bum fuck Poughkeepsie?"

"Her mug is all over the TV because she wants to take Simonetti's job and be the Bronx DA. I think she wants to cultivate this image as a fighter for the people of color in Bronx County." Matt took some files off one of the chairs and motioned for Sam to sit. "You should've seen it, it almost turned into a riot with the Brown Lives Matter people. They had to call in more court officers. Fitzmorris threatened to clear the courtroom. It was a shitstorm. I think that's what helped convince Fitzmorris to send the case to Poughkeepsie.

"By the way, Bankman wants you to go to Millie's job. She works at South Bronx Realty. It's a real estate management office in a little shit hole of a building right on Fordham and Webster. Go there and introduce yourself tomorrow. Make arrangements to take the Hudson River line to Poughkeepsie."

They probably didn't want him driving her up there in his piece-of-shit minivan. It was all a bunch of bullshit anyway. Nobody gave a shit if Millie Santos showed up in Poughkeepsie tomorrow, but Bankman was paying; and if that's what Bankman wanted, that's what he would get. They were really desperate to get some dope on Kevin.

Matt rubbed his eyes with the palms of both hands. "It's uncomfortable living up there since I got this case. This was Vera's and my big escape from the city to the suburbs, where the schools are great and you don't have to worry about your neighbors. That's all gone to shit. The whole town knows that the firm I work for is suing Knowles. It's especially hard on the kids. These people in the town look at me like it's my fault Kevin was indicted. Unbelievable."

After living in Maplewood, it didn't surprise Sam that the town was reacting this way. "It's all going to blow over soon, and it'll be a thing of the past. You'll see."

"Yeah, I guess you're right." Out of the corner of his eye, Matt looked at the sandwich on the wax paper.

Sam guessed that the minute he left, Matt was going to demolish the remains of the hero. He looked like the classic case of the anxious eater.

"I'll show you out."

In the hallway, Matt lingered by the fish tank that was dug into the wall of Bankman's office. Half of it was in Bankman's office and the other half in the hall. Gorgeous blue and yellow saltwater fish swam among a sunken ship and treasure with water bubbles coming from inside the wreck.

"I should've stayed a court clerk with a nice civil service pension and not moved out of my rent-controlled two-bedroom apartment on Mosholu Parkway. I'll tell you, the American dream with a house and a mortgage is killing me. Look at me. I'm fucking almost three hundred pounds. One of these days they're going to find me in a puddle of drool on my desk blotter."

"I really think you don't have anything to worry about." Truth be told, Sam couldn't be sure what Kevin would do.

"Yeah, you're right. I think I been watching too many of those true crime shows."

Sam waited for the elevator. The door to one of the other offices on the floor was open. There was a view south to New York Harbor and the Statue of Liberty. The Freedom Tower, which replaced the World Trade Center, towered over lower Manhattan.

Chapter Fourteen
Sam Free

Matt Prey was right. South Bronx Realty and Management Company was a little shit hole one-story building on the corner of Webster and Fordham. The black gates on the windows matched the ones that covered the front door. It looked like a fortress wedged between a CVS and a Toys "R" Us. Its gray siding was stained with the remains of purple graffiti.

Sam had to reach between the gates to ring the buzzer. Some of the gold stenciled letters on the front door had fallen off so that it read *Sout Bronx Realt and Management Com.* He put his hand over his eyes and tried to look into the smoky glass windows.

"Yeah?" an angry, muffled voice asked over the intercom.

"I'm looking for Millie Santos."

"Just leave your rent in the mail slot in the door."

"I'm not here to pay rent. Mr. Bankman, her lawyer, sent me. Is she here? I need to talk to her."

He waited there for a good ten to fifteen minutes. Whoever had spoken to him must have forgotten about him. On the other side of the Webster was the campus of Fordham University, surrounded by a tall metal gate with spiked ends. Should he ring again? He didn't want to aggravate the person behind the door. The voice sounded pretty agitated already.

The door began to open. It stuck to the frame.

"Shit!" The man on the other side struggled with the door and pulled it open, and in the process, it must have nailed him.

"What if there was a fucking fire?" He bent over and rubbed his shin, and when he stood straight, his shoulders were stooped and his gray hair was wrapped around the top of his bald head. "I'd be burned to a crisp. I can't even get out of my own fucking office."

"Who're you?" He straightened his smudged reading glasses perched on the edge of his nose and studied Sam; and then, instinctively, he looked past Sam onto Webster, which was a madhouse of traffic and pedestrians. He was a ferret emerging from his hole, sniffing about like he was guilty of doing something.

"I'm Sam Free. I'm an investigator. I work for Bankman, Millie's lawyer. He sent me up here to see Millie." He felt he had only a few seconds of the man's attention before he went back in and shut the door in Sam's face.

"I'm Lapidus. Millie works for me." He held the door for Sam. Sam followed him inside, and they stood in the narrow, dimly lit hallway.

"Millie!" The rest of the office was partitioned off by a counter of the same smoke-colored glass. "So did Bankman mention me?"

"No." He stared down at the little man. Why would Bankman mention him?

"You know, me and Bankman used to be law partners."

No way. This slob Lapidus, who looked like he slept in his clothes, and obsessive compulsive, religious, neat freak Bankman partners? Clearly Lapidus was talking out of his ass.

"Don't look so surprised." He looked up at Sam. How could he see through the lenses on the glasses perched on his brow? They were caked with dirty fingerprints and God knows what else.

Where was Millie? He wanted to get out of here and not get caught in some insane conversation with this weirdo.

"Don't let that religious, holier-than-thou OCD vibe that Bankman puts out fool you. It's all repressed." He giggled to himself and shuffled his feet as he snorted with satisfaction.

It was too late. Now Sam was compelled to listen to this little dweeb while he waited for Millie.

"We graduated from Brooklyn Law School together. I'll bet you didn't know that?"

Lapidus' breath was terrible, and, of course, it was worse when he spoke. It smelled like food gone bad from lying in the sun. He had probably had a bad stomach.

"Bankman and me, we made so much money, but we got greedy. The Feds had me on tape hiring Russian mobsters in Brighton to orchestrate car accidents and dig holes on the sidewalk for people to trip on."

"That doesn't sound good."

"No shit, Sherlock." He gestured to himself with both hands. "Look at me, living the fucking dream, working in some shit hole in the South Bronx selling title insurance and mortgages and collecting rents for the slum lords, and Bankman has an office around the corner from the Empire State Building. What the fuck happened?" He opened the door that led into the office. "Millie!"

Millie appeared. She was tiny. Sam recognized her from the video he had seen at Feldman's. At first, she looked like an eighth grader, with her hair in a long braid that reached her bottom. That was until he looked closer and saw the lines in her face and the crow's feet around her eyes.

"Here's Millie." Lapidus did his best impression of Ed McMahon.

"Bankman sent you?" She squinted at Lapidus with a hard look that said for him to scram or else. Lapidus turned quickly and went back inside, leaving her and Sam alone in the hallway.

She was small but tough as hell. The toughness probably came from the fact that she got picked on a lot. Because of her size, she had to be a hard rock.

"Yeah, Bankman wants me to take you to court in Poughkeepsie tomorrow."

"For what?"

"They moved the trial."

"I ain't going to Poughkeepsie." Millie had dark, almond-shaped eyes, and she smirked at him. "What're you, crazy?"

"I'm not crazy, Millie. Bankman hired me to take you up there. If you don't want to go, I can't force you."

"Isn't it too soon for the trial to start? Kevin only just got indicted."

"I don't think the trial is starting. It's pre-trial."

"Are you kidding me? I ain't going to no pre-trial proceeding to sit around all day and do nothing. I know about court." Like a little girl, she smiled, closed her eyes, and shook her head. Her long black braid swiveled like a serpent. When she smiled, he could see her back teeth were missing.

She pointed up at him. "Don't get me wrong. I'm with Bankman one hundred percent. Bankman is the man. Bankman knows this is not about justice. These upstate white people are gonna walk Kevin Knowles, but it don't matter because this is about dollars and cents." She said "dollars" without the "r" sound. It sounded like *dollahs.* "It's about getting paid, son. You tell Bankman that I'll go to the trial, but not to waste my time with this pre-trial bullshit." Abruptly, Millie turned and went through the same door Lapidus went into, and she disappeared behind the smoky glass.

That went well. What was he going to tell Matt? He was glad Bankman's check had cleared.

Millie was right. He knew it from his own experience of going to court while on the job for all those years. Nothing happened in these pre-trial proceedings. Everybody just sat around with their finger up their ass. That's how court worked most of the time anyway. It was a lot of waiting to get a chance to stand in front of the judge for two minutes.

Clearly, Millie was a tough home girl from the 'hood. Sam was relieved that she refused to go. She was pretty obnoxious, and he didn't look forward to the start of the trial, when he'd have to take the train with her up to Poughkeepsie.

He stepped outside, called Matt, and told him what Millie said.

"What am I going to tell Bankman?" His voice was squeaky with panic.

"Tell Bankman that I'm going to check out 1275 Webster, the scene of the shooting." He noticed the red Hyundai parked across the street.

"I guess."

"Tell him I'm going to interview some witnesses to the shooting." He knew no one at 1275 was going to talk to him. They were all afraid of being branded as snitches. That was a stupid way to live, but in the South Bronx, it was the way of their world.

"Okay, I'll let him know."

He drove north on Webster. 1275 was only a few blocks away.

From that look on Lapidus' face, it was obvious he got pleasure out of trashing Bankman. He blamed Bankman for everything. It was Bankman's fault that Lapidus got pinched by the Feds. A defendant always blames someone else for getting locked up. It was a common theme when Sam was dealing with perps. It was always someone else's fault. It was easier to blame someone else for their own fuckups.

He was a block from 1275 in the right lane, behind a late-model Camry with two men in the front seat.

When they were diagonal to 1275, there was a group hanging out in front of the building. One of the girls had a baby carriage.

The Camry sped up and made a U-turn. The man in the front passenger seat held a small Intratec nine-millimeter machine gun out the window and sprayed the crowd. The girl scurried with her baby carriage, and a young man fell from the hood of the car. Just like that, the Camry was gone up the side street.

Sam pulled over. The boy that had a fallen from the hood of the car was not moving, and the pool of blood that formed around him in the gutter got larger. Somebody on the southbound side stopped their car. He was a big weight lifter type. He walked over to the fallen boy and spoke into his cell phone. Two young girls appeared, holding each other and crying. Traffic stopped on both sides of the street. There was the frantic cry of police sirens as they approached.

With his past, the cops were going to break his balls about why he was there in the middle of a drive-by. Bankman was not paying him enough to dodge bullets.

Holy shit! The Bronx was getting worse. When he was on the job, drive-bys like this usually happened at night. Interviewing witnesses at 1275 would have to wait for another day. A crowd started to gather on the sidewalk. Somebody had spray-painted graffiti on the door of the bodega next to the building. The store had closed, and its windows were covered.

On the corner, there were the remnants of a no-parking sign. The end where the sign should have been was sheared into a point, like a spear sticking out of the cement. That was the sign he had seen in the video of the beating.

How did Nooney get that video?

In his mind's eye, he saw that picture of Nooney when he and Frank found him. The scene was staged. It was fucking crazy. The way Nooney sat there with both eyes blown out like he was watching something with no eyeballs.

The sirens were just behind him, coming from Fordham Road. He drove away and made a left on 199th and followed the side streets west to the Concourse.

He ended up by the empty Reservoir. Iris' parents' building was right there.

He thought about the haunting screams of that beating in that video. "*Pig Buddies.*" Was that a cop that was getting beaten?

He should give Iris a call. Then he saw her up ahead. He recognized her walk right away.

"Hey." He pulled over and called out to her.

Iris turned and smiled. She walked over to the driver's side. They were right in front of Bronx High School. When they were teenagers, they had a little spot where they would fool around in the bushes behind the building.

"How's your dad doing?"

She took a deep breath and started sobbing. "I'm afraid he's on his last leg."

"How's your mom doing?"

"You know. They're married fifty years. How's everything at home?"

"Good. I'm losing weight." When he said it, he realized how ridiculous it sounded. Her father was dying, and he was talking about losing weight. What a stupid thing to say.

There was an awkward silence. He wanted to ask her when she was coming back.

Sam had witnessed the end of both his parents' lives. The way death takes a methodical, terrible course and where there once was a person was now just a hole. Sure, she had been through it with his parents, but it was different when they were your own parents. Poor Iris.

"You want to get something to eat?"

"I've got to get back. I just needed some fresh air."

"Listen, take your time. Take care of your dad. Tell your mom and dad I send my best."

"Thanks, Sammy." She leaned in and kissed him on the mouth, and turned and walked back to the building.

He wanted to give her a hug, but instead he drove away.

He drove down the hill to Broadway and parked at his parking spot in the lot. After he parked the car, he sat there a moment.

What the fuck had happened to his life? Like Lapidus, he asked the same question. He went from a cop to a bum. His troubles were his own doing. He put up a wall between himself and Iris and the kids, and he hid behind it so that they wouldn't see how scared and shaken he was. Truth was, he couldn't forgive himself for how he'd fucked things up.

Those kids caught in the drive-by and the boy who was shot were so young, with the girl dodging bullets with her baby in a carriage, watching her friend gunned down. What the hell was going on with this world? It probably wouldn't even make the news.

Chapter Fifteen
Kevin Knowles

With Charlie in tow, Kevin looked out onto the expanse of fields behind Maplewood Junior High. With the end of winter, Dobbs had called to set up Little League practice. They were early.

Because Dobbsy was the Commissioner of the Little League, they always practiced on the best-kept field. A flock of robins on the infield watched them approach the empty dugout.

"Do you wanna help me set up the bases?" Kevin looked for his son. Charlie sat, swinging his legs back and forth, in the dugout on the farthest spot on the bench from where Kevin stood. Charlie was consumed with some air ship battle fight between two sticks he held with fisted hands. He made the sound of gunfire and then imitated the voices of the pilots as they battled.

Kevin walked around the diamond and placed the bases. Charlie had no interest. Everyday after school he had played catch with Charlie in the backyard until his back hurt, but nothing helped.

Charlie cried when he wasn't allowed to take his video game to practice. Kevin told himself that he didn't want to be one of those asshole fathers who pushed their kids too much. At the same time, he was angry at Charlie for not being a jock like he was. Why couldn't Charlie just have fun playing baseball instead of playing those fucking video games?

He watched Brian Dobbs approach from the parking lot. Brian Junior helped his dad carry the duffel bag packed with bats and the plastic pail filled with hard balls.

"Go help Coach Dobbs and Junior with the equipment."

"I don't want to, Dad. That kid hates me."

It was true, little Brian was a prick to Charlie. It made Kevin want to wring the little bastard's neck.

Dobbs' limp was more pronounced. He wore his Mattingly Yankee pinstriped jersey. His gut was bigger than Kevin remembered.

Dobbs stopped to talk to another man, and they shook hands. Someone else passed and slapped Dobbs on the back. Brian Dobbs was the guy that everyone loved.

"Hey, Wheels." Dobbs was winded from carrying the bag. The aluminum bats clanged when he dropped the bag on the concrete floor of the dugout.

Some of the other kids and their dads appeared. Junior and the other boys went to the outfield, and they threw high flies to each other.

Kevin watched Petey Dwyer's dad raking down the mound. Sal Alonzo's dad spread dirt around home plate. Mickey Conner's dad filled the puddles in the base paths with top soil. There were still remnants of snow in the shaded area beyond the fence that circled the perimeter of the field. It was funny to watch how all the dads were trying to do anything to get on Dobbsy's good side, so that he would give their kids more playing time.

Dobbsy loved to get his ass kissed. He stood next to Kevin in the dugout with his arms crossed, smiling. "We need to have a meeting to go over the signs for stealing, bunting, and hit and run."

"Hey, Coach Dobbs, you want me to coach first again?" someone's dad asked.

"Yeah, sure."

"How 'bout me? Do I still get the job on third?"

Dobbs turned to Charlie. "Hey, Charlie, how's it going?" He gave Charlie a high five. "Now get your butt out there and warm up with the rest of the crew."

Slowly, glove in hand, Charlie walked to the infield. He stood there tentatively, waiting for someone to throw the ball to him.

Dobbs held a clipboard that contained the roster. "How many kids did I pick?"

"Twelve." Kevin looked over his shoulder. Dobbs counted the kids out on the field. "Then how come there are only eleven? Who we missing?"

From between the gap in his front teeth Dobbsy emitted a shrill whistle. "Bring it in, boys, bring it in." He cupped his hands over his mouth.

Something about Dobbs gnawed at Kevin, and he couldn't quite put his finger on what it was that was bugging him. Maybe if Dobbs hadn't been so persistent in having Kevin coach with him, then Kevin wouldn't have forced Charlie to come to practice. Why was Dobbs always acting like he and Kevin were such big buddies. Sure, it was Dobbs who encouraged Kevin to apply to Narcotics. Yes, Dobbs was the lieutenant in charge of the squad, but they were never friends on the job. It was only when Kevin moved up here, and after all that had happened, that Dobbs insisted they become friends, and coach the boys in basketball league in the winter, and coach the boys in the baseball league in the summer together.

The kids and their fathers stood in a semi-circle around Dobbs and Kevin outside of the chain link fence that encircled the dugout.

Dobbs waited until they had all gathered around. "Listen up, fellas. Those of you who were with me last year know that all the other teams are gonna be gunning for us because we won the championship."

Kevin watched Charlie, who was playing with the loose laces on his mitt and was a million miles away, not hearing a word Dobbs was saying. Dobbs would always give the Narcotics squad pep talks before they went out on a buy and bust. He was good at that.

". . . And when you're the champion, everyone wants to bring you down. So that's why this year, we're gonna have to work extra hard; that means, when you come to practice, you need to put out an effort and work your butts off. Because the way you practice is the way you play in the game. If you slack off, I'm gonna sit you. There are no favorites on this team. The best players play. Now first thing I want to do is have everyone line up on the mound and pitch to Mr. Dwyer. Junior, bring a pail of baseballs out to the mound."

Each kid got to throw a few pitches. Charlie was the last in the line. If it wasn't for Dobbs bothering Kevin to coach Little League with him, Kevin wouldn't have forced Charlie to play this year. Why was it so important for Dobbs to have Kevin be his assistant coach.

A man in a suit and a boy hurried toward the field. The man was heavy.

"That must be the twelfth kid." Dobbs watched the boys pitch.

When they got closer, Kevin recognized the suit as Millie Santos' lawyer, Matt Prey, from the deposition. Kevin couldn't forget him after spending a couple of hours in a room with the guy, being peppered by questions.

After those hours of questions, Kevin had wanted to punch him in his fat face.

Kevin wanted to laugh at Matt Prey's expression. When he approached and recognized Kevin, it was like he said "Oh fuck!" to himself.

Matt Prey stood outside the field. His rosy features had turned scarlet.

"No hard feelings. Listen, you got a job to do. I don't hold that against you. This is about the kids. Let's leave all that other stuff out of this." Kevin still had a bad feeling in his mouth. He still wanted to throttle Prey.

Dobbs had walked over to the mound. He was giving one of the kids instructions on his windup.

"I appreciate that." Matt rubbed his hands together and looked at the ground. His black Oxfords were caked with mud from the field. "This is Dylan." He put his hand on his son's shoulder.

"Well, Dylan, get out there and show us what you got."

Prey turned to watch his kid pitch.

Some kids just have it. The way Dylan held his glove. His stance on the mound. His windup was perfect. He threw like a mini version of Luis Severino. Petey Dwyer's dad's glove popped when he caught the ball that Dylan threw.

"Your kid brings it pretty good." Out in the open, Kevin got a good look at Prey. He wasn't behind some desk, like he was at the deposition. What a lard ass. He needed to lose forty pounds.

"He loves baseball."

The silence was awkward, and then Prey checked his watch.

"How long does practice last?"

"We'll be here an hour."

"I have to pick up my daughter at soccer, so I can leave him?"

"Sure." Not in a million years would Kevin leave his kid with someone he just met. Especially someone he was suing.

After Prey left, Dobbs approached from the mound. "Who's the guy in the suit?"

"That's the lawyer that's suing me." Kevin said it as kind of a joke. The criminal case scared the shit out of Kevin, not this stupid civil lawsuit bullshit. If he lost the civil suit, the city would pay. If he lost the criminal case, he would go to jail.

"Motherfucker suing you over some scumbag junkie that got what he deserved," Dobbsy said under his breath, and his blue, bloodshot eyes bulged with anger. "Payback's gonna be a bitch for that asshole. I'm going to run his ass out of town."

"Why you so bent out of shape? Cops are always getting sued for this or that. It's really the city that's on the hook. I don't give a fuck."

"I dunno, he just bugs me is all. Fucking asshole." He took his glove and went to the mound to pitch batting practice to the kids.

Kevin umped. For a moment, he forgot his troubles. He enjoyed the sounds of the boys and their dads lined up behind the cage. "Good cut." "Wait for a good one." And the ohs and ahs when the crack of the bat sent the ball out on a fly.

It felt good to be out in the air, but after a while, his back hurt from squatting behind home plate, and one of the other dads was quick to jump in.

Kevin stood in the dugout. He watched Charlie in the outfield stare up at the sky while he used his glove to shield the sun. It was like there was a fly ball, but the batter hadn't even swung. At least he was getting ready just in case, Kevin tried to convince himself.

He watched Dobbs pitch to the boys. Why the outburst about Prey? What was going on? Dobbsy was scared of something. It was so out of character. It made him wonder. Dobbs was the commissioner, and he got to pick whatever kids he wanted. Why would he pick Prey's kid? Everybody in town knew that Matt Prey was the lawyer who was suing him. Maybe Dobbs felt that he should keep his friends close but his enemies closer. None of it made any sense.

From working with Brian all those years in Narcotics, Kevin knew that Ray Santos was Dobbsy's CI for years. Maybe he forgot that Kevin knew? Why didn't Dobbsy mention that? Why did he say all of those things? *"Scumbag junkie got what he deserved."* Had something happened between Santos and Dobbs? Why had he referred to him that way? "*Run his ass out of town.*"That was a little strong. What had Prey done to Dobbs to make him so mad? Was Dobbs worried about Prey? For what?

Dobbs started coming around to take him for coffee to Ralph's or the Dunkin' Donuts. It was almost like Dobbs was trying to find out what Kevin knew.

Then, he started calling Kevin about the basketball league and the Little League that they should coach together?

Kevin knew that he was paranoid, but he trusted his instincts. Sure, Dobbs could just be a nice guy trying to help his neighbor and old coworker out. Maybe, like Dobbs said, he just wanted to show his support for a brother in blue. Yeah, but Dobbs wasn't that nice.

Kevin knew him from all those years working in Narcotics. Dobbs always had an ulterior motive.

Maybe Dobbs felt guilty. Maybe Dobbs felt that if he hadn't recruited Kevin into Narcotics, none of it would have happened. Yeah, but Dobbs wasn't the type to feel guilty about anything. Kevin just didn't understand why all of a sudden Dobbs wanted to be his best friend.

Charlie got his turn and struck out, but at least he got some good swings at the ball.

The clocks hadn't changed, and the sun still set early. It was around four and everything started turning gray and colder.

"Let's wrap it up." Dobbsy again gave that shrill whistle, and the kids surrounded him at the mound. Kevin walked over to the group. "I don't know how many nice days we'll have, but we'll try to get a few practices in before the start of the season. Maybe I'll see if we can use the gym at the junior high. Good job, men!"

"How was it?" Kevin asked Charlie as they walked back to the car.

"Glad it's finished."

"How about we get a slice of pizza at Mario's before we head home?" He rubbed Charlie's head.

"That sounds like a good plan, Dad." Charlie ran ahead to the car.

Chapter Sixteen
Kevin Knowles

It was the middle of the night when Kevin, his T-shirt soaked with sweat, woke wide-eyed and out of breath. He would wake some nights like this in a panic, and then he wouldn't be able to get back to sleep. In the bed next to him, Sue snored softly, under the influence of her nighttime cocktail of Lunesta and Zinfandel.

Through the bedroom window, Kevin could see the full moon as it illuminated the night sky. When they first moved out to the 'burbs, he was amazed at how much light the full moon gave off. Its rays lit the hallway on his way to check on the kids.

Charlie had thrown off his covers. His handheld computer game was on the bed. Kevin put it on the shelf and covered him.

In Erica's bedroom, he stood over her and watched her as she rolled from her stomach to her back, opened her eyes for an instant, and looked at him sharply before she drifted off again. Erica looked just like her mother.

Downstairs, his hands shook as he poured a glass of water from the fridge. He sat in the armchair in the living room and stared out the bay window into the moonlit yard. His insomnia was always worse with the full moon.

Suing you over some scumbag junkie. Those words that Dobbsy used filled his head.

Was he becoming more paranoid? With the stakes this high, it was especially important to wrap up all the loose ends and not leave anything hanging. After all, wasn't his life, his kids' lives, his wife's life, all hanging by a thread. First he needed to get to the bottom of what the fuck was going on with Dobbs. He had a plan for that.

"Keep your friends close, but your enemies closer," he whispered to himself as he drifted off.

* * *

He woke at dawn and went to the garage. There, in the far corner, was a locker he had taken from the squad when they decided to replace the old ones at the precinct. It was green, and on the vented door, he placed a huge lock that was unbreakable. He took the key out of his wallet and opened the locker.

Back in the day, Narcotics had been doing an investigation with the Organized Crime Task Force for the DEA. Those DEA guys had some tools. After the operation had finished, he had scooped up one of the GPS systems they used. It was high-tech shit that the NYPD didn't have the budget for.

On the bottom of the closet, he found the unopened box for the whole GPS kit. Next to the box were two weapons. The first was a Beretta .22 he had taken off a fourteen-year-old who was pitching crack on Davidson. The other weapon was a Lorcin .38.

The Lorcin .38 had a story to it. It had been over on Elder when he was plainclothes, and he watched two idiots beefing. One had the Lorcin, and at first, he had tried to shoot the other one. And then, when the gun jammed, he used the butt of the gun as a club to beat the other bloody. From his surveillance post, Kevin saw the fight, but he didn't want to break it up because that would have blown his cover. Then he saw he had no choice because it looked like the one idiot was going to beat the other to death. He couldn't watch a murder and do nothing.

He kept the gun and took it apart and oiled it, and it worked like a charm. Drug dealers used Lorcin .38s. With the serial numbers removed, this one was untraceable, just like the Beretta. Sometimes, like now, he had a need for these things he kept hidden in his locker.

GPS in hand, he spoke out loud to his image in the mirror that hung on the back of the door to the locker. "*Never forget to listen to your instincts. And let me tell you something else"*—he gestured at the mirror—*"being paranoid is not such a bad thing."*

Sue and the kids were still asleep. He liked alone time like this, when the house was completely quiet. He put the box with the GPS on the front seat of the Explorer. He was being eaten alive on the inside. It was the fear of getting convicted and being locked up with the perps he had locked up.

* * *

He passed the lake on the way into town. Its water was dark, like the sky, and the wind churned white caps on its surface.

Dobbs' beige Escalade was parked in front of Ralph's, and there was a vacant parking spot right next to it. Kevin parked in the empty spot.

This early, it was quiet on the street. He crawled underneath his Explorer like he was checking something out, and from there he was able to reach under Dobbs' Escalade and stick the magnet attached to the GPS to its chassis.

"Hey, Wheels." Dobbs was standing there holding his coffee when Kevin pulled himself out from underneath his Explorer.

"Hey, Brian."

"Car trouble?"

"I thought I had an oil leak."

"Bring it over to Petey Dwyer's dad. He has a shop over by Longwood."

"It keeps running low on oil." Kevin stood and brushed himself off.

Dobbs put his hand on Kevin's shoulder and gave it a gentle squeeze. "I feel for what you're going through, my brother." He looked Kevin in the eye. "Lemme know if you need anything. We're all behind you."

"Yeah, thanks."

"I'll call you about getting a practice in this weekend. It's supposed to be nice." Dobbs stood there and watched Kevin pull out.

Kevin drove over to the Dunkin' Donuts on Route 6 and stayed inside his SUV in the parking lot, sipping his coffee and watching Dobbsy's SUV, which was a little blip on the monitor. For a while, it stayed blinking, unmoving, like a stationary Pac-Man.

Then he watched Dobbsy move. If you want to find out about a body, you have to keep tabs on the body to know where it goes and what it does. Now he was going to find out. *"Where you going, Brian?"*

Dobbsy was traveling on Route 6 right past him. Kevin had plenty of time. He didn't need to tail Dobbsy when he could watch Dobbsy on the GPS heading toward the highway and south.

Kevin's phone lit up with a text. *Got everything you need.* It was from McBride and Ryan.

That was good news. *Great. In the Bronx later, catch you then,* he texted back.

He guessed Dobbs was headed to the Bronx. He was on the Deegan. Was he heading to Yankee Stadium? No. Dobbs got off before the exit to Yankee Stadium at Fordham Road.

Fordham was always a slow go with the lights, the buses, and gypsy cabs darting in and out of the traffic. It was the fucking shopping mecca of the South Bronx running west from the border of Manhattan to the Bronx Zoo. There were always crowds. He followed Dobbs up the hill on Fordham, past where the Grand Concourse cut across it, and from there, downhill to Webster. On Park Avenue behind Webster, Kevin found a spot where he had a clear view of Dobbs' Escalade.

Chapter Seventeen
Brian Dobbs

Dobbsy double parked his Escalade in front of South Bronx Real Estate and put on the flashers. He texted Lapidus. *Here.*

Before he could get out of his SUV, an RMP pulled up and the cop rolled down his window.

"Sorry," Dobbsy told the cop, and he showed him his PBA card.

"No problem, Lieutenant."

"Thanks, guys, I'll just be a minute. I got to pick something up."

He gave the uniforms a thumbs up as their patrol car pulled away.

Lapidus stuck his head out of the gated doorway. He held the door for Dobbs, who left the Escalade and jogged inside the fortress. They stood in the hallway.

"Did you know there was a drive-by at 1275?" Lapidus asked.

"Another one?"

"Yeah, and the super wants to quit because he's afraid of catching a stray bullet in one of these shootouts."

"I'll talk to him."

"You better give him some more money. Fucking battle pay is what it is. And look what just came in the mail." Lapidus smirked as he showed him the subpoena. He loved to aggravate Dobbs.

"Lemme see that." He snatched the paper out of Lapidus' hand.

Dobbs studied it with his beady blues. "Is this from Millie's lawyer?"

"That's what it says."

"Motherfucker! I hope you didn't give him anything."

"Don't get so excited. The subpoena doesn't mean shit. For one thing, it isn't signed by a judge, and then he sent it by mail. It's not valid unless a process server served it on us with an eighteen-dollar check. Everybody knows a subpoena isn't valid unless it's accompanied by a eighteen-dollar check. It's in the statute."

"I don't want that fat twerp Matt Prey digging around in my business."

Lapidus waved his hand at Dobbs as if to dismiss him. "He'll stop when the city pays out on Millie's lawsuit."

"Would you believe that fat fuck lives in my town, and his kid plays baseball on my team?"

"I'm sure he's gonna get a lot of playing time." Lapidus rolled his eyes.

"What does he want to know?"

"He subpoenaed Ray Santos' employee file for DB Holding Company."

"Does he know DB Holding is my company?"

"Probably, it's public record. Anybody could look up who owns a corporation through the New York State Office of the Secretary of State."

"I'm getting really sick of that fat fuck. Do you think he knows that I own 1275?"

"If he doesn't know it now, he can easily find out. All he has to do is go to the County Clerk, run the ownership records on 1275. Anybody could find it out." Lapidus handed Dobbs an envelope filled with rent checks and cash.

Dobbs stuck the envelope in his pants pocket. "Where's Millie?"

"What's it to you? What, you got the hots for Millie?"

"For Christ's sake, Lapidus. I don't need you to break my balls."

"I can't find anybody else to collect the rent at 1275 since Ray was capped. I asked the super to do it. He looked at me like I had two heads. I have to collect it myself and take my life in my hands going over there."

"That's why I pay you the big bucks."

"You're kidding, right?" Lapidus arched his eyebrows over his smudged reading glasses. Dobbs turned to leave. "For the pennies you pay me, you can have somebody else manage that rat hole. With all the shootings going on over there, I'm taking my life in my hands. I told you that's why the super wants to quit."

Dobbs turned to Lapidus. He held the door open and eyed his double-parked Escalade. "I told you I'll go over there and smooth things out with the super, and I'll find someone else to collect the rent. Take it easy, will you?"

Lapidus caught the door behind Dobbs. "By the way, Dobbs, has anyone told you you're getting fat? Man, take a diet for Christ's sake." he shouted after him.

"Fuck you, Lapidus!" Dobbs turned and screamed above the din of the busy street.

Chapter Eighteen
Kevin Knowles

On the monitor, Kevin saw that Dobbs had driven from the South Bronx Real Estate Office on Webster to 1275. Kevin found a parking spot where he could see the building with his binoculars. The Escalade was double parked in front of Ray Santos' late-model red Mercedes, which had parking tickets stuffed inside the front windshield wipers. There was police tape in the gutter.

He could make out Dobbs standing on the sidewalk talking to a short, dark man who was wheeling a trash bin to the curb with a hand truck.

Except for Dobbs and the man he was talking to, the block was empty. In the aftermath of the shooting, no one wanted to leave their apartment and risk getting caught in another drive-by. Better to let things cool down. The vibe left behind by the violence was like a shockwave.

Fueled by a vacuum of power, it was all caused by the dealers beefing over who would take over the spot. It was a business dispute, but this one was settled with automatic weapons.

What is your ETA to the diner? The text came over Kevin's phone.

Be there in ten, He texted McBride and Ryan back. This was one more piece to the puzzle.

He left the monitor on. When Kevin got to Broadway, the bleeping dot that was Dobbsy headed north, probably back home to Maplewood.

Why was it that the more Kevin uncovered about Dobbs, the more Dobbs dug a hole for himself to be buried in.

Kevin spotted McBride and Ryan in the parking lot of the Riverdale Diner. They were as big as lineman, dressed alike in khakis, golf shirts, and windbreakers with Docksides. They had been partners so long they looked alike, except that McBride was bald and Ryan had a head of curly red hair that was mostly gray.

Across from the diner, under the El, sparks from the passing trains fell onto the blacktop.

"Hey, how you doing?"

With Ryan at six-foot-eight and McBride at six-foot-nine, the two of them were so large they filled up all the space around them. Kevin was tall, but these two made him feel like a dwarf.

"We got what you wanted."

"I knew it from the text. Thanks."

McBride held pictures in his big mitt. He handed them to Kevin.

"That's Primo and Lurch."

Kevin was grateful that they had found these two pieces of shit that had ruined his life for him. Now he could finish it.

"You sure you don't need any help on this?"

"No. It's fine, really, I'll take care of it," Kevin reassured them.

"You sure?"

There were photos with the number of the building, 199, on Hillside Avenue in Jamaica that the duo were entering. It was ideal.

"Morons think they leave the Bronx and move to Jamaica, Queens, that we're not going to find them." McBride guffawed.

"I think these idiots think Queens is another country," Kevin said.

"After you beat the case, you'll come back to the squad." Ryan studied Kevin to see what Kevin's reaction would be.

Kevin didn't say anything. He didn't know what to say in response to that. He wasn't thinking about that. All he could think about was violently seeking retribution. The thoughts of what he would do to Primo and Lurch were soothing.

"Really, how you doing, Kev?" Ryan put his hand on Kevin's shoulder as the three of them stood in a semi-circle.

"I'm good, Ry, once I take care of this."

The surveillance was a piece of cake. Kevin found a spot on the other side of the Hillside across from 199. Hillside was a big, wide stretch. Kevin would be hard to spot. In the Explorer, he pushed his seat back. Kevin always possessed the kind of patience that was needed in surveillance. It didn't bother him to sit and wait and watch. He brought a plastic gallon jug to pee in.

He thought about the tools he needed to get this done. Lurch and Primo were bruisers. He needed a burner with force. In the wheel well of the Explorer there was a compartment for the spare tire, which had a lot of extra space, and he had hidden a Stoeger Uplander sawed off shotgun there. He was always worried that the perps he had locked up would seek him out for revenge. He kept it there for protection. The Stoeger was an equalizer if there ever was one. He was going to need earplugs and goggles as well.

The neighborhood was rundown. The building had a plexiglass door leading to the lobby. The owner probably got tired of replacing broken glass and the lock on the door. Two men in hoodies and jeans so low and baggy they showed their underwear pushed open the unlocked lobby door. He watched them. Unfortunately, they were not Primo and Lurch.

Chapter Nineteen
Matt Prey

James Donovan, the city's attorney, and Prey waited in the hall outside Judge Eldridge's chambers.

Donovan stood on the balls of his feet, ready to do battle, and he stared sharply at Matt. "You're not going to be able to prove negligent hiring against the city, and the judge is going to toss your case on my motion for summary judgment." He mimicked throwing a football and lifted his arms to signify a touchdown and then slapped his thigh in glee. "I fucking can't wait," he said to himself.

Donovan had a reputation as one of those defense attorneys that fought everyone tooth and nail. He acted as if any money the city might pay in a lawsuit was coming out of his pocket. Throughout the case, he would play mind games with his adversary by talking shit and acting as if the case had no merit.

It was douche bags like Donovan that made Matt question what had possessed him to go to law school. His past life in this courthouse as a clerk was a walk in the park compared to this crap.

Who needed this stress? It wasn't like if they won the case he would get any benefit other than keeping his job. He had ditched the civil service gig for law school because he was chasing the dream. And yes, now he had achieved it, with the house and all the trappings that came with life in the 'burbs. Yeah, but nobody ever told him what a headache it would all turn out to be.

"The judge will see you now," the court officer told them.

The chambers were wall-to-wall plush burgundy carpet. The judge sat at the head of a shiny long oak table. He was small and thick like a fire plug with short arms. He wore black suspenders and a polka-dotted bow tie with a purple dress shirt and gold cufflinks. His sleeves were rolled up, exposing arms that were covered with a carpet of thick curly hair that reached the knuckles of his stubby fingers. He motioned for Matt and Donovan to sit on either side of him. In front of him, on the table, lay the subpoena Matt had served on the police department requesting Kevin Knowles' personnel file.

"Do you have a good faith basis to subpoena Detective Knowles' personnel file?" Judge Eldridge surveyed Matt with mean, lively black eyes. In the corner, there was an overstuffed recliner that matched the carpet and the drapes. The judge had a big round head, and what seemed like an endless carpet of black hair sprouted from underneath his shirt to the back of his neck.

"How can I have a good faith basis if I don't know what's in the file?" The minute those words left Matt's mouth he regretted them.

Eldridge squinted at him and then turned to Donovan. Of all the pro-plaintiff Democratic judges in the Bronx, it was Matt Prey's shitty luck that this case had to end up with Eldridge. Plaintiff's lawyers called him "Death Ridge." He was a plaintiff's nightmare. Any ruling that Eldridge could make to sabotage a case he would gladly do.

"This isn't some fucking fishing expedition." The judge made the motion of casting a line from a rod.

Donovan covered his mouth to hide the smile and his enjoyment of this whole scene.

"The fair thing to do would be to have the court examine the personnel file of Knowles in camera to determine if there is anything in there relevant to a negligent hiring claim." Matt tried to reason with him.

"That's denied," the judge snapped at him.

Donovan seized the opportunity. "Judge, they have nothing to support their baseless allegation that the city was negligent in hiring or retaining Detective Knowles."

"If you think it's appropriate, and you believe that the plaintiff does not have a good faith basis to support her claim against the city, bring the motion to dismiss the complaint." Eldridge drummed his fingers on the table's shiny surface, like he was playing the scales on a piano.

"I'll get on it right away, Judge." Donovan was poised for the kill.

"That'll be all," Eldridge told them.

Matt felt the room closing in on him. Eldridge and Donovan were squeezing him into a corner, and he was fucked in every which way.

He walked to the other side of the building, away from Donovan, who wanted to torture him some more, and found the bathroom. He closed the door to one of the stalls. Fully clothed, he sat there, and he could feel the sweat soak through his T-shirt. If this case was dismissed, Bankman was going to kick him to the curb. His only hope was Sam Free. Wasn't he supposed to be such a hotshot detective before he got himself all jammed up? Sam Free had to dig something up on Knowles, anything.

Chapter Twenty
Sam Free

"Not for nothing," Matt told Sam. "It's on you if I get fired behind this. I did you a solid by getting you this gig because I knew you were having a hard time finding work, and this is what I get in return? I wanted to give you a break, and now you've come up with nothing on Kevin Knowles. Have you done anything to try and get some dirt on Knowles? What's the problem? Everybody knows he's dirty."

Sam's first reaction was that he wanted to tell Matt to fuck himself and then hang up the phone, but he might lose this gig if he did that. Matt was full of shit. Sam didn't get this job because Matt recommended him. Bankman hired him because he knew that Sam had been on the job with Kevin.

In a way, Matt was right. They were paying him good money to come up with some dirt on Kevin, and he was getting nowhere. "Give me a couple more days, I'm sure I'll come up with something."

After Matt hung up, Bankman called. Bankman and Matt were putting on the full court press. Bankman wanted to know if there was any progress. Sam had to tell him that he hadn't come up with anything on Kevin Knowles. Bankman was quiet on the other end of the phone. Then he said, "Keep me posted," and he hung up. Sam didn't like the sound of that.

Sam's thoughts were stuck on the video that he and Frank found on the phone in Sean's hoody. Nooney had given Sean the video before both of Nooney's eyes were blown out. Sam couldn't get it out of his head. The cut-off sign by the corner in front of 1275 was the same as the one in the video. In his phone, Sam wasn't able to find the copy of the tape Frank had emailed him.

He had to call Frank, and that was how they ended up in Frank's red Hyundai across from 1275 on Webster, watching the new crew who had filled the power void sell drugs on the block.

"Look at this shit," Frank said. "This is a classic set. What do we have here? A black female wanting to score some product. We have a male Hispanic wearing a red du rag approach her and take her money. Oh, look, John Doe du rag goes up the block with the black skank's money to the kid in the Cleveland Indians jacket who gives him product for dollars." Frank pronounced it *dollahs* without the R.

During their years of doing the buys and busts and locking up knuckleheads, he had heard Frank do this same play by play. When they got transferred to Homicide, Frank had less opportunity to engage in this stupidity, but still, every once in a while, when they stumbled on a drug spot, Frank would break out into this play by play of the street dealing. It annoyed the shit out of Sam.

"Ladies and gentlemen," Frank continued in his announcer voice. "We can't forget about the junior high schoolers in North Face bubble parkas acting as lookouts. And pitchers are busy and the business is brisk."

No wonder there was so much beef over this block. It was a gold mine of a drug spot.

"Frank, please stop the play by play bullshit. It's ridiculous. Can you play the tape?" They were parked right across the street from the sign, which was still cut in half. It stood out like a spear stuck in the sidewalk. Sam was sure that it was the same one as in the video.

Frank held the phone in his gnarled misshaped hand and with his busted, bent index finger that never healed right, and he pressed play.

The beating didn't get easier to watch. If anything, it seemed worse every time. Those haunting screams were why Sam couldn't get it out of his head. There were those awful screams again, when the two goons beat him, and the one stabbed him with the broken ends of the two-by-four. It was awful. Frank played it over and over again to the spot where they dragged the man, rolled up in the rug, onto the street. And there it was, that fleeting image of the street sign cut in half.

"It's right there." Frank pointed to the sheared pole sticking out of the cement.

"But where did the rest of what happened on this tape go down?"

"I'll bet it was there in the bodega that's closed," Frank said.

"Your pig buddies?" Sam repeated what the men said in the video. "What does that mean?"

"Did Nooney shoot this?"

"Who the fuck knows?"

"Look at this." Frank looked in his rear-view mirror. "What're they trying to do? Intimidate us? Oh no. No fucking way." Frank got out of the car.

Sam turned and saw that McBride and Ryan had pulled up behind them. Their combined weight had to be five hundred pounds or more. And when they exited it was like their vehicle breathed a sigh of relief. Sam got out too and followed Frank.

"What're you two idiots doing here?" McBride towered over Frank, but Frank didn't give an inch.

"It's not like you're on the job." Ryan said.

"Say, I'll bet you two gorillas have done a buy op right here on this block," Frank said.

"What the fuck you talking about?"

"Fuck you, Ryan."

"Get the fuck outa here."

"Before we lock you up," McBride finished his partner's sentence.

"When I heard that you two got busted back down to Narcotics from Homicide, it was one of the happiest days of my life. You two pieces of shit deserved it." Frank clapped his hands in glee.

"Hey, Frank, why don't you and your convicted felon partner go fuck yourselves."

McBride and Ryan got back in their car. Frank threw them the bird. "Assholes."

With McBride behind the wheel, they drove off, just missing Frank.

"Did you see how he looked at me when I mentioned them doing a buy op here at 1275?"

"No fucking way." Sometimes, because they'd worked together for so many years, Sam could tell what Frank was thinking.

"You remember the back door. Remember how we would jam a piece of cardboard in the door so it wouldn't lock; that way we could sneak in and out of the squad without Dobbs finding out."

"I'm not sneaking into Bronx TNT. That was a long time ago. I'm sure they fixed that door by now."

"I wonder if they got a file on 1275?"

"You're nuts. I'm not doing it."

"Whatever you say, Sam." He gestured dismissively with the back of his hand, as if to say, "Forget about you."

They sat in the car and Frank asked him, "Don't you want to know what kind of mess Nooney got himself involved in? Who knows, maybe you could get some info on Kevin to give to that big shot lawyer? You never know where this shit might end up. You might be helping yourself on this."

"I told you, no fuckin' way, Frank. You must be deaf or something." Sam mumbled. "I swear to God."

Chapter Twenty-One
Kevin Knowles

These two thought because they moved to Jamaica, Queens, they would be free and clear like they had moved to Jamaica, Jamaica, or something.

On and off for a couple of weeks, he watched 199 Hillside. Primo and Lurch would leave around six for the subway station and return about three or so. They must have had some kind of construction job because they wore hard hats and Timberlands. When they returned, they were covered with dust and paint, their gait slowed by a day of labor.

No doubt that today was the day. It was cold and raining. Ideal weather because there weren't too many people out on the street, and, also, he wouldn't stand out wearing a raincoat and a ski mask. In his garage, he put on the white surgical gloves before he loaded the weapon to be sure not to leave any prints on the slugs.

Stoeger Uplander. Even the name was powerful. She was tucked into the pocket of his raincoat. He had lifted her from work too. The SWAT guys liked them because they were short, effective weapons. She was a nasty, powerful, and compact little bitch. Easy to transport and maneuver in cramped spaces.

When it had gone missing from the SWAT inventory, there was a big hullabaloo. They had seen him on video in the area where the sawed off shotguns were kept, but he made up some bullshit excuse and stood by it. *Deny, deny, till you're blue in the face.*

When he found a space right in front of the building, the rain turned to ice. The weather couldn't decide whether or not to leave winter behind. One day might be nice and springlike, and the next cold and nasty. It was like that this time of year, and then suddenly it would turn to summer swelter.

They were approaching the building. He could see them in his rear-view mirror. His long frame was scrunched down low in the seat. They had no clue. They were smiling and laughing. They passed him and walked toward the lobby, pushed through the broken door, and stood with their backs to him waiting for the elevator.

He had to time it just so. He reached into the pocket of his raincoat and grabbed the sawed off. He could feel its hourglass shape and the two huge nostrils on the muzzle of the gun. She was a wicked lady with two triggers, one for the left muzzle and one for the right. He had selected high brass shells. Kevin put in his earplugs.

He could see into the lobby. Their backs were to him as they waited for the elevator. Just as the elevator door opened, he exited quickly from the Explorer, and walked before the cameras that were placed on the outside of the building and those in the lobby. Subconsciously, he hunched over and covered his face, even though he wore the ski mask. They stepped in the elevator, and it began to close. He came from behind them, entered the building, and pressed the button so that the elevator door opened again.

He had practiced with the Stoeger in his backyard, shooting at a piece of cast iron target he had found in the junkyard. The gun's blowback required him to hold it with two hands.

As the door reopened, they turned toward him. He pointed the weapon at Lurch's chest. There was a huge explosion that came from those awful dark snorting nostrils of the Stoeger. Lurch, the taller and thinner of the two, was pushed against the back wall of the elevator. The hard hat he wore flew off his head. There was a huge hole in his chest, and the car was filled with flying bits of tissue, bone, and flesh.

It was fleeting as the lights inside the elevator car were blown out with the muzzle blast. Even with his earplugs, the blast made Kevin's ears ring in those close confines. He had a very brief glimpse of Primo in the dark elevator from the light that came from the lobby.

It didn't seem to register with Primo. One second, he was having a conversation with his friend, and then, in the next, his friend had a hole blown through his chest. Primo's face and hard hat had pieces of Lurch's tissue on it. In those precious few seconds before Kevin pulled the second trigger, Primo looked at Kevin, and he seemed to grin slightly as if Kevin was a familiar face. He couldn't possibly recognize him because Kevin wore a ski mask and goggles. Then Primo reached for the pistol in the waistband of his jeans just before Kevin pulled the second trigger on the right side of the nozzle. This slug passed through the side of Primo's face and the hard hat sat at an odd angle on his face before it was thrown against the elevator's back wall.

In the dim light, he caught an image of Lurch's one lifeless eye. The blood puddles on the tile floor grew. It was so quiet that Kevin thought he could hear the stream of red above the ringing in his ears, like a leak or maybe ice cubes melting. Kevin recognized the stench of one of them letting go and of blood and bone and tissue.

He let the door go, and the elevator closed behind him. Quickly, he walked back to his SUV. He slipped on the icy sidewalk and fell onto the sawed off. He grunted and jumped up quickly. Boy was he glad the gun chambers were empty or it might have gone off. He was probably going to have a bruise on his ribs from where he fell on it.

There was no need to worry about the shotgun shells on the floor of the elevator mixed with bits and pieces of Lurch and Primo. He reassured himself that they couldn't be traced as long as he was careful not to leave any prints on them, which he was. He pulled out into traffic on Atlantic Avenue and headed toward the White Stone Bridge, and pulled off the goggles and the ski mask. At the entrance to the Van Wyck Expressway, screaming police cars passed him in the opposite direction. He watched them in his rear-view mirror, and noticed there was some blood spatter on his forehead. He wiped it away and cleaned his hand on the coat.

The Long Island Sound below was hidden under fog. He hid the Stoeger under his seat and pulled off the raincoat and his bulletproof vest as he waited in the EZ Pass line. He stuffed the coat and the vest into a plastic garbage bag on the floorboard of the passenger seat.

With his ears still ringing, Kevin didn't want to listen to the radio.

* * *

Sue and the kids weren't home. He found the lighter fluid in the garage and dumped the raincoat, goggles, earplugs, and surgical gloves into the barbeque pit in the backyard. He squirted the lighter fluid to start the flames, and they hissed through the frozen rain. The smell of burning plastic from the goggles gave him a headache. The ringing in his ears lessened. He took off his sneakers and jeans and threw them into the flames. He was in his boxers, shivering on his deck while watching the flames.

Barefoot, he went into the garage and placed the Stoeger back into the rear tire well of the Explorer. There was a box of shells in the compartment as well.

He paused there in his garage for a moment and took a deep breath. True, that dull ache of vengeance that he felt in the pit of his stomach had lessened, but it hadn't gone away completely. Those two got what they deserved, but he wasn't finished.

Chapter Twenty-Two
Sam Free

Sam had breakfast at the donut shop, where the older Spanish lady at the register winked and flirted with him.

He had come out onto the street after wolfing his eggs, restless but not knowing whether he should go with Frank to break into the Narcotics division. He didn't know if Frank was serious. Frank had some crazy fucking ideas.

He was lonely as hell without Iris. After twenty-five years of sharing the bed with her, it was tough to sleep alone, and he wasn't getting used to it. It had started raining yesterday, and it went through the night turning to ice, and now the sun had come out, and the thin layer of ice on the sidewalk and streets had melted. The air felt clean the way it always does after the streets get a good soaking and some of the city's soot is washed away.

He saw Frank parked at the curb up ahead, and he got in. For a moment, the two of them sat there not saying anything and staring straight ahead. Frank pulled away from the curb.

Two alleged members of a Marielito Street Drug Gang that had terrorized residents of the Morrisania section of the Bronx for years were gunned down by a lone assailant in Queens today. The all-news station filled the silence in Frank's car.

"Nobody is gonna weep for those two scumbags." Frank turned to him and took his eyes off the road as he always did. Sam steeled himself.

"Who's to say . . ." Frank continued.

"For Christ's sake, Frank, look at the road. You don't have to look at me every time you talk to me. When we were on the job, how many times did you crash before I stopped letting you drive?"

"Who's to say that when McBride and Ryan were bumped back down to Narcotics they didn't go back to their old tricks?" Frank asked rhetorically. "All I'm saying is that door could still be open."

Sam knew where Frank was going. He didn't feel good about this. It was stupid. They had cameras at all the entrances.

"That's what I need, Frank, to get pinched breaking and entering into the TNT office." He shook his head.

"I forgot that you're a convicted felon." Frank smirked.

Why did he get in the car with Frank this morning?

It was because he was desperate. He wasn't getting anywhere looking into Kevin's background, and Bankman wasn't going to keep paying him without results.

This was a bad idea. Frank was right that back in the day, when he and Frank worked Narcotics, they would keep a piece of cardboard wedged in the back door so they could leave without anyone knowing. That was more than ten years ago. Frank was stupid to think that the piece of cardboard wedged in the back door was still there.

The funeral for slain Highway Officer Sam Smith who was struck and killed by a drunk driver as he stood outside his vehicle on the LIE will be laid to rest in Huntington today. Police from all over the area and the fifty states will be attending the funeral. Traffic on the LIE for the morning commute is a mess.

"How about that?" Frank turned to him. They were on the Mosholu Parkway sailing past Clinton High School and the scary, looming, dangerous Tracey Towers, which looked like another tall dungeon. The traffic light turned red just as they entered the whip curve where the Grand Concourse began. Again, Frank had to slam on the brakes not to rear end the Camry Gypsy cab stopped ahead.

Had Frank had planned the burglary of TNT headquarters to coincide with the time when all the cops were attending the funeral of the cop in Huntington.

"Frank, this is a stupid idea."

"Yeah, yeah. I know, you told me that already. If you didn't want to come with me, you didn't have to. Nobody is forcing you." Frank drove quickly and ate some red lights on the way. Cops never gave ex-cops tickets.

* * *

They stopped at a red brick building that housed a satellite branch of the Human Resources Administration that oversaw the North Bronx. In its basement, the Tactical Narcotics Team's Bronx Division had its office.

The building occupied the last patch of land in the Bronx. Westchester County and the City of Mount Vernon began across the street.

Frank drove past it.

Sam let out a sigh.

It was inconspicuous. By the looks of it, you couldn't tell that the basement of the building housed the Bronx Narcotics and Tactical Narcotics Team (TNT).

Frank parked a few blocks away in a residential area with small homes, all of them different—some stucco, some brick, some shingle. The one-family houses were so close together there was only a driveway or a small walkway between them.

Frank handed Sam a flat-top Yankee cap. Sam pulled down the rim and it covered his face. He hunched his shoulders and pulled up the collar of his jacket. They left the car and separated. Frank walked ahead.

Sam watched Frank walk toward the rear doors of the building on a narrow walkway off the sidewalk. Frank opened a door and disappeared inside.

Sam wanted to keep walking away from this. If he got caught, for sure he was going to jail. "Fuck," he murmured to himself. Despite everything that had happened, he couldn't let his old partner go in alone.

Frank was right. If he hadn't wanted to come with him, he should have said so. It was too late to walk away. He went to the door that Frank had opened. He could feel the black angry bulb of the camera above him in the cement overhang. It seemed to peer down his neck, and he fought the urge to look up at it.

The entrance that Frank went through didn't have a door knob. With his fingers he had to dig into the gap between the opening and the side of the building, and he pulled it open. It was an exit at the back of the office, and there it was, where the latch was—somebody had jammed a piece of cardboard taped into a ball so that it wouldn't catch. Fucking Frank was right again.

In the hallway inside, he and Frank stood next to each other. Was someone else there or had they all gone to the funeral of the cop killed on the LIE?

This was crazy. Frank went to the file cabinet in the conference room.

The whole layout was prefab, with assembled cubicles in a circle around a common area with a conference table and a coffee maker and a fridge. Against the far wall was the file cabinet that Frank bent over. He pulled hard on the sliding shelf and the whole cabinet rocked back and forth against the wall. "Fuck."

Sam looked around. He couldn't believe it. Nothing had changed since he had worked here twenty years ago. The sergeant's office, with a safe where they kept the contraband and weapons, overlooked the common area. It was laid out like a prison, where the common area was overlooked by the booth with the CO in it. The elevator opened here. The floor numbers blinked on the monitor.

"It's fucking locked."

"Of course it's locked, genius."

"Do you still carry those keys?"

Frank had remembered that Sam carried a special set of keys. It had come in very handy when they were on the job and needed to open a desk or cabinet, and they didn't have time or probable cause to get a warrant.

Most locks on file cabinets and desk drawers were similar. On his key chain, Sam kept a couple of exemplars, and one or the other usually did the trick, even though he hadn't used them in years.

Frank watched as Sam tried the keys on the lock in the file cabinet. After he found the one that fit best, Sam gingerly twisted it until he felt it catch, and then he applied a little strength. The key caught some more, and he twisted it again, and the file cabinet opened.

Just like back in Sam's day, they still kept the files of the different buys and busts catalogued by neighborhood. Highbridge, Kingsbridge, Morrisania were separated by file tabs and then the neighborhoods were further broken down by street and building numbers.

There was 3211 Kingsbridge and 188th Street, 1403 Davidson and 190th Street. They looked for 1275 Webster, but there was no file.

"I know there had to be a buy and bust there."

"Then where's the file?" Sam's hands shook. Sure, the office was empty, but who knew when they were coming back?

"There's no record of a buy and bust at 1275 because it wasn't sanctioned by the department and because they didn't want anybody to know."

Sam was ready to leave. Was there no record because it wasn't official? They ripped off the dealers in a fake buy and bust.

"Come on." Frank went into the first cubicle on the left. This was their old office. Now there was a pair of size 15 Docksides under the desk. "Those apes took over our office." He shook his head in disgust and gestured with his head at Sam and the desk.

"I don't want to go to fucking jail."

"You're not going to jail." He said it like Sam was being irrational. "Let's just take a quick look around." He pulled on the drawer. The desk was one of those small Formica-topped jobs they sold in Office

Depot. McBride or Ryan were too fucking huge to fit into these chairs or the desks. The desktop was clear except for a postcard of a trawler stuck into the corner of the blotter.

That was McBride and Ryan's thing. They liked to go out on the party boats for the blues off City Island. Their master plan after they retired was to buy a trawler in the Keys and charter it out to the tourists. Sam remembered that they talked about it incessantly, but who was going to tell those two monsters to shut the fuck up?

"Frank, this was really stupid. Let's go." He looked at the elevator.

"Sam, I'm not leaving until we check out these desks."

"Fucking Frank." Sam got out the key ring. The drawers of the first desk were empty. In the bottom drawer, he found a box of 9 mm shells.

There was a blue nylon jacket with NYPD emblazoned in white letters on the back hanging off the door. It had to be as big as a beach blanket to fit either one of those galoots.

He did the same thing with the second desk. Both desks faced each other, just like when he and Frank worked there. It was the same thing as the first desk he rifled. It was empty. When he pulled out the side drawer, there was box of .22 shells and some cuffs. There was a piece of white paper on the bottom of the deep drawer. Sam pulled it out and realized it was a photo. He turned it over, and it was Kevin's face swollen twice its size, and his eyes were black and blue and shut. His head was wrapped in gauze. He had tubes coming out of his nose.

"Holy shit." Sam gasped.

Frank had his cell phone out. He took pictures of the photo.

Sam heard the elevator ding, and the arrow indicated it was coming down. With that, he went back to the rear of the office and out the door he came in. Frank was right behind him.

On the street they separated, and Frank walked ahead.

Sam tried to walk casually. He was almost giddy with relief that they had made it out of there, but he couldn't shake that image of Kevin when he turned over the photo. *What the fuck?*

From across the street, he watched Frank. Frank's hands were stuck deep in his pockets, and he bent over as he walked, staring at the ground like he was afraid what else he might see if he looked up.

They both walked toward the Hyundai, but they were still apart, across the street from each other. Frank got into his car first. He sat there in the driver's seat, staring straight ahead as if he was in shock. When Sam got in, Frank pulled out his cell phone, and they looked at the pictures he had taken of the photo of Kevin. He left it on the console between them with the picture of Kevin staring blankly, beaten up to a pulp, on the screen. They couldn't take their eyes off the photo.

"My God!"

"I know." Frank pulled away from the curb, and he headed south to the West Bronx. He found the highway and got off on Broadway, on the Yonkers side.

"Maybe Kevin got into a fight at a bar or something?" Sam was tired and he'd had enough of Frank.

"Too much of a coincidence."

"Maybe?" He needed to process all of this. This steady income from Bankman was nice, and he didn't want it to end. He thought he knew a way to put this all together, but he needed time to think it through.

"My nephew has a tape of a body getting the shit beat out of it, and then we stumble across a picture of Kevin all messed up." He turned to Sam. It was good the car was stationary because Frank seemed lost in thought.

"Too much of a coincidence. Too much." Frank mumbled under his breath. He kept repeating it to himself.

It sounded like a low growl. This was how Frank got when they were deep in a case. He would talk to himself underneath his breath so that Sam almost couldn't hear what he was saying.

"What was Nooney doing with that tape?" Frank seemed to come out of his trance.

"I think this was a buy and bust nobody knew about because McBride, Ryan, and Kevin were up to their old tricks and decided to get paid out of the proceeds."

"You don't know that, Frank. You don't know that Kevin is the one in the video getting his ass kicked."

"Then how come they used the words 'pig buddies?'"

"Who knows?"

"I'm telling you, this was not a legit undercover gone bad."

"You don't know anything. All you got is suspicions." Sure, part of it was that he liked to get on Frank's nerves and question everything Frank said. He needed proven facts to be sure. Speculation meant nothing. They had pulled up in front of Sam's building.

He saw he was getting a text from Matt Prey on his cell, but he didn't want to look at it, because he didn't want Frank getting nosy and look over his shoulder. He'd wait to read it after Frank dropped him off.

"I hope they don't recognize us on the video." Frank studied Sam's face. He wanted to see how scared Sam was of getting caught.

Funny how they had been partners all these years and the two of them didn't care much for each other. What they liked to do was aggravate each other. Maybe that was why Frank didn't stand up for him when Sam needed him most.

"Thanks, Frank. I feel much better now, asshole." He stepped out and studied his building. He wasn't in the mood for his empty apartment.

He crossed the street on his way to O'Sullivan's, and he read the text from Matt Prey. *Kevin Knowles' trial starts tomorrow. Pick*

Millie up at South Bx. Realty at 8:30 and take her to court in Poughkeepsie. Call me when you get this.

At the bar, he watched ESPN on the TV.

"Hey, Sam. Where you been, sweetie?" Janey, the forty-something curvy barmaid asked him.

"Around." He smiled. She still looked great in her jeans.

"What can I get you?"

"Jack Daniels on the rocks."

She bent over in front of him, and he could see down her loose-fitting Yankee jersey with its top buttons opened.

The baseball season had started. With the sound turned off, images of Aaron Judge, Gary Sanchez, and the Yankees' latest acquisition, Giancarlo Stanton, filled the screen. He never followed the Yankees this early in the season. It didn't matter how good the team was in the spring. Where they were in October was what really mattered.

Janey put his drink on the bar and then went over to serve someone else. It was quiet, right after the lunch crowd had left.

On an empty stomach, he sipped his drink. This could be what Bankman could hang his hat on. Maybe Kevin wasn't fit to go back on the job after being attacked. Did the city know? Were they hiding it? Maybe they didn't know. Maybe Kevin covered the whole thing up? Maybe McBride and Ryan were in on the scheme, and it blew up in their faces?

It didn't matter. He was going to keep this info about the beating under his hat for now. It was too soon to let Matt Prey and Bankman in on what he had uncovered. He could milk this for a while. If he spilled the beans too soon, his gig with Bankman would end because they wouldn't need him anymore. It could blow this case wide open.

His cell phone vibrated in his pocket.

"Bankman wants you to take the train with Millie to Poughkeepsie. He wants the press to see the grieving widow. It adds value to the case." Matt Prey was all business.

It was all about dollars and cents. "I think I might have found something about Kevin Knowles." He needed to give Matt a morsel to whet his appetite.

There was a brief silence on the other end.

"What is it? Is it good?"

"Could be? I need to do a little more digging. I'll let you know." He needed to find the hospital that Kevin was treated at. He downed the last of the bourbon, sucking on an ice cube. "I'll let you know. I don't want to talk about it over the phone."

"I hope it's good. I'm trusting you, Sam. Don't let me down. I recommended you for a job when no one else would. I vouched for you."

"I know, you told me that bullshit a number of fucking times. How am I going to pay for me and Millie to take the train back and forth to Poughkeepsie? The round-trip ticket isn't cheap, especially if you multiply it by two."

Matt Prey let out a sigh on the other end. "I'll put some cash in your bank account to cover your expenses."

Sam gave him his account number.

The camera caught Judge in a perfect swing, and it followed the trajectory of the ball as it flew into the stands. Judge seemed to shake his head in disbelief as he rounded the bases, amazed at himself. Stanton waited for him at home plate, and the two sluggers high fived.

"Janey, I'll have another round and a cheeseburger."

Burgers were all they served here, with fries.

He would enjoy a cheeseburger after living on tuna and white toast sandwiches for the last few weeks.

Chapter Twenty-Three
Kevin Knowles

Trial starts soon, can you come to my office today at 2:00?

After all those messages he had left for Gold, his lawyer, finally Gold had texted him back. When he saw the text, Kevin took a deep breath and exhaled. He tried not to panic, but sometimes it got the best of him. It wasn't so much the pressure of the upcoming trial that made him go bat shit, it was knowing that if he lost the trial he was going to jail. He couldn't escape it.

He had met Gold twice, once at his arraignment in criminal court and then at his arraignment in Supreme Court, after that bitch Celeste Santiago had indicted him.

The first time in criminal court the bail was posted through the union. With Gold at his side, Kevin was in front of the judge for a minute, and then he was released through the back door of the court. On Sheridan, McBride and Ryan were waiting in their car, and they took him home. He got to avoid the press that way.

The second time he met Gold at his office, they had walked over to the Supreme Court. He had followed Gold through the back entrance off Walton Avenue. It was the same thing. Gold had barely said a word to him or the judge, and the court officers escorted him out a back door of the courtroom away from the crowd.

The front row was packed with the press.

The only other time he had spoken to Gold was when the trial had moved to Poughkeepsie. Gold had called him with the news, patting himself on the back on what a good job he had done.

With his NYPD placard on the window, Kevin was able to park right in front of the Family Court, the same spot McBride and Ryan had picked him up the night of his criminal court arraignment.

"Fuck," he said to himself. Even though he had been in Gold's office before, he couldn't remember which one of the strip mall storefront law offices was his.

Up and down the block he read the names on the doorways.

In one of the windows, a fluorescent sign blinked *bail bond 24 hrs* in red ink. He would have remembered that if this had been Gold's office.

There was one office where the lettering was faded, and he couldn't make it out. The secretary with the bee's nest hairdo buzzed him in. He remembered her.

"Who are you?" She wore the cat-shaped glasses.

"I'm Kevin Knowles to see Mr. Gold."

"Oh." She seemed to recognize the name. Maybe from the news or maybe because Kevin had called so many times. She buzzed the intercom on her phone. "He's here," she said into the receiver.

"Oh, he's waiting." She pointed down the hall at the door at the very end.

The narrow, paneled hallway was covered with a deep green '70s shag carpet. Fluorescent lights embedded in the paneled ceiling buzzed above. Kevin couldn't remember coming here, even though he knew he had been here. It was a place he would want to forget. It was like a cave too narrow for two people to pass side by side.

The smell of pipe tobacco came from the back. He paused when he walked by an office and saw old man Feldman sitting behind the desk cleaning his pipe. Feldman's hooded eyes looked down at the pipe cleaner and the marble ashtray like a saucer filled with tobacco.

After he had passed Feldman's office, Kevin stepped back and stood in the doorway and watched him. He looked ancient and small behind the desk, and he moved like a sloth with a pipe cleaner in hand, trying to dig the debris out of a pipe. Amazing that old Feldman ran the Bronx from this little shit hole.

When the old man looked up and saw Kevin standing there, he waived at him impatiently to keep going. Like, what the fuck are you looking at.

Kevin found Gold standing in front of his office.

Inside the desk and the floor were piled with files and papers.

"Good to see you again." He was thin and wiry like Kevin but not as tall. "Good news. We got the trial moved up to Poughkeepsie. It has a much better jury pool."

"I know. Don't you remember that you called me and told me the trial's been moved?"

"I did?" Gold gave him a bemused look. "A jury in the Bronx would've crucified you. We've got a much better shot with a jury from upstate."

"Why's that?" Kevin stood close to him. Gold tapped the toe of his left foot, and then Gold took a step back.

"Huh?" Gold asked. He removed some files from one of the chairs and motioned for Kevin to sit. Gold sat in the other seat in front of his desk.

Kevin brought the chair real close to Gold. He wanted to be in his space and keep him uncomfortable.

"It was a long drive down here." Kevin's knees were almost touching Gold's. "So why do you think we got a better shot with a jury from upstate?" Of course, he knew the answer. It bugged him a lot that Gold hadn't returned his phone calls, and now, the night before the trial, he called him in.

"Common sense . . ." Gold started to explain.

"I'm not stupid, Golden Boy." That was a good name for him. It evened the playing field.

"Excuse me?"

Kevin could see that Gold was taken aback. "You don't have to explain to me why it's much better that this case was transferred upstate. I get it. I'm just a little pissed off, Golden Boy, that you haven't returned my phone calls."

"I'm sorry, I've been so busy."

It pissed Kevin off to be bullshitted to.

"See, that's the thing, Golden Boy, I'm not just another perp on your busy calendar. This case is a special case for you, and you need to work real hard on it. You feel me, Golden Boy?" He paused. "If I lose, I go to jail with all the perps I locked up, and Golden boy, you are not going to let that happen. Because if I lose, you lose." He made a slicing motion across his throat. Kevin gave Gold a sheepish look when he said it. Like he'd be reluctant to do it, but if Gold lost this trial, it was curtains for them both. This was the way it was going to be. No one had a choice. Gold stared down at his desk and his hands fidgeted on top of the desk blotter.

"I'm not worried about your case." Gold pushed his chair back away from Kevin and stood. "Most of the people that live in Poughkeepsie or thereabouts are blue collar, and a lot of them are cops, firemen, corrections officers, and court officers, and they're going to love you." Gold talked with his hands, gesturing and pointing at the air when he spoke. "Your case is a slam dunk."

"That's what I like to hear, Golden Boy."

"This is all about appearances. You show up tomorrow in your suit and tie with your wife. You'll see how these people on the jury look at you. When you get on the stand and testify, and you tell them that you were afraid for your life and that's why you pulled your gun." Gold continued with his hands, unconsciously pointing with his index fingers, stabbing at the air.

"I thought his cell phone was a gun, and he reached for it from his waistband. . .

"Exactly. Reasonable grounds to use deadly force based on what you saw, and that video doesn't hurt you. This jury is going to relate to you."

"Okay, Golden Boy." He patted Gold on the back. "Do your best, and you don't have to worry." Kevin felt bad that he had come on so strong to make his point. Sometimes all the pressure got the best of him.

"You have to testify at the trial. These people on the jury have to hear from you. I think you'll make a good witness." Gold's tone was soothing and confident. He went to pat Kevin on the back. Instead, he held his hand there but didn't touch Kevin. He was feeding him a line.

"You're going to prepare me to testify?"

"Of course. There's going to be a lot of time during the trial for us to sit down and go over some stuff. What's your wife's name?"

"Sue."

"I'll meet with you and Sue tomorrow at the luncheonette that's across the street from the courthouse at 8:45. Remember, it's all about appearances. It starts the minute those jurors get a look at you in the hall before jury selection. People make up their minds on a first impression." Gold didn't look at Kevin.

How could he blame himself for frightening Gold? He was desperate because his life was in Golden Boy's hands. And he could go to jail. He needed to drive that home.

He didn't get up to leave. He wasn't ready.

"Of course, I'm going to work like a maniac on your case. I don't look at your case like just another. There's a reason you got sent to me." Gold's voice rose in pitch.

That was good. Gold got the point, and now Kevin could leave.

In the car on his way home, he took Morris to Park and ended up on Webster. He passed 1275. There was a squad car parked in front of the building. Ray Santos' Mercedes was no longer double parked in front of the building. It must have been towed.

Chapter Twenty-Four
Sam Free

"Are you kidding me?" Millie asked Sam when she opened the door to the minivan and slid into the passenger seat.

"What?" He towered over her from the driver's seat.

"You work for Bankman, and you drive this piece of shit? Come on, white boy." She shook her head, rolled her eyes, and looked straight ahead onto the morning traffic of Webster.

"Just because I work for Bankman doesn't mean I have money."

"Don't tell me you're driving me to Poughkeepsie in this heap."

"No, we're taking the Metro North."

"So, let's go. What're you waiting for? Chop, chop, gringo." Over the edge of the seat, her tiny legs swung back and forth over the floorboard.

Sam remembered last night when Matt Prey had called and given him Millie's cell phone number. He said, "You have to text her because she doesn't answer her phone." When he was about to hang up, Matt said, "Have fun." He laughed when he said it. Sure, hanging out with Millie promised to be tons of fun.

"Can you get me a tea and a toasted bagel? I had to get up so early, I didn't have enough time. There's a place right up here on the right." She pointed to the store with the yellow flashing bulbs that spelled Cuchifrito.

"Tea?"

"Yeah, tea with milk and sugar. What, you think just because I'm from the South Bronx I don't drink tea? And a plain bagel, toasted dry, no butter, no margarine, nothing on it."

Sam left her in the van with the engine running. The store was part Cuchifrito and part supermarket. He followed the smell of bacon to the back. There was a small man with a hair net and a spatula who nodded when Sam ordered. The bagels in the bin display looked stale. Nothing about this place looked fresh.

She nibbled on the bagel. "Jeez, it's like a rock. I should have told you to get me toast." She pulled back the plastic cover and slurped the hot tea. "Ah." She turned to him. "What's wrong with you?" She said *which* instead of *with.* It sounded like "What's wrong wich you? Why aren't you eating? Are you sick or something?'

"Maybe I'm just not hungry."

"Don't be so testy, white boy."

"Do me a favor, don't call me white boy."

"I didn't mean it as an insult. Don't get so tight."

"I'm not tight."

"If the shoe fits." Millie shrugged and looked out the window.

They rode in silence as she finished each slurp of the tea with a resounding "Ah." "You musta been a cop too?"

"Yeah."

"I can tell. All youse got that five oh look." She said it with disdain. "I could pick out a cop in a crowd." Millie didn't look at him when she spoke, instead preferring to look out the window at the East River as they reached the end of Fordham Road, crossed the bridge, and entered Manhattan up Broadway to where the island ended at the 207th Street Bridge and then they were headed back into the Bronx.

"I don't get why Bankman wants me to go up there and check out this trial. Does he really think it's gonna make a difference that the widow of the stiff is in court? Sure as shit, Sherlock, these upstate yahoos are gonna walk that Loco piece of shit Kevin Knowles for capping my Ray."

"You never know what can happen at trial." Sam found it funny how she called Kevin Knowles by his street name.

"Oh please. Don't bullshit a bullshitter."

"I hope Bankman don't think I'm going to be going to this trial every day. I don't mind showing my face, but not every day." She wiggled her nose when she said it.

"I don't know, Millie. Why don't you and Bankman work it out?"

"Did you know Ray?"

"No. Not really." He wondered if she knew Nooney. Did she know what happened to him?

"Well, you ain't missing much. He wasn't the nicest person you would wanna meet. Check this out. Look at my mouth. You see, I have no back teeth." Millie grimaced in a protracted make-believe smile so she could show him. He turned from the traffic to look at her. "That's 'cause Ray knocked out my teeth. At least something good is coming out of my marriage."

"What?" He didn't know how to take what Millie was telling him. Was she being serious? He couldn't figure her out.

"This pay day, this lawsuit. If I wouldn't have married Ray, I wouldn't be able to collect."

They had reached the Spuyten Duyvil train station, and he found a spot in the parking lot.

"Listen, don't pay me no mind. I'm just shooting off my mouth. Sometimes I don't make much sense. I just say things to see people's reaction. I wanted to get a rise out of you is all." She followed him to the train platform. "And besides, I figure you can't say nothing to no one on account of the attorney-client privilege."

"I'm not a lawyer, Millie."

"You work for a lawyer. It's the same thing, my gringo friend."

The platform overlooked the spot where the East River met the Hudson in a confluence of currents that gave the brown running water an angry look. The surface swiveled with the ripples formed by the currents and an undertow.

The platform was empty. They could see the rear of a train headed south into Manhattan. They were opposite rush hour, and there would be empty seats on their train to Poughkeepsie.

On the New Jersey side, the cliffs of the Palisades loomed over the Hudson River in hues of red and brown rock. There, colors changed as the sun got higher in the sky.

On the river, it was cold. Millie zipped up her jacket and hopped up and down in her lifts. She wore the same azure-colored North Face with her long braid stuffed inside.

"You got kids?"

"I don't want to talk about my family with you. My job is to take you to the courthouse in Poughkeepsie so that you can watch the trial and show your face like the poor concerned widow."

"That's not a very nice thing to say to me. I could report you to your boss Bankman. I'm worth a lot of money to Bankman." She waited for Sam to react. He didn't. "You don't worry because you know I wouldn't rat you out to Bankman. Besides, all those things I said before, I was just kidding."

"No worries, Millie. It doesn't bother me."

"I don't have kids because I wouldn't want to bring kids into this world."

They could see the lights of the train approaching. It sounded its horn as it approached.

The minute he and Millie stepped onto the car, there was Celeste Santiago with her chin on Desante's shoulder, and they were reading something on a laptop. They didn't see them, and Sam decided to keep it that way. He motioned to Millie with his head pointing at the door to the other car.

"That's the cop that was there with the DA lady when Ray was murdered."

He listened to the way Millie said Ray *was murdered.* She said it like she knew something. A secret, maybe?

They found a seat in the other car. She sat facing him. She liked to sit with crossed her ankles above the floor.

"They seem too cozy, like they're in each other's pants." With that, Millie turned to the window and was silent as they traveled north alongside the Hudson.

Chapter Twenty-Five
Celeste Santiago

Celeste Santiago saw Sam and Millie on the platform as the train entered the station. She didn't mention it to Robert Desante; instead, she rested against his shoulder and studied the laptop. It was the autopsy and toxicology report for the deceased Ray Santos. She read the part of the report that listed the labs and toxicology data collected, and there it was—opiates were found in the deceased's blood.

"You think Gold saw this?"

"Of course, he did." Celeste knew Gold. They had dated and battled each other at trial a few times. Of course, he was going to see the toxicology report.

If Kevin Knowles wasn't acquitted, it would be a miracle. In a few hours they would be starting the trial, and she didn't want to think about it. She thought instead about Desante's cologne. She still liked it, and she had convinced him to limit his intake of garlic and use mouthwash, and that had gotten rid of his garlic breath, which made him more palatable. He closed his eyes and put his arm around her.

She shook off her stilettos and put her pantyhose feet up on the seat. She studied the loose skin around his neck. She'd have to get used to it if she was going to be with a man who was more than twenty years her senior. Celeste liked how grateful he was to be with her.

The Metro North Railroad stopped in Yonkers, Hastings, and Dobbs Ferry. This far north, there was still ice on the Hudson. The train skipped the empty platform in Ossining.

Celeste drifted back to last August when she and Schneiderman took the LIRR out to Amagansett. In their ocean-front condo, with its majestic view of the Atlantic Ocean, he broke it to her about moving out. What an asshole. "It'll be just temporarily," Schneiderman told her. "Until I work through this issue I have with commitment." What a load of crap that was. He was giving her the "it's not you, it's me" line of bullshit.

She knew something was up with him for weeks before their trip to the Hamptons. He had been acting aloof and distant since he got appointed as a judge to the Court of Claims, and he was going to Brooklyn. It was his opportunity to make a great escape.

Why couldn't he have just waited until they got back? Because he was a self-loathing fuck who felt guilty about breaking her heart, or maybe he didn't like her very much. Her choice in men was always poor. She wasted three years of her life on that asshole. Maybe the solution was for her to be with an old man like Desante.

"You okay, kid?" Desante sat up and looked at her.

"It's all good." She smiled. "I'm just thinking about this trial in Poughkeepsie." He was going to be her ballistics expert in the trial.

"I can't believe the judge sent this case up here from the Bronx."

"Judges can do whatever they want. Nobody wanted this case in the Bronx. They don't want a circus of Brown Lives Matter, the Puerto Rican Legal Defense Fund, and Hispanics Across America parading on the courthouse steps demanding justice for another killing of an unarmed man by the police."

"So now what are you going to do?"

Celeste laughed at Desante's strong Bronx accent. He sounded like he was from Arthur Avenue. "What am I gonna do?" she mocked Desante, and then she felt dejected. She couldn't believe that she had gone into Levin's office and begged for this case. She was going to be a big shot seeking justice for the poor unarmed super or building manager gunned down by the white police officer. "I'm gonna have to go up to bum fuck Poughkeepsie to try Kevin Knowles for shooting a man with drugs in his system. After they find him not guilty, they're going to congratulate Knowles and wish him the best. They're probably going to give Knowles a party." The toxicology report from the medical examiner had found heroin in Ray Santos' blood. Gold was going to parade that toxicology report in front of the jury.

Desante threw up his hands in mock despair. "What can you do? You do the best you can and get through it."

She had the trial folder in her blue cloth shopping bag, and she thought about taking it out and going over the file one last time before they got to court. She had slept like crap. All night she checked the clock radio. She was gripped with some irrational fear that she was going to sleep through it and not wake up to catch the 7:03 to Poughkeepsie.

Soon, she was going to be at the courthouse picking a jury. She didn't want to think about it. She needed to close her eyes for a few minutes, and she did. She drifted off for a few minutes on Desante's shoulder.

"Hey, kid." Desante nudged her awake. "We're here."

When they exited the train, they walked to the cab stand. Desante carried her bag with the trial folder. There was a long line of cabs. The drivers were all Haitian, and they spoke French as they stood together in the cold spring day.

Celeste saw Sam and Millie approaching the cab stand.

She walked up to Millie. "How are you? Did you get my messages? I've been trying to reach you. Are you going to the trial?"

"I don't know why in God's name I would be here otherwise."

"Why don't you ride with Detective Desante and me? I want you to sit in the first row when we're picking a jury. You don't mind, do you?" Celeste looked through Sam as though he weren't even there. "No need to hang around." The way Sam hesitated when he saw her, like he wasn't sure what to do, Celeste could tell that as big as he was, Sam Free was still afraid of her. Sure, she had tried to have him thrown in jail, but that was a long time ago. She had almost forgotten about that. She had much bigger fish to fry.

"You know what. Maybe I'll just wait until you adjourn for the day, and I'll make sure that she gets home." He looked away when he spoke to her.

"Well, if you want to hang around all day, be my guest. They're not going to allow you to sit in the courtroom during jury selection."

Celeste had heard that the famous Bankman was representing Millie in the civil suit against the city, Kevin Knowles, and the New York City Police Department. She guessed that Bankman probably sent Sam up here with Millie to make sure she got to the trial. The publicity of having the widow attend the criminal trial would only help the civil case. Bankman was probably going to make another couple of million when he put poor Millie Santos in front of a Bronx jury and told them how the police had murdered her unarmed husband.

It just didn't seem fair that the personal injury lawyers made all the money and lawyers like her struggled to make ends meet on a civil service salary. She was going to use some of that sympathy for the widow by walking into the courtroom with poor Millie Santos.

"I guess that's what I'll have to do," Sam told her.

Desante waved them over to the cab as he held the door open.

Millie turned and looked at Sam and shook her head in disapproval as she left in the cab.

It was only a few blocks to the courthouse.

Poughkeepsie had a sad feel about it. They had tried to spruce it up with new street signs and bright awnings on the stores. Maybe once, long ago, it was different, but now it seemed as though a depression had set in. It was a weekday morning, and Market Street, in the center of the city, was empty, like a ghost town.

Millie sat with Celeste in the back seat. Desante sat up front with the driver.

Up ahead a few blocks, was the courthouse, an old limestone building, sandblasted clean, adjacent to the Dutchess County Department of Social Services. There were TV trucks in front of the courthouse. Celeste fixed her face in the compact mirror she removed from her purse. She checked her makeup in the rear-view mirror of the cab. Maybe the rear-view mirror was closer to the perspective of a TV camera. She studied Millie and brushed some stray hairs from her face. She had fine, perfect, doll-like features with big coal-colored, almond-shaped eyes. Millie would be pretty with a little makeup. She thought about touching her up.

There was a stand with microphones in the square of the courthouse entrance and a flurry of reporters when she exited the car.

"Ms. Santiago, as a prosecutor, are you concerned the case was moved up to Poughkeepsie?"

"No, not at all. As Judge Fitzmorris stated, in his opinion, he feels the defendant can get a fair trial up here."

"So, are you saying you agree with the judge's decision to move the trial up here?"

"I wouldn't go that far."

There were some laughs and some guffaws from the crowd. Some held "Brown Lives Matter" or "Don't Shoot" signs. "Stop killing us!" someone shouted. "No justice no peace," others in the crowd chanted.

Celeste turned and entered the courthouse. Behind her, she could hear the chants of "Don't shoot" growing louder.

She recognized the court officer at the manometers. He had a mountain man beard. He had transferred up here from the Bronx. A lot of the court officers lived up here, and it was an easier commute. "What floor is Gallagher?"

"He's on four."

Last night when she couldn't sleep, she had Googled Justice Lanell Gallagher. He was a right-to-lifer who Governor Pataki appointed to the Court of Claims. Before that, he was the town justice of the Village of LaGrange, a tiny dot on the map outside of Poughkeepsie.

In the hallway, Celeste passed Brian Dobbs as he spoke on his cell phone. He looked at her and then at Millie and Desante. She wasn't sure if he recognized her from when he was a member of Bronx Narcotics, or maybe he was giving her the cold shoulder because she was prosecuting a cop. With the phone glued to his ear, he paced the hallway. He had a bad limp and a huge gut.

Desante and Millie followed her to a small courtroom with new sterile gray commercial carpet. Gold and Kevin Knowles were at the counsel table. Gold smirked slightly when he saw her. She had lost track of how many trials she and Gold had been in. Gold looked skinnier than when they had dated. She wondered how she looked to him. His smirk annoyed her. It was like he had this one in the bag.

Kevin looked uncomfortable in his ill-fitting suit. She got a creepy, dangerous feeling from him. It was a feeling that stayed with her since Kevin had been with Bronx TNT, and she had been a prosecutor with the Narcotics Division of the Bronx District Attorney's Office. She could never put her finger on it. Whenever she dealt with Kevin, there was always that feeling that he was not right, that there was something off with him; and now, seeing him sitting next to Gold, she had that same feeling again. There was a woman sitting behind him in the first row of the audience section of the courtroom. It was probably his wife.

Desante and Millie sat in the first row behind the prosecutor's table, which was the counsel table closest to the jury box.

Celeste entered the well through the wooden gate.

"Ms. Santiago." Judge Gallagher had thick, close-cropped hair and a beard neatly trimmed. The hair and the beard were all snow-white like a polar bear. He stared at her. "We do things differently around here. It's not like Bronx County where the court gets going at ten o'clock, ten-thirty, or maybe even eleven o'clock. In my court, we start promptly at nine-thirty."

The clock on the wall behind the bench was at nine-fifty.

“I’m sorry, Judge. I won’t let it happen again.” Now she knew why Gold was smirking. It was because Gold had the lowdown that Gallagher was one of those judges who was a stickler for time, and that Gallagher was going to let her know about it.

“Let’s get the jury,” Gallagher told his clerk. “You will each have ten minutes to address the panel. I expect to have a jury by lunch time.” Gallagher rose and went back to the robing room.

Gallagher was probably pissed off that he had to try a case sent up from the Bronx. In Dutchess County, defendants rarely went to trial, because up here, juries almost always convicted. Best thing to do if one got pinched was to take a plea. Unless you were a white cop who shot a Hispanic man who had drugs in his system and who you thought had a weapon on him.

Chapter Twenty-Six
Kevin Knowles

"I'm glad it's starting." Kevin was too nervous to drive. "It's the waiting that's worse than anything."

"We're in this together." Sue had a way of watching him from the corner of her eye when she was driving.

Kevin didn't know why Sue was so devoted to him. It was probably because she needed him around to be a father to the kids and a breadwinner more than anything else. He wasn't even sure she still loved him.

He wasn't sure what she knew about him and what she didn't, or maybe what she chose to ignore, or block out, or admit to herself.

His mind went back to when they were first dating in the Bronx. How he would hold her so tight on the whole way back to her apartment building in Woodlawn, by the vast cemetery. In the cemetery they found an empty shed that the gardeners used, with shovels and pick axes and wheelbarrows, where they fooled around. It was creepy, and they were clumsy and fumbling. He remembered how, late at night, he and Sue would walk past the baseball fields and over the train yard where they would watch the carpet of sparks from the subway cars in the yard fall onto Jerome Avenue from the El above. He thought he was thinking about the past because he couldn't stomach what was happening to him now. All of that happened so long ago that it seemed to him to have happened in another life.

When he and Sue had gone shopping for suits, it hit him like a shot to the gut that he was going on trial, and if he lost, he was probably going to jail. Alone in the dressing room, he started sweating real bad, and he had to sit on the bench for a few minutes because he felt he was going to pass out. Sue came to check on him. He told her he was fine, but he wasn't.

Kevin put on a show for everyone. He acted like he was strong and that he was going to get through this with the help of his family, but it wasn't true. Inside, Kevin felt himself falling apart as the trial grew closer.

He was so frightened that he held his hands together to hide that they were shaking. He stared out the window. They were going the opposite way, north, and the rest of the world was going south to work. In this direction, the highway was empty.

He watched Sue. He was the one who got up early with the kids and got them ready for school. She needed that extra time in the morning to shake off the after effects of that cocktail combination of Lunesta and a couple glasses of red wine that she consumed to fall asleep. Now that the trial had started, they needed to leave earlier than usual, right after they put the kids on the bus. Sue seemed okay to drive.

Up ahead a bunch of deer grazed on the shoulder of the Parkway. He spotted a doe and a fawn, and he thought the mother and daughter made eye contact with him. He was paranoid like that. He always thought people were looking at him or were after him. How stupid that he thought the deer were looking at him too. Their mangy winter coats were gray and dingy like the forest. It hadn't been warm enough to bring the green out in the forest. It didn't help that every few days a cold front hit that halted spring's progression. On some days, like today, it felt like winter.

Sue followed Route 44 into downtown Poughkeepsie. It looped around the civic center past the Section 8 multi-family tenements.

They passed the courthouse, and he saw the news trucks and the protestors with their signs.

"We'll get through this like we get through everything else," Sue told him as she pulled into a spot in the municipal lot. She stared straight ahead when she said it.

Gold waited for them outside the coffee shop.

In the cold, Kevin noticed that he still had no feeling in the right side of his face underneath his eye. It felt numb.

"Are you ready?" Gold as usual was talking with his hands. It was like he was pulling words right out of the air.

"The more important question is if you're ready?" Kevin asked.

Kevin, Sue, and Gold crossed the street. Kevin grabbed Sue's arm, bracing against the onslaught of the crowd and the protestors. The court officer with the mountain man beard and the others formed a human barrier around them, and together they walked quickly into the courthouse and passed through the metal detectors.

"So, you ready, Golden Boy?" He asked again as he and Gold waited for Sue to pass through the manometers. He liked the way Gold cringed when he called him that. He liked to bust his horns.

They took the small elevator up to the fourth floor. Except for a court officer reading the paper, the courtroom was empty.

"Sit here." Gold showed Sue where he would like her to sit–in the first row behind the counsel table, which was usually reserved for attorneys. Because she was the wife of the accused cop–"wrongfully accused"–she got a bye.

Kevin followed Gold into the well. They sat at the counsel table. Gold opened his bag and took out the file.

Kevin's knees were shaking. He put his hands on them to make them stop.

Kevin could hear the court officers laughing from the back room, and he could hear one of them talking. To them it was just another trial.

" *When these people hear that Knowles killed a man with a record for selling drugs because Knowles thought he had a weapon, they are going to take five minutes to find him not guilty and give him a standing ovation.* "

He turned to Sue in the first row. She winked at him and smiled.

He wished the nausea would fade. He poured himself some water from the pitcher on the table.

"Don't drink that," Sue whispered.

She was right. No one knew how long that water had been in that pitcher, or where the water had come from.

"Here," Gold said, and from his trial bag, he removed a bottled water that he put in front of Kevin.

Chapter Twenty-Seven
Sam Free

He was supposed to bring Millie up here for the trial and then bring her back to the Bronx, and now she had left with Celeste Santiago. He didn't want to mess with Celeste. Based on their past dealings, Sam did not want a beef with her. He thought it best to hang out by the courthouse until court adjourned for the day and then catch up with Millie. If Bankman found out about this, it probably would be the end of the gig, and Sam did not want that.

By himself, he took a cab to the courthouse. It was a madhouse of reporters and TV trucks. After a few days, they would disappear. There was always a better story that viewers would be more interested in.

When they were picking a jury, they didn't let people in because there was no room—the courtroom was filled with potential jurors. They let Millie stay because she was the dead guy's wife.

He looked for a spot to wait until he saw Millie come out of the courthouse. He was trying to do what Bankman told him to do, which was to shadow Millie up here so that she could show her face and get a little publicity as the grief-stricken widow. Celeste Santiago was getting in his way.

He looked around Market Street, where the courthouse was, for a place to wait. There was a coffee shop across the street, and he went in and waited in line. He was behind a very shapely brunette in a sky-blue dress suit that fit her well, like a glove, and she had gorgeous silky hair. She turned, and she was pretty, with an upturned nose and dark skin and big brown eyes that made his knees shake a little, but she needed to lose a couple of pounds.

"Are you here for the trial? It seems like everybody is." When she turned and smiled at him, he could see her front teeth were crooked.

"Yeah, sort of." He felt an instant attraction for her. Wow, an electricity of sex that he felt deep in his loins. He hadn't felt that in a long time. It never happened to him. He thought she felt it too, but he wasn't sure. The way she looked at him, like she was hot for him. He wasn't sure if he was making it all up in his head because he had been so lonely.

"I'm here for the jury."

"Really?"

"Swear to God, and I hope they pick me."

"Why's that?"

"Huh?" She stared up at him, wide-eyed.

He laughed. "Why's that, that you hope they pick you?"

"Oh." She giggled. The line had moved, and she didn't realize it because she was facing him, and he didn't realize it either.

She walked to where the line stopped again and turned to him. "I'm probably the only one sitting there who wants to be picked for the jury. I guess it means that my life must be pretty sad if I prefer jury duty over it."

"I don't find it sad." He saw that even though she was heavy, she was shapely. He tried not to act like he was checking her out.

"Not having to travel ninety minutes each way to try to get the attention of a bunch of inner-city sixteen- and seventeen-year-olds would be a vacation for me." It was a cafeteria line that passed trays filled with scrambled eggs, sunny side eggs, and boiled eggs. Beyond that were the trays filled with toast, French toast, sausage, and home fries.

He followed behind her as she got her tray and plate and went along the line. He sat with her at the table.

"Linda Esposito." She held out her hand. Her nails were perfect and polished purple. She held his hand a little longer than necessary.

"Sam Free."

"Are you here for jury duty too?"

"No. I got work here."

"Oh," she said, and she leaned in. "I heard they're starting the trial for that cop that killed that super in the Bronx. I hope they pick me for that."

"That's funny. I never heard someone say that they wanted to be picked for jury duty."

"I told you, Sam Free, my life is that pathetic." She sipped her coffee and then put a plastic lid on it. "I got to get going, they said that everybody has to be back in ten minutes."

Sam took his tray to a table by the window, and he watched the protesters and the news trucks, and the court officers trying to keep order.

Chapter Twenty-Eight
Sam Free

Sam caught sight of Millie Santos in her pale azure parka as she left the courthouse with the lunch crowd at the one o'clock break. His hands shook from all the cups of coffee he had drank waiting for her.

Because she was so small, he lost sight of her as she made her way through the protestors, court officers, and lawyers.

From outside the coffee shop, he searched the crowd and then she reappeared. He thought about Linda Esposito and the attraction they had to one another. He didn't feel like he was stepping out on Iris. What was he to do? Iris was the one who was pushing him away. How long was Iris going to punish him? He hoped Linda Esposito was picked for the jury and that he would see her again. Did he have the guts to fool around with her? Did she like him that much or was she just flirting? He wasn't sure.

He crossed the street, and when Millie came out of the crowd, he was there.

"What're you, like, my big brother picking me up after school to see that I get home safe?"

"What happened to your new friends?"

"Stupid DA." She shook her head in disgust. "These people they picked for the jury are all a bunch of rednecks. They adjourned. Over lunch, the lawyers had some meeting with the judge. It's a mess." She rolled her eyes. "It's a good thing you were here waiting for me because Bankman would've been pissed if he found out I had to go home alone from Poughkeepsie." She laughed at him.

They made an unlikely pair; he was a big bald white guy with blue eyes, and she was tiny with those doll-like features and the long braid stuffed into her parka.

A bunch of Haitian cab drivers that he saw at the station were hanging around the courthouse, and Sam and Millie caught one back to the station. The train to the city was there when they arrived.

"I ain't coming back for a while, you tell Bankman that. This is all a bunch of bullshit anyway." She sat across from him.

"Whatever you say, boss."

"Oh my God, please don't talk down to me."

"I'm not."

"Just don't call me boss."

"Okay, I won't call you boss."

"When Loco testifies, I'll come to watch that shit." She giggled and rubbed her hands together in anticipation.

There she went again, referring to Kevin as *Loco*. That's what the dealers called him.

"I used to take this train all the time to see Ray when he was locked up."

"To Poughkeepsie?"

"No. It was to one of the prisons farther away, up the line. I don't remember if it was Coxsackie or Dannemora. It was one of them. I had to catch a bus after the train let me off. It was bum fuck middle of nowhere."

"Sounds like a blast."

"It was a complete riot." Millie sat up straight and pursed her lips together. "Prison changed Ray. He came home mean. Now, don't get me wrong, Ray was always a tough guy. He was little like me—we got to be tough—but when he came home from prison that first time, I saw a change in him. It was like a sadness that he had seen the worst things people do to one another, he told me that." She said *told* without the "d" so that it sounded like *tol*.

She shook her head in disgust. "After that, every time Ray got locked up, he would act all nice and devoted until he got released, and then he would start the same shit all over again. And then finally, when he decided he's going to get a job and live a clean life, he gets snuffed. Ain't that some shit?" She looked out the train's window as they followed the Hudson River south.

They rode in silence for a while.

"That DA, the Spanish lady with the skinny legs, she's gonna lose this case bad."

"Why do you say that?"

"That jury is gonna take five minutes to find Loco not guilty."

"I don't understand why you keep saying that."

"Because, Ray was a functioning addict."

"What does that mean?"

"I'm saying that when they did the autopsy, they found traces of dope in his system."

"How do you know that?"

"Because, when I rode in the car with that DA and the detective, she told me that."

"What else did she say?"

"I'm saying that lawyer for Kevin is going to parade that in front of this upstate cracker jury, and they're going to walk him." She stared out the window at the Palisades cliffs on the New Jersey side of the Hudson. "Ray was no saint, and me and Ray were no match made in heaven." Millie paused for a minute. "When you were a cop, did you know Dobbs?"

"Why are you asking me about Dobbs?"

"'Cause, I seen him in the hall at the court today."

"No shit. Are you sure?"

"Cross my heart and hope to die." She smiled sadly.

"So how do you know Dobbs?"

"Why are you asking me that? Is Dobbs a friend of yours or something?" It was as if she was asking Sam that to be sure that he wasn't Dobbs' friend before she gave him the goods.

"Dobbs was my boss on the job. He was never a friend of mine." He wiped the back his hand across his mouth. He did it subconsciously, as if to wipe away the bad taste of thinking about Dobbs.

"When Ray came home from prison, he became a CI for Dobbs. Those were dangerous times. Ray hustled, but at the same time, he ratted out the competition."

He wondered why she was telling him this. Did she think that he knew it already? She knew he worked with Dobbs. He wanted to see what else she knew, and he knew she wanted to know what he knew.

He also wondered what she knew about Nooney. If Ray was Nooney's godfather, Millie must have known him, but she didn't say a word about him.

"I'll tell you a story about that fat piece of shit Dobbs." She leaned forward and lowered her voice. "It was the last time I seen Dobbs before today." Millie Santos didn't look at him when she spoke; instead, her eyes focused on the passing river, tinted silver by the afternoon son. "Ray was strung out, and he begged me to pick up some drugs from Dobbs." She laughed. "The reason Ray couldn't get any dope was because the cops, Dobbs, and his crew busted all the dealers. It was a drought."

It was always the cops that had the best product.

"Ray had arranged for Dobbs to meet me at a cop bar on Bainbridge. When I got there, Dobbs told me to follow him to the bathroom. He was drunk. In the bathroom, Dobbs locked the door and forced himself on me. At first, I tried to fight him off, but he was too big and strong." She sighed. "Then I just let him do his business so that I could get it over with and get out of there with Ray's junk."

At that moment, he thought of his Tamara, his baby girl. Sure, she was a grown woman, but when Millie told him what Dobbs had done to her, it made him want to find Tamara and hold her tight.

For a while they didn't say anything, and then, as the train entered Yonkers, he could see Millie's clenched jaw loosen. She was relieved to be close to home. She laughed again.

"You shoulda seen Loco Kevin Knowles sitting in the court with his lawyer. He was all suited up. He doesn't look like a psycho at all. He's playing it up to the max. His wife is a skinny Irish lady, and she sits right behind him. You could see the jury watching them. Unbelievable! They look like they're in church."

The train pulled into Spuyten Duyvil.

He was going to call Tamara and Justin the minute he got home.

He looked over at Millie as she held her cell phone, and he caught sight of the screen. He could have sworn he saw a message from Loco, but Millie put the cell phone away fast. He was almost sure he saw those letters *LOCO* in her text.

Chapter Twenty-Nine
Kevin Knowles

It was late. The metal gate that covered the front of the office was pulled halfway down, and Sheila's secretarial station was empty.

"We are going to go over every question I'm going to ask you and every question Celeste Santiago is going to ask you on cross examination. This way you'll know what to expect."

He and Gold were in Feldman's office. They came in here because there was no room to sit in Gold's office, as the floor, chairs, and desk were covered with paperwork from his trial.

The round marble ashtray sat on Feldman's desk blotter with pipe cleaners and a pipe. The potpourri smell of tobacco filled the office. Gold sat behind the desk in Feldman's chair.

"The trial is going so fast, Golden Boy."

"After you testify tomorrow, we do summations, and then the jury gets the case."

"Oh my God." He took a deep breath. He held his stomach, hoping the nausea would pass.

"When you're on the stand, put them in your shoes. Make them feel what you felt when you thought Ray Santos was pointing a weapon at you." Gold was poking away at the air as he spoke. "You've got to get their blood pressure going. Tell them what you saw—that you came into that building to investigate drug activity, and you saw this man who you thought was pointing a gun at you, and you fired." His hands formed a pistol. "Do you think you can do that?"

"It's the truth."

"Reasonable grounds to use deadly force."

It annoyed Kevin when Golden Boy used those words. Does anyone know what that really means? It was lawyer mumbo jumbo from someone who didn't know what it was like to be out on these streets locking up the bad guys.

He saw Gold about to say something and he cut him off. "So you think we're in the clear if my testimony goes well tomorrow?"

"I'm not saying that."

"Well, you must be confident."

"I'm worried about their expert, Desante, who says that after that initial shot, you shot him twice at close range."

"But your expert says he was not shot at close range."

"But there was stippling from your gun on his clothes."

"You know what, Golden Boy? Your negativism is really starting to aggravate me. Just shut the fuck up and prepare me to testify tomorrow. Okay?" He looked at Golden Boy's hands, and they were shaking. "Ah, jeez, stop being nervous. I'm not going to hurt you yet. We're in the middle of the trial. Why would I hurt my own lawyer? If we lose, and I have to go to jail, than it's a different story." He felt himself caged in, like an animal pacing back and forth.

"I got it, Kevin. You don't have to threaten me. I know how important this case is. I think this jury loves you, and they love your wife Sue sitting in the front row. I see them looking at her. It's going good, so don't worry."

Golden Boy was a pro. Kevin could see that in the way Gold handled this situation. Golden Boy was right. He did notice the jurors, and they were making eye contact with him, and some of them were looking at Sue sitting behind him.

"That bitch Celeste Santiago is going to cross examine me and try to make me look like liar."

"Don't worry, we're going to go over all of it."

And they did. Gold grilled him like he thought Celeste Santiago would. Gold tried to give him the same questions Celeste would ask, and then he would suggest to him how he thought Kevin should answer. Gold prepped him until it was very late, and when Kevin drove home, the Parkway and Route 6 were dead.

He was too wired to sleep, too worried about testifying tomorrow.

He tossed and turned in bed with Sue, and even in her usual semi-comatose state behind her cocktail of red wine and Lunestra or Ambien, she began to moan and complain.

He went downstairs and managed to get a little sleep on the loveseat looking out at his yard and the woods that backed his split-level.

In the morning, when he got ready for court, he felt like an automaton. His hands wouldn't stop shaking as he buttoned his shirt, and then they got so bad he couldn't make his tie. Kevin hated that Sue had to tie it for him.

The feeling that he was doing everything as a robot lasted the whole ride to the courthouse. He felt like he was on automatic pilot when he and Sue walked from the parking lot to the courthouse, through the path made by the wood barricades, through the crowds of Brown Lives Matter protestors that were much thinner than the first day of the trial. There was only one local TV truck. Again, as soon as the court officers saw Kevin and Sue, they surrounded them and escorted them into the building before the protestors could do or say anything.

It was like he was watching someone else go through this. It was really the only way he knew to go through this and not fall apart. When they got to the courtroom, Gold was at the counsel table and the judge came in, and they all stood. Before Kevin knew it, he was walking to the witness stand and swearing to tell the truth.

Kevin looked down on everyone in the courtroom. His hands still hadn't stopped shaking. He held them together on his lap. He caught Sue's eye. A few more rows over to the left, behind Celeste Santiago, was Millie. All the way in the back was Dobbsy. What was he doing here?

Kevin turned his chair to the jury box, just like Gold told him to do, and the way Desante, the ballistics expert, had. Kevin had heard that Desante was banging Celeste. McBride and Ryan knew someone in the department who knew. Linda Esposito, the healthy juror he had seen getting close with Sam in the coffee shop, wasn't making eye contact with him. The others were. He tried to remember their names as Gold walked over to the podium alongside the jury box with his notes.

There was Albright, the mailman. The guy sitting next to Albright was the Con Ed worker. He couldn't remember his name. Next to him were the two fat ladies. He couldn't remember their names either, nor could he remember the name of the juror with some growth on her cheek, who worked in Walmart. The corrections officer was Yaris.

He could feel the whole courtroom's eyes on him.

"Are you married?" was Gold's first question. "Do you have children? How many? How old?" It was just like they went over last night.

Then they got to the shooting.

"I told him to freeze." Kevin looked at Gold. He wanted to look out onto the sea of faces, but then he was afraid that he would panic, and he focused on Golden Boy instead.

"In that moment, I was sure that he had a gun. I was so sure of it. I could see the glint."

"What did you do next?" Gold asked, stabbing at the air the way he did when he got animated.

"He ran from me, and I kept telling him to drop it." Kevin was so afraid. He couldn't keep the thought out of his mind that if he lost he would go to prison. That fear was always looming and gripping. It was just too much for him, and he began to weep.

"So what did you do?" Gold tried to make him stay focused.

"I didn't know he was hit. I could have sworn he spun toward me holding what I thought was a weapon, and I fired two more rounds because I was afraid for my life. I swear to God that the cell phone and the holster. . . In that hallway of that building. . ."

The court officer brought him a box of tissues.

He watched Millie's tiny frame rise from the front row and leave. They could hear her sobs as she rushed from the courtroom.

The corrections officer, Yaris, was all choked up too. His face got all red, and he kept clearing his throat.

Kevin was glad Gold picked Yaris and the Con Ed guy, who patted Yaris on the shoulder.

"Worst day of my life."

Kevin waited for another question. Gold shuffled through his papers on the podium. He saw that Gold didn't have another one. He was waiting before he sat down to let the raw and ripe moment linger and simmer in the minds of the jurors.

"Do you have another question for this witness?" The judge impatiently leaned forward on the bench, staring down at Gold.

"I'll live with this for the rest of my life," Kevin told the jurors. He wasn't sure if he was seeing things or wishing them in his mind, but he was almost sure some of them were nodding.

"Nothing further, Judge." Gold sat down.

"You may proceed," Gallagher told Celeste Santiago, and for a moment it was like she hadn't heard him because she just sat there and stared at Kevin.

She was letting him stew. He tried not to show her how nervous he was, but how could she not tell by the way he held his hands together so they wouldn't shake. He sat with his knees pressed together so they wouldn't bang against each other. The courtroom was completely quiet.

In her stiletto heels, Celeste walked with ease toward the lectern. She held her legal pad, covered with scribbled notes, like a Frisbee between her index finger and her thumb. Her nails were pink.

Her legs still looked great in her form-fitting black dress. With her deep auburn hair pulled back, the lines in her face were deeper, and there was loose skin on her chin and arms.

"When you entered the lobby, was it empty?"

"Other than this person approaching and reaching for his waistband, it was empty."

"Was it noisy?"

"I don't understand."

"It's a simple question, Kevin. Was there a lot of noise in the lobby?"

"I don't remember. My attention was focused on this man that I thought had a gun."

"Well, did you hear any radios?"

"I don't remember. I wasn't paying attention to that." "Did you hear any shouting? Were you paying attention to that?"

"I'm not sure." He was doing what Gold had coached him to do. If you're not sure, say "*I don't know*" or "*I don't remember.*"

Celeste walked up to him and stood about three feet away from him. She was facing him with one side of her body, and the other side was also facing the jury. "Well, when Mr. Santos was approaching you, before he reached for his cell phone, do you remember hearing this?" She pressed the cell phone, and the courtroom filled with a salsa ringtone. "Did you hear that?" The phone's melody was non stop.

Gold didn't prepare him for this. He was trying not to panic and say something stupid. "No. He must have had the phone on vibrate."

She walked up to the witness stand, and she rested her skinny arms on the surface. Her freckled face was flushed with anger. "No, he didn't have it on vibrate, because I was there when he was dying on the floor of that lobby, and his phone was ringing just like that."

"I didn't want to shoot him. I swear to God, I thought it was a gun."

Celeste walked back to the podium. "When you fired the second and third shots that you fired, how far away from him were you?"

"I don't know. All I know was that I was afraid that if I didn't shoot him he was going to shoot me." Just like Gold had told him to say, *that he was afraid for his life.*

"Were you three feet away?"

"I don't know.""Were you two feet away?"

"I don't know."

"Were you a foot away?"

"I don't know."

Judge Gallagher stretched his arms out over the surface area of his bench and he leaned forward as if to pounce. "That's enough, Ms. Santiago, move on."

Celeste walked from the lectern to her table and began looking at some of the papers spread out there. "Before the day that you shot Ray Santos, had you ever been to that building?"

The pace of her questions shifted. What was she getting at?

"Objection. Whether my client was at the building on a previous occasion is not relevant."

"It goes to his state of mind, Judge." She looked up from the prosecutor's table.

"I'll allow it," Gallagher said, sounding like he didn't want to.

"Had you ever been to that building?"

"I don't remember." He was being evasive like Gold had coached him.

"Did you know that building was a drug prone location?"

"That was why I went there. We had complaints from the community about drugs being sold there."

"But you went there alone. Correct?"

"That was so I wouldn't attract attention."

"Do you think you might have overreacted and shot Ray Santos because you were in a drug prone location by yourself?"

"I didn't overreact, because I thought he was pointing a weapon at me in that hallway."

"Maybe if you weren't so afraid you would have realized it was a cell phone and not a weapon?"

How dare she question him? Who was she to second-guess him? Kevin could feel himself burning with anger at this bitch trying to throw him in jail.

"It turned out I was right to be afraid, because I found out that Ray Santos had a long record for drug dealing."

"I move to strike this witness's last statement. It's non-responsive to the question."

She stared up at him. She was so angry that she took short breaths, and she gripped the side of the table as if she was going to throw it over.

"Well, Ms. Santiago, you were the one that opened the door to let this in, and just because you're not happy with his answer, I'm not going to strike it. The answer stands."

Kevin saw the self-satisfied look on Gold's face. Gold tried not to show it as he stared down at the floor and shook his head in agreement. Kevin had done what Gold told him, to somehow get out in front of the jury that Ray Santos had a long record for drug dealing.

"I'm finished with this witness," Celeste told the judge as she stared at him.

He could feel everyone in the courtroom watch him as he rose from the witness stand, walked toward the counsel table, and took his seat.

"Does the defense rest?"

Gold stood in the well. "Yes."

The jurors looked at Golden Boy as he walked over and sat next to Kevin at the counsel table. He whispered in his ear, "That was good that the last thing the jury heard was about Ray Santos being a criminal."

"I think now would be a good time for the jurors to take a break as the lawyers and I need to take up some housekeeping matters." Whenever Gallagher addressed the jurors his tone was avuncular, like they were his children.

"I saw the jurors' faces after you said that about Ray having a record. They looked at me, and they were looking at you a lot."

"I hope that's a good sign." Kevin wanted to tell himself that no matter what happened, no matter what verdict the jury came back with, he was going to take it like a man and not crumple into a weeping mess, like he had seen defendants do after they were found guilty, but it wasn't true. No, he was not going away for this. No matter what he had to do. He wasn't going to take it like a man. Truth was he didn't what he would do if they convicted him

Chapter Thirty
Sam Free

Again Sam couldn't get a seat in the courtroom.

"It's full," the court officer told him. Sam thought that Celeste Santiago had arranged this. Had she told the court officers to make sure Sam was kept out of the courtroom? She still hated his guts from way back when he refused to lie on the stand for her and she lost her first big murder trial behind that. Then she had him locked up and tried to send him to prison. Of course, it could also be that Celeste wanted to parade Millie Santos before the jurors as much as she could, and having Sam sit with her in the courtroom wasn't practical. It would take sympathy away from the poor little widow seeking justice for her dead husband if some galoot like him was shadowing her.

He ended up in the coffee shop across from the court where he had a vantage point at the window and could watch when Millie came down.

He was pouring himself a cup at the self-serve counter when he felt someone standing next to him, and he turned. There was Linda Esposito, smiling at him. This time she was in a tight purple dress that showed significant cleavage.

"Hey, there you are. What's your name again?" She giggled and slapped his chest and pushed him lightly and giggled more. "I'm kidding. Of course, I know your name."

He was caught by surprise. "Sam Free." He didn't believe that she remembered his name. "How you doing, Linda?"

"They picked me for the jury of the cop."

"Really?"

"I'm getting my much-needed vacation."

"That's funny."

"You probably want to know which way I'm leaning?" She leaned against him as she poured her own cup.

"I'm curious. Who wouldn't be?"

"How do I know you won't rat me out? We're not supposed to talk to anybody about the case."

He acted like he was thinking about it. "I guess you don't know that I won't rat you out."

"I seen you bringing the widow to the courtroom. What are you doing up here?"

"I work for the civil lawyer of the widow. I bring her up from the Bronx on the train to watch the trial." He probably should not have told her that.

"Yeah. It's probably not a good idea that I'm seen talking to you. What are you, an investigator or something? I figured you were a cop too. I tend to get involved with cops." She looked longingly into his eyes.

"You think?" He laughed.

"Put the widow on the train and I'll pick you up at the station, and we can hang out and nobody will know."

He looked out the coffee shop onto the small plaza in front of the courthouse and watched Millie walk toward the coffee shop.

"Wait for me later at the station, my friend." She touched his arm, and went to the cashier to pay. "Soon as we're done here, I'll come scoop you."

* * *

"So, what's up? You and the fat juror got a thing?" Millie asked as he stood with her outside the courthouse and hailed one of the Haitian cabbies.

Sam ignored her. "Take us to the train," he told the driver.

"Tomorrow the jury decides." She looked out the window.

Today there were no Brown Lives Matter protestors holding signs outside the courtroom. Tomorrow, when the jury was deliberating, they would be out in force.

Just when they reached the station, the train approached, and they rushed to the platform to catch it.

"I'm going to hang out for a while." He gave Millie her ticket and some cash.

"Uh-huh, I knew it." She looked at him like he was a misbehaving child. "Don't go playing around with that juror."

"You could catch a cab when you reach the Bronx. There are always cabs at the station."

"A cab is better than riding in your stinky minivan. Text me tomorrow, I probably ain't coming. I told you, these cracker jurors are going to walk Loco."

* * *

When the train with Millie pulled off, he had a moment when he thought he should have gone with her. What was he doing waiting around for Linda Esposito to pick him up? He laughed to himself and shook his head.

She came in the blue Blazer. The seats were covered in blue leather too. The car smelled like her, like flowers.

"So, what do you want to talk about?" He wanted her to tell him which way the jury was going and what she thought was going to happen to Kevin. Were they going to convict him or walk him?

"I know what you want to talk about, but I'm not saying anything. I'm not telling you what I think. I don't think that would be proper."

"All right, we'll talk about something else then." Maybe later she'd let on what was going on in that jury room.

He looked at her as she drove. She gave off that lonely vibe, just like he was. "What's up with you, Linda Esposito? You got kids, husband, etc.?"

"My story, in a nutshell, is that I believed my husband when he said we should move up here from the Bronx because he could afford to buy a house on a cop's salary up here and we wouldn't have to worry about crime. We moved up here with the kids, and then he left me."

She wasn't upset when she told him. It was almost matter of fact. Sam guessed that enough time had elapsed that she could talk about it this way.

"And what about you? Married?"

"Separated." It was the first time he had said that and he surprised himself.

They drove away from the train station past the blocks of one-family houses.

"You got to tell me what you think."

She hesitated. "I don't like him. The cop, Kevin, whatever his name is. He's all dressed up in a suit, but he's creepy. I'm probably the only one who thinks like that. Maybe because my ex, Hal, was a cop, and I told you what happened."

"You're supposed to judge on the facts and not your prejudices."

She pulled over and parked on a street. "That is all a bunch of lawyer nonsense that they tell you. Oh, you got be fair and not be prejudiced against one person or the other. They have to prove their case beyond a reasonable doubt. What does all that mean anyway?" She touched his face and kissed him on the lips.

Sam was surprised. He tried to kiss her back, and she pulled away. "So tomorrow you decide?"

"I feel sorry for his wife."

"Sue?"

"You shouldn't tell me anything about her. I'm a juror under oath." She grabbed him by the lapel of his jacket and pulled him toward her. She kissed him hard and long.

"The first shot maybe was an accident, but the second and the third–so close–he had to have seen the cell phone, especially that Latin music ringtone it made. He had to know it wasn't a gun." She was short of breath as she spoke.

He rubbed his mouth. He didn't have anything to say.

"Yeah." She smiled. "Maybe I should get home? It's going to be a big day. We get to hear the lawyers. I like them both. I feel bad for the Spanish DA. She's a pretty redhead. She looks like she's been through the ringer. I don't think she stands a chance with these jurors. I also like the nervous lawyer for Kevin too, the way he talks with his hands. Sometimes he's poking in the air, it's like he's reaching for words."

She brought him back to the station.

"Will you meet me tomorrow after we reach a decision?"

"Yeah, sure." He wasn't sure if Millie was going to want to go, but he'd come up here to meet Linda for sure.

"Here's my number, text me tomorrow. I'll let you know when we're done."

The sun was setting over the Hudson as he waited on the platform. What must Kevin and Sue be feeling now? They were probably scared shitless. Who knew what these twelve people were going to do?

Chapter Thirty-One
Kevin Knowles

If they convicted him, would the judge let him stay out pending sentence?

Sue and the kids kept their distance when he was like this, scary and brooding. She had put the kids to bed and was in bed herself finishing the second large juice glass of red wine, that washed down her meds. Soon she would be gone to the world.

Tomorrow the jury would decide, and he was panicking. He felt like he was crawling out of his skin and the walls closing in on him. He had to talk to Sue about what would happen if they came back with a guilty verdict. He paced the living room. He saw the way those jurors looked at him, like he was one of them. It looked good, but he couldn't be sure. He had seen it happen before in court with some of the perps he had testified against. It seemed clear that they would get off, but the jury came back with a conviction. It could happen. You could never tell what these people were thinking.

He needed to get out of the house for a while. It was still early, and he knew he had the whole night of worry and anguish ahead of him. It could be his last night of freedom. Holy shit, he shouldn't think like that.

No doubt Judge Gallagher was going to put him in if he went down for this. He was a no-nonsense judge. Out would come those cuffs with that sound they made like grinding gears and the judge would remand him to the custody of the Department of Corrections, and they would set a day for him to be brought back to court to be sentenced. Then he would be inside with the knuckleheads he had locked up.

As all of this sunk in, Kevin felt himself shrink under the weight of it all. He was like a little bug, of no consequence, about to be squashed.

He thought about Dobbs. Why did he show up at the trial? Oh, he knew what Dobbsy would say: *We need to show support for a brother in blue in this witch hunt by this crazy prosecutor who wants her name in the news.*

It was bullshit. Something was not right. Dobbsy was worried about something and that's why he kept popping up. For some reason he wanted to be around Kevin. Why?

Was it all in Kevin's head? Maybe Dobbsy did care? Yeah right. Was he thinking about Dobbsy because it took his mind off tomorrow when the jury was going to decide whether to send him to jail or not? Did he blame Dobbs for all of this because it was Dobbs who first recruited him to Narcotics?

It was still getting dark early.

He went to his garage from the kitchen. He went inside his Explorer and opened the glove compartment and took out the GPS tracker, plugged it into the charger, and it came on with Dobbs' Escalade beeping in the picture. He had been tailing Dobbs on the GPS, but nothing had come of it. The worst Dobbs did was go to the strip bars in Newburgh and then take one of the girls back to his Cadillac for some head. He went to his properties up there or down in the Bronx or in Brewster. Tonight, on the tracker, he saw Dobbs heading toward Croton Falls. There was no way Kevin was going to get any rest tonight.

Maplewood didn't have a train station. The closest one was Croton Falls. Dobbs had parked in the train station over there.

He was probably picking up his wife, who took the railroad into the city for the day.

Kevin opened the garage with the remote and backed his Explorer out.

Chapter Thirty-Two
Brian Dobbs

Dobbs waited in his Escalade in the parking lot of the station for Matt Prey to arrive on the 7:50 out of Grand Central. Dobbs knew what train Prey took because he had been watching him for a while. He parked right behind Prey's Honda.

He reached under the seat and found the half pint of Wild Turkey. He half expected his wife might have beat him to it and thrown it out. He was so tired of her always searching his car for his stash. That was why he locked it and wouldn't let her use it.

He made up the excuse that he didn't like her driving his car because she was always changing the seats and the mirror. Why did she have to drive his car anyway? For God's sake, he had bought her one of those Lexus SUVs.

Today, on his way over, he decided he was going to do a little more to Prey than just watch him. He made that decision after Lapidus told him about Prey serving the subpoenas. Dobbs was going to leave Prey in a crying heap of pain courtesy of a couple of taps from the black jack to his knees and shins. Maybe a couple whacks to the back as well? He just didn't want to mark Prey's face up because that would attract too much attention. He moved stuff around in the glove compartment, looking for the black jack. It had been a while since he'd taken a knucklehead down a notch or two with a series of whacks from the black jack, but Dobbsy had no doubt that his skills with the club were still there. He found the lead piece. It was thicker in the grip portion, and then the weapon flattened out to give more surface for a beating. It was just the right weight and balance to mete out some certain punishment.

Like clockwork the train arrived, and the quiet parking area became flooded with suits.

Dobbs spotted Matt Prey as he walked the same lane of cars he walked every night. Most people were creatures of habit. Usually Dobbs parked father away than he did tonight. He got out of his Escalade and prepared to be on Prey with that small lead rod. He had it poised in his hand at his side, obscured with his coat sleeve.

He could never be too careful. He took a three-hundred-and-sixty-degree turn around to make sure, and there he spotted Kevin's white Explorer sitting a few rows behind.

"What the fuck?" Dobbs asked himself.

Prey approached, yapping away on his cell phone, oblivious.

Dobbs got back in the Escalade and drove away. Was Kevin watching him or was he just waiting to pick someone up at the station? Kevin probably didn't know it, but he saved Prey a beating.

Driving out of the parking lot in the line of traffic, Dobbs thought back. The minute he got to know Kevin, he wanted him on the Narcotics squad. When he had last gone to the Bronx, Dobbs was glad that he'd given Lapidus the CD to mail with the video recording from that lobby of the building in Queens. It was just in case something should happen to him, so that somebody would know. Back then, Kevin was just a young kid in uniform, but Dobbs recognized the fearless soldier in him. There was nothing Kevin wouldn't do, and that turned out to be Kevin's undoing.

Chapter Thirty-Three
Sam Free

That morning, when Sam left his building, he saw Frank double parked in front.

Sam walked out into the street and over to the driver's side of the red Hyundai. "Why are you bothering me again?" he asked, as Frank rolled down the window. "Didn't my business with you finish?"

The sun was behind where Sam stood so that when Frank looked up at Sam he had to squint. "Don't you need to find out whether Kevin was the one in the video getting beat up? With that type of beating, he had to have been hospitalized. We just gotta canvass all the hospitals. We need to ask the guys in the security to see if they recognize Kevin from the photo."

Sam snorted, as if to intimate that Frank must be out of his mind to think that Sam would help him out. "What's this with using the word *we*? You and me don't work together." Deep down, Sam was relieved to see his old partner parked there. Truth be told, he could use Frank's help, but never in a million years would he admit it.

Frank shook his head. "I need to find out if Kevin murdered Nooney."

"What's your point, Frank?"

"I thought we could help each other out. Watch each other's backs like the old times."

"Oh shit. You must be delusional. You threw me under the bus and I'll never let you forget that you did..."

"I know, you told me like a million times already. Can we just go and take care of this and stop the bullshit."

"I'm so tired of you coming around and bugging me to help you out." Sam got into the front passenger seat.

They started at the hospitals they were familiar with in the Bronx. There was Lebanon, Jacoby, and Lincoln. Over and over again they showed the photo of Kevin all beaten up to see if the security guards at any of these hospitals recognized someone who was brought in looking like that. They came up with nothing.

"Let's move north to Westchester; maybe they brought him to one of those hospitals up there."

The next closest hospital to the Bronx was in Mount Vernon.

Mount Vernon Hospital was set on a quiet block behind the police station and City Hall.

There was an old guy sitting on a folding chair at the entrance.

The old guy wore a blue windbreaker with "security" in white letters written on the back. His glasses were tinted and rectangular, and he wore a gray cap with a kangaroo decal. He crossed his long legs as they approached.

"How long you been here?" Frank asked. He was frustrated that they had come up with nothing.

The old guy gave him a once-over. "You mean, how long I been working here?"

"Yeah, that's what I mean."

"Shit." He said the word so that it came out like "Sheeet." He stood and towered over Sam. Tufts of gray hair formed a goatee on his chin. He looked like Bill Russell, the famous center from the Celtics.

"You are fucking tall." Frank looked up at him. The length of the security guard's legs was about Frank's height.

"Almost seven feet, brother. What you need?"

Frank showed him the picture on the screen of his cell phone.

He took the phone and studied it. "Hmm." He looked up at Sam and Frank. "You two cops?"

"Used to be."

"Yeah, man, I seen these two big cops bring this one in all beat up." He pointed at the photo. He had long fingers, and his nails had clear polish on them.

"When was this?"

"A while ago. The two cops who brought him in were mean and as big as fuck. They scared the shit out of everybody. They wanted the whole thing hushed up, to be kept very low-key." He pointed to the image on the cell phone screen. "He was in bad shape. The doctors didn't think he was gonna make it. He needed surgery to fix his face. Oh man, he was fucked up. He had broken ribs, and his whole body was busted up. Somebody had thrown him a fierce beating." He squinted like he had seen something awful.

"Do you remember his name?"

"Wheels was what they called him. Kevin something. Can't remember his last name."

"Holy crap." Sam clapped his hands and then held them together.

"What else do you remember?" Frank pressed him.

"That's all, little man." He looked down at Frank. "You a fierce little brother, aren't you?"

* * *

"McBride, Ryan, and Kevin were up to their old tricks, and it ended up biting them on the ass." Frank grabbed the steering wheel as he drove.

"Kevin was kidnapped, and the city hushed it up."

"How did Nooney get messed up in this?"

Sam wasn't listening to his ex-partner. He texted Matt Prey. *Very important info on the case. Need to see you.*

I'm in court. Bankman's at the office, was the text back from Matt Prey

Chapter Thirty-Four
Sam Free

"This is the tape I was telling you about." Sam handed Bankman his phone with the tape of Kevin's beating. From across his desk, Bankman took it and pressed play on the screen. Kevin's screams filled the room. Impassively, Bankman's beady eyes studied the tape of Kevin's beating.

"This is a picture of what Kevin Knowles looked like when the drug dealers found out he was an undercover police officer." Sam took his phone back and showed Bankman a copy of the picture they had taken from the desk drawer in the Bronx TNT office.

"The city was hiding something. I knew it." Bankman stood and began to pace. "Email me this, will you? We aren't going to let the city or Judge Eldridge know we have the tape or the picture. If this case goes to trial, we'll spring it on them. It'll blow their minds. They won't know what to do. Wait until I show this tape to Matt."

He stopped in front of the gleaming tank filled with those yellow, purple, and blue fish. "How did they know he was a cop?" Now his beady eyes through those fancy designer black-rimmed glasses were focused on Sam.

"I'm not sure." Sam wasn't going to tell Bankman that he thought the buy and bust that Kevin got beat up and kidnapped in wasn't legit. That it was a setup to rip off some dealers that backfired. After all, Bankman didn't need to know everything.

"You impress me. You broke this case wide open for us. I'm going to tell Mr. Feldman what a good job you did."

"Thanks, Mr. Bankman," From the 48th floor, the sidewalk below, spotted with umbrellas, was a long way down. Spring had been like this. It was mostly shitty cold days and then one nice day, far and few between. He wanted to get out of there; Bankman was a little creepy, with those black beady eyes that followed his every move. He preferred dealing with Matt.

"I had a few more questions about this." Bankman wasn't ready for Sam to leave. "Did Kevin work with an informant?"

"I don't know."

"Maybe his informant gave him up?"

"I don't know. I haven't worked with Kevin in years." Did Bankman know that Ray Santos, Millie's dead husband, had been Dobbs' CI? Nooney was Ray Santos' godson. Was Nooney a snitch too? Was Nooney shot in both his eyes and his body staged like that because he had seen too much?

"Do you think this was a buy and bust where Kevin was made for a cop and that was why he was beaten up?"

"Could be." Bankman studied him. "This was really good work." Bankman went behind his cavernous desk, and out he brought the shiny leather pouch that contained his checkbook. "Say, was there a verdict? I tried to call a lawyer I know up there and I wasn't able to reach him."

Sam checked his watch. He remembered that he had to text Linda Esposito. He could drive up there. "I think they're still deliberating."

The check was for ten thousand dollars. "I will certainly keep you in mind for other work. I still may need you to tie up some loose ends on this one."

Sam didn't like the way Bankman said that. What did he mean by loose ends? He was fucking thrilled with the ten-grand check, but he wanted this job done with.

Chapter Thirty-Five
Matt Prey

They were in Eldridge's chambers with its plush burgundy wall-to-wall carpet and matching drapes.

"Judge, based on this new information that we've uncovered through our *own* investigation"—Matt Prey looked right at Donovan, the city's attorney, when he said this—"we have a good faith basis to believe that the city covered up that Kevin Knowles, one year before this shooting, was viciously assaulted and was left near death when he was working as an undercover police officer. The entire incident was brushed under the rug. At the very least, Judge, we should be allowed to get these records from Mr. Knowles' personnel file. This would support our claim that the city should not have kept him on the job. That he was not emotionally fit to be a police officer. Surely Kevin Knowles must have suffered some form of post-traumatic stress disorder as a result of the attack, and this should have prevented him from going back on the job as an undercover detective with Bronx Narcotics. I know we asked for this before, but we are now making a second request that you so order the subpoena for Kevin's personnel records, including the records from Mount Vernon Hospital where Knowles was treated after the attack."

Donovan seemed to sink into his chair. After what a hard time the city attorney had given Matt the last time they were in front of Eldridge, it felt good to give it back to him, especially since his boss Bankman was there too.

"I should point out that as we sit here, a jury is deliberating Kevin's fate in his criminal trial," Bankman added. He sat at the opposite end of the table facing Eldridge.

Millie's wrongful death case against the city would be worth more if Kevin was convicted.

The judge was more subdued today and so was Donovan, who sat across from the judge at the oak table with his head down and hands clasped together on the table.

"I'll hear what you have to say, but I don't think I have any choice but to sign the subpoena, otherwise I'm sure Bankman here will go over my head to the Appellate Division, and nobody wants to be reversed by the Appellate Division." Eldridge was somber.

"Hey, Donovan," Bankman continued. He couldn't resist laying into him. "Think of what a Bronx jury will say. A Bronx jury that already hates the police department. Donovan, think of what they'll say." Bankman stood, paused, and put his index finger and his middle finger to his chin in a pensive pose. "Think of what they'll say when at trial they find out that the police department kept a cop on the job who had been traumatized and left for dead."

Bankman continued his pose as if he were still lost in thought. "Anybody would agree that Kevin Knowles can't be right in the head after something like that happened to him. He isn't suitable for the police department." With that, he pointed to his temple and made tiny circles with his index finger. "I'll bet there are psychiatric records in the file. Remember, Donovan, these jurors are going to be people from the South Bronx who are constantly watching their neighbors, brothers, sisters, cousins beat down and jailed by the police. . ."

"All right, Mr. Bankman." Eldridge banged on the table surface. "Save your summation and histrionics for the trial. What do you have to say for the city, Mr. Donovan? Did you know about this?"

"This is the first I heard of this, when I got the Affirmation in Opposition from Mr. Bankman's office fighting my motion to dismiss this case. I swear it, Judge. "He began to stammer.

Matt could see the gears in Donovan's brain working, trying to come up with something else to say. It was great to watch the little prick flounder.

As Judge Eldridge picked up the pen and was about to sign the subpoena, he turned again to Donovan. "Are you sure you didn't know anything about this when you came in here all sure of yourself that they couldn't prove negligent hiring and retention by the city?" His voice rose, and he slammed the pen down. Donovan, startled, jumped a bit out of his seat.

Matt Prey wanted to laugh. He remembered how Donovan had been so sure of himself.

"The first I heard of this was when I got the response to my motion to dismiss. I swear, Judge. I would never have represented that they couldn't prove their case against the city."

"Yeah, sure, Donovan. I believe that like a hole in my head." This time he picked up the pen and signed the subpoena. Eldridge wrote something else on the face of the subpoena. "I'm directing the city"—with that he eyeballed Donovan—"to turn over Kevin Knowles' entire personnel file, including any and all psychiatric records, within forty-eight hours."

"And do me a favor, call up the Comptroller's Office and get some settlement authority before you get hammered with a huge verdict from a Bronx jury."

"It turns out that I did get a chance to conference the case, and I do have some settlement authority." Donovan's voice was low, and when he spoke, he looked down.

Prey now knew that Donovan was a lying bastard. Because if the city didn't know about Kevin, why did they conference the case?

"You're full of surprises. So what you got?" Eldridge drummed his stubby fingers on the conference table.

"Seven hundred and fifty thousand."

Bankman made a choking sound of disbelief. His beady eyes behind those black designer glasses took aim at Donovan and Eldridge. "Can you imagine the jury's award just for pain and suffering? We know from the ME's report that Ray Santos didn't die from the first shot. As part of this wrongful death reward, they can consider the pain and suffering."

Bankman crossed his arms over his chest, as if he felt the pain of Ray Santos. His eyes got bigger. He was convincing.

Matt knew that Bankman became a changed person when he argued his case. Bankman was consumed with it. Matt believed everything he said. That was why the juries gave him so much money—because he had that gift of being able to convince others.

Bankman continued, "As he lay there in that hallway, reaching for his cell phone to call his wife, he ended up dying like a dog. She found him there surrounded by the police who killed him."

Bankman shook his head in disbelief. "The cop that killed him was himself left for dead by a group of drug dealers on another occasion, not too long before he executed my client's husband. This cop should not have been on the police force after what had happened to him. This is outrageous." The skin that hung over Bankman's collar, held so tightly by the gold tie bar, was red with fury. Bankman acted as though he struggled to control himself at this realization of how outrageous this was. It was perfect.

"I'd ask forty million. May not stand up on appeal, but who cares?"

"Santos was a drug dealer." Donovan was dejected.

"Who was trying to turn his life around," Prey answered him. Bankman arched his eyebrows and looked at Prey. Maybe he shouldn't have said that. Was he stealing Bankman's thunder?

Eldridge drummed his fingers some more and looked across at Bankman. "What will you take?"

"6.2 million."

"That's a little high. Settle the case for 4.7 million. You guys are going to get buried on this," Eldridge told Donovan.

"I have to talk to the Comptroller's Office."

“Do it before your office is completely taken to the cleaners and then vilified in the press.” Eldridge rose and made a motion with his hands that they should leave.

* * *

On Walton Avenue, across from the courthouse,
Prey stood with Bankman in front of the court deli that used to be a kosher one,

“Would you like to join me for a late lunch?”

In ten years of working for Bankman, Prey didn’t know if he had ever seen Bankman eat anything much less gone to lunch with him. “Can we take a rain check? I’d like to get home and watch my son’s baseball game.”

“Sure. Sure, go right ahead.” Bankman paused. “But Matt, I’m serious, let’s make it a point sometime next week to have lunch. I’d like you to have a more prominent role in the office.”

What the fuck did that mean? A more prominent role in the office? He didn’t trust Bankman. Prey didn’t want a more prominent role. He wanted things to die down in Maplewood about this whole suing Kevin Knowles thing. Maybe now that the civil case was settled, and the criminal case would soon be over, his neighbors would stop treating his family like outcasts. Maybe now they would let up a little.

Matt didn’t need a bigger role; he needed a piece of that 4.7 million settlement that Bankman was going to collect on. His fee was a third of the recovery. How much did Bankman actually net in the end? What ended up in Bankman’s pocket when the smoke cleared, after he had to give a piece of his fee to Lapidus and Feldman?

What about Millie? What would she walk away with? He whistled softly as he did the math. Millie would probably end up with about three million, tax free. What was she going to do with that? Was she going to blow it on cars, more cars, jewelry, parties, business ventures that went belly up? He had seen it before with other clients in the office. They got a big settlement, and in a year it was all gone.

Chapter Thirty-Six
Sam Free

He had texted Linda Esposito, but she didn't respond. He decided to drive up and wait for her at the railroad station.

On the long drive up the Parkway, he switched the radio to the all-news station.

A jury in Poughkeepsie is deliberating the fate of Bronx detective Kevin Knowles for the shooting of an unarmed super in the Bronx. Knowles claimed that the super had what looked like a gun, which turned out to be a cell phone.

The broadcaster gave the weather report, which predicted more rain and cold temperatures. When was spring coming?

The road was wet, and it was dark. He took his time on the drive.

He started to lose his nerve and was about to turn around and head back. The jury could be out a long time. He made himself keep driving. What else was he going to do? He had texted Millie to see if she wanted to be there when they came back with a verdict, and she didn't respond either.

He saw a text from Matt. *Millie's case was settled. How much?* Sam texted back, 4.7 *million.*

Holy shit. After Millie got word from Bankman about her settlement, she was probably having a party.

Following the GPS on his cell phone, he arrived at the train station. There was the line of Haitian cab drivers waiting for the next train. He parked at one of the meters.

The drizzle turned to downpour, and the steady drumming of the rain on the hood made him drowsy. He turned off the radio. He woke to tapping on his driver's door window.

"Wake up, Sam." Linda was wearing a London Fog raincoat open at the chest. She got in the passenger seat. "Did you hear what happened?" She leaned over and kissed him on the mouth.

"What?" He was distracted.

She giggled. "We couldn't reach a verdict."

"Didn't the judge want to deliberate more?"

"I think he saw how deadlocked we were and thought it wouldn't do any good."

"It was a hung jury?" He was in disbelief. For sure he thought they were going to walk Kevin. "So, what was it?"

"You're not going to believe this." She moved in close to him, pressing up against him.

"It was eleven to one." As quickly as she was on top of him, she moved away. "I was the holdout."

"Holy cow." He looked her up and down with amazement. She ran hot and cold. "They must have wanted to lynch you."

"You have no idea."

"If you were the lawyer, would you have put you on the jury?"

"No way." She pushed him in the chest playfully and smiled.

She liked that he asked her that.

Was she turned on again? He couldn't tell. She licked her lips.

"Do you know the minute they selected us as jurors the first thing those assholes did was break into cliques, and they wouldn't include me." Linda made a face like she'd tasted something bad. "They would play their stupid card games and not once did they invite me to play. The only thing I could do stuck in that room with all those he-haws was look out onto Market Street. I spent hours in that room with those people, and I grew to hate their guts. I guess we just got on each other's nerves, and I couldn't say that Kevin Knowles was not guilty. There was just too much. The cell phone ringtone. How come he didn't hear that?"

She looked at him like she wanted to devour him.

"They called me a liberal schoolteacher, bitch, and every other name in the book."

"You shouldn't have to put up with that."

"I know. They thought I hated cops because I wanted to convict Knowles. I hate my ex-husband, but I don't hate all cops." She put her arms around Sam's shoulders. "I like you and you were a cop." She kissed him again for a long time. "Did you like that?"

"Not bad." He blushed.

"Tell me how you like this."

She went for his zipper. She smiled as she unzipped it, and she went down on him. "So?" She giggled.

"That was . . . Wow!" He had trouble speaking.

Linda snuggled against him. "The women on the jury made me the maddest. They would ooh and ah over the photos of each other's grandkids, but they wouldn't give me the time of day. They were a bunch of nasty, self-righteous bitches."

He was at a loss for words. What could he say in response? The one holdout in the case was sitting in his passenger seat. Gold made a big mistake keeping her on the jury. He'd seen that before. A juror is good-looking and the attorney keeps her on the jury without thinking. If she wasn't good-looking, would Gold have kept her? Probably not.

"You want to go have a cup of coffee?"

"Yeah, I do, but can we take a rain check because I have a long drive home."

"Oh, so what are you, one of those slam, bam, thank you ma'am type of guys?"

"That's not it, Linda. I'm a little overwhelmed is all."

"It's not a problem." She looked away. "I've got to get up early tomorrow and get to work. My vacation is over." She smiled sadly as she exited the passenger door and disappeared into her truck. It roared away.

"Holy shit." Sam left the railway station and found the Parkway back to the Bronx.

Chapter Thirty-Seven
Celeste Santiago

"Hey, kid, what're you doin?" Desante was in the waiting area of the Dutchess County District Attorney's Office. They had let Celeste Santiago use one of their cubicles during the trial.

"What are you doin?" Celeste mimicked him. She wrinkled her nose when she smiled. Celeste was in a surprisingly good mood. She was wheeling her trial bag out behind her.

"Nobody expected you to win this." Desante walked alongside her.

She shrugged her shoulders. "Whatever. I'm just glad to get out of Poughkeepsie." She whispered the last part in his ear, and she smelled his familiar cologne. She didn't mind it. He had an avuncular air about him, and it fit with the smell. She wondered whether it was because her father wasn't around much, that she was looking for a fatherly figure.

"To me, that's a win for you."

"Oh, that's sweet." She stopped and turned to him. "You know, it's probably not the smartest thing for you to hang out with me. I don't think I'm one of NYPD's favorites."

"Who gives a shit? I put in my papers. I've done my thirty years."

They started walking again past the courtroom where Gold, Knowles, and his wife were on the bench. At first Knowles didn't even seem to notice her.

When their eyes did meet his were lifeless. His stare was dull. He had no expression.

She felt Gold stare at her.

"Schneiderman was a fool to walk out on you. I'll bet he kicks himself in the ass every day for doing that."

Celeste didn't feel like thinking about Schneiderman anymore, and she didn't know why Desante would bring him up. Desante sounded a little desperate when he said it. It was a turn-off, and she saw it in Desante's eyes when he realized he shouldn't have said that. Her stiletto heels clicked as she walked down the hall.

"It was eleven to one for an acquittal. The schoolteacher, the one who came to court in the tight dresses and gave Kevin Knowles dirty looks throughout the trial, she was the holdout. Gold should never have kept her on the jury."

"You think they're going to want to try him again?"

"They should try that bastard Knowles again. He always gave me a bad feeling, even when I worked with him in Narcotics. They're probably not going to with eleven to one for acquittal. Those are not very good odds. Who knows if something else pops up, and we get some new evidence? Unless that happens, my boss isn't going to want to try this asshole again."

"Really, Celeste, you should be proud of yourself." He faced her. They were by the elevator bank.

She wasn't sure what she wanted to do. Desante sensed it in her. Is that what a rebound affair was? Celeste just wanted someone to hold her, and to not be alone. "What will you do?"

"I'll probably visit my daughter in California. You know, I have grandkids I haven't seen."

That wasn't what she meant.

She didn't want to be lying alone in her cold bed. She needed another body next to her. She smiled at him.

Chapter Thirty-Eight
Sam Free

Sam had the windows on the minivan open as he pulled into the lot of the brick building that housed the elementary school. Finally, spring had arrived. The air had that perfect perfume-like smell that it brings. It just put him in a good mood to finally have a beautiful day after all the cold, wet, nasty weather they had been having.

Bankman had Matt Prey email him a release that Kevin needed to sign before the city would send Bankman the check for 4.7 million.

When Sam saw Bankman the last time and Bankman was gloating over what a good job Sam had done, Sam had a feeling that he wasn't done with him. That somehow Bankman was going to hit him up to do something else on this case, and lo and behold he got this email out of the blue from Matt Prey starting with *Mr. Bankman wants . . .*

Sam didn't want to bother Kevin at home, and surprisingly, when Sam texted Kevin and asked if he could meet Kevin at the baseball field to sign this release, Kevin agreed. Sam thought Kevin was going to give him a hard time about being bothered at his son's baseball game. From the parking lot, Sam walked around the school to the sand playground that was on a bluff that overlooked the vast expanse of baseball fields.

He texted him, *Here in the playground with the paper for you to sign.*

He tried to find Kevin out there in that beehive of activity of kids with different uniforms and coaches and parents moving in a million different directions.

He watched a little kid shriek with delight as another child, probably eleven or twelve, pushed him mightily on the swing. It flew so high that it seemed it would come over the bar at the top of the chains.

The little kid on the swing was tiny—he looked three, maybe four—and he seemed too small to be able to hold on, that he would be sent flying through the air face-first onto the asphalt parking lot. He emitted terror-filled, gleeful screams as he held on for dear life. His legs were like sticks, and he slid around the shiny surface of the metal swing seat. His hands were clenched fists wrapped around the chain.

He watched a figure of a man approach him at the playground, and he realized that it was Frank Cortez. What the hell? Why was Frank here?

Then he saw Kevin's tall frame approach, with his long strides, up the hill. Sam stood.

Frank arrived first.

"What are you doing here, Frank?"

"I'm here to talk to Kevin. I went to his house, and Sue told me he was here."

"Do me a favor. Just let him sign the paper before you start with your third degree?"

"Did you know that Dobbs owns 1275 where the shooting happened?" Frank breathed heavily from coming up the hill.

Kevin arrived. "Hey, Frank, what's going on?"

"Let me ask you. Did you know that Dobbs owned 1275 Webster?"

"What's this all about? My son is playing baseball, and I'm nice enough to meet you here to sign a release, and now you start with some fucking interrogation?"

Frank and Kevin stood toe to toe.

The lady whose kids were playing on the swings came and got them and hurried from the playground.

Sam could see that some other arrivals in the parking lot stared at them.

"What's going on, Kev? Did you and McBride and Ryan do like youse did back in the day? What was it gonna be, a big payday? What was the take supposed to be? A couple kilos?"

"I have no idea what the fuck you're talking about. Sam, do you want me to sign the paper? Or I'm going to leave right now and get back to my son's game."

"Here." Sam got between them. He held a folder and a pen, and he showed Kevin where to sign on the release.

"Kev, what you do is your business, but when it concerns my family, then you got some questions that I need you to answer." Frank stood in Kevin's way and wouldn't let him leave. When Kevin stepped in one direction, Frank was there.

Kevin held up his hands like he didn't want to be touched.

"I think Nooney was your CI, and he dimed you."

"Frank, I don't know what you're talking about."

"I hear things out on the street." He cupped his cauliflower ear as if he were listening. "Did Nooney blow your cover? Was Ray Santos in on it too? Is that why he bought it too?"

"Frank, you're out of your mind."

"Kevin, I swear to God, if I found out that you capped my nephew... I think you did, but I can't prove it yet."

"I got nothing to say to you if you think I would do that. Maybe you should think about shit before you make accusations. Maybe you should think about the fact that you're looking at the wrong person. Maybe you should be looking at Dobbs as your shooter. Didn't you just tell me that 1275 is owned by Dobbs?"

Frank was taken aback for a moment, and Kevin used the opportunity to sidestep Frank and walk back down the hill to the baseball game.

"Fucking asshole. Maybe I will ask Dobbs!" Frank shouted after Kevin.

"Come on, Frank, now's not the time." Sam tried to put his hand on Frank's shoulder, and Frank shook it off.

A little girl entered the playground and went to the apparatus shaped like the shell of a turtle attached to a spring and buried in the sand.

"It ain't right what happened to Nooney. He was just a kid."

Sam wished that they could have sent someone else up here to have Kevin sign the release.

He walked Frank back to his red Hyundai.

"I'm going to get to the bottom of this. You know I will."

"Just not today, Frank."

"All right. I hear what you're saying, but I am coming back. I'm going to find Dobbs and ask him about what he knows. I know you don't give a shit because you got paid, and your case is done and over with. I'm not resting until I find out who killed my nephew."

"Okay, Frank."

When Frank pulled off, Sam looked at the release to make sure Kevin had signed it in the right spot.

Chapter Thirty-Nine
Kevin Knowles

Kevin woke in the living room. Again he had gotten up in the middle of night. His T-shirt was soaked through with sweat. This time in his nightmare, Frank Cortez was leading him out of his house in handcuffs. In the unmarked police cruiser that was parked in his driveway, Celeste Santiago sat in the front passenger seat. He walked to the front of the house and looked out onto his driveway. It was empty.

Frank Cortez could be the one to sink him. He had worked with Frank in Narcotics, and Kevin saw that once Frank started working on a case he didn't stop until he locked up who was responsible. Frank was a pit bull. He was a good cop. When Frank and Sam worked together in Homicide, their statistics in closing cases, solving murders, were among the top for detectives in the city.

He needed to get Frank off his back. It had to be Dobbs.

In his sweatpants he went to the garage and drove over to Dobbs' street. He passed Dobbs' house.

There was a path through the woods to Dobbs' house. Dobbs had shown it to him once when they had been here for a barbecue. He had seen Dobbs take the garbage can from his driveway to the curb on the garbage pick-up days. Dobbs had complained to him that his wife refused to do it, and that Dobbs had to wheel the cans the length of his long driveway with his bum leg.

Fucking Dobbs was going to get his. He drove off and found Falls Road, the side street where the path through the woods led to Dobbs' property. Son of a bitch Dobbs was to blame for all of this. If Dobbs hadn't recruited Kevin to Narcotics when Kevin had joined the force, Kevin would have stayed in uniform and none of this would've happened. It all started and ended with that motherfucker Dobbs showing him the ropes.

There was no other way to get Frank off his back, to stop Frank from digging around, unless Dobbs was dead.

It would make sense to Frank that Dobbs had killed Nooney. What could Frank do? Investigate a dead cop?

Dobbs wouldn't be able to defend himself. Everybody would think that it was payback from one of the bad guys Dobbs had locked up when he was a cop. It would put the whole thing to bed.

What choice did Kevin have? He needed to do this or he was really going to get locked up and it wasn't going to be in his dreams.

Chapter Forty
Kevin Knowles

When Kevin parked his Explorer in the woods off Fall Road, it was pre-dawn, still dark out, with the sky changing from gray to blue in the east. He followed the path that led to Dobbs' house.

"Double jeopardy," he said to himself in the quiet forest. It sounded like some kind of word game, maybe like a form of Scrabble. "It wasn't double jeopardy because the jury deadlocked."

A mistrial meant he could always be tried again. That thought choked him, like a noose pulled tight. If he had to go through another trial, he wouldn't make it.

He approached the back of Dobbs' house. The pool was covered. He watched the light come through the trees, and the bird song filled the forest.

It was desperation that was making him do this. With Dobbs gone, would Frank think it was Dobbs that murdered Nooney? Would that take the suspicion away from Kevin and get Frank off his back? He was convinced it would. Frank had to be suspicious of Dobbsy. With Dobbs gone, Frank wouldn't be able to confirm or deny his suspicion. It was a walk for Kevin on Nooney's murder if Dobbs was no more. There was no other way to get around it.

He looked down at his feet and noticed that with the advent of spring a fine carpet of green pushed through the earth. Kevin began again, and walked with purpose into the thicket that surrounded Dobbs' large colonial.

Like the good cop he was, Kevin had checked all of this before. He knew that Thursday, which was today, was Dobbs' trash day. Kevin carried the Lorcin .38 in the breast pocket of his windbreaker.

How appropriate that this was the pistol he had taken off the knucklehead who was beating another to death with it. He stopped again and stood in the thick brush that bordered Dobbs' house.

On the top branch of a pine, a cardinal, in full ruby luster, unleashed a full-throated aria.

From where he stood, he could hear the automatic garage door open and the wheels of the garbage cans along the blacktop. He was able to see Dobbs come around the curve, limping with the trash in tow.

Kevin waited until Dobbs reached the mailbox, painted with an American flag, before he stepped out of the tree line and stood behind Dobbs.

When Dobbs turned to return to his house, he jumped when he saw Kevin.

"Hey, Wheels, you scared the shit out of me." Dobbs was out of breath.

"It was you."

"What?"

"It was you."

"I'm sorry? I don't understand what you're saying. Are you okay?" Dobbs surveyed Kevin with a slack-jawed blank look.

Dobbs reacted just as Kevin thought he would, with that *I don't know what you're talking about* line. Kevin reached inside the windbreaker and felt for the trigger of the Lorcin with his index finger.

Dobbs' eyes went to Kevin's hand inside his jacket. Kevin could see Dobbs' mind going a mile a minute. Dobbs looked toward his house. Dobbs was thinking that he should run for it, and he could make it back to the house.

"I've been following you."

"You're making a big mistake, Kevin,"

"I don't think so. In fact, I know so."

"You're not thinking right."

"My thinking is as clear as day." He watched Dobbs look toward the road. Dobbs knew he couldn't make it back to his house in time, but could he make it to the main road to get away from Kevin. "Remember that day at the baseball field when I told you that Prey was the lawyer that was suing me for shooting Ray?"

"No, I don't remember you telling me that."

"Now you're just being full of shit. Remember what you said? *Motherfucker suing you over some scum bag junkie that got what he deserved.* I don't know how, but at that moment, when you said that, I just knew it was you. You blew your cool too easily. Something was up with you. You gave it all away. After that, I knew that it was you who ratted me out to those drug dealers."

"Stop, Kevin. Realize that what you're saying doesn't make sense."

"Were those drug dealers paying you rent for that storefront? Was that it?"

"I would never hurt you, Kevin." Dobbs inched closer to him. Kevin saw that Dobbs had decided that instead of running he was going to fight. "It was Nooney who told Ray Santos. I never thought they were going to do what they did."

"You never thought I was going to live through it. Was that what it was?" Kevin was seething. "Did you think you were going to lose your precious building if they found out you rented to drug dealers? Was the city going to bring a forfeiture proceeding against you? Me and McBride and Ryan weren't going to tell anyone. We were just going to take their drugs and money is all. It's what you taught me to do. I was on your squad. I had your back. I did anything you asked me to do."

"You were like my kid brother, Kevin." Dobbs looked at Kevin mournfully.

Dobbs was trying to lull him so that Kevin wouldn't be ready for it when Dobbs pounced. "At first, I refused to believe what I saw with my own eyes. You kept coming by. Was it because you felt guilty? Did you want to keep me close to you in case I found out it was you?" Kevin was waiting for Dobbs to lunge. He wrapped his finger around the trigger as he inched closer. He watched Dobbs tense up, ball his fists, and ready himself. All those years as a cop taught Kevin how to read a perp's body language. When he got ready to lock them up, he knew if they were going to fight him or not. Developing those special skills on the job probably saved his life.

Dobbs' weight gave him an advantage, and when he rushed Kevin they fell to the ground with Dobbs on top. He could smell Dobbs' horrible liquor morning breath. Dobbs was grunting in desperation as he scratched at Kevin's hand and fingers, trying to reach into the breast pocket of Kevin's windbreaker for the pistol. Kevin was trying to point the pistol at Dobbs before he pulled the trigger, but Dobbs was pushing the barrel away from him and was reaching for Kevin's trigger finger .

With Dobbs still on top of him, Kevin used his left hand to feel around in the dirt for a rock. He found one that was round and fit nicely into his hand and used it to pound Dobbs in the face. With each blow, Dobbs grunted, and blood poured from Dobbs' nose and ear. Dobbs couldn't protect himself because his left arm was stuck in the breast pocket of Kevin's jacket. Instead, he bit at Kevin's face, and Kevin could hear Dobbs' jaws snapping like he was a fucking dog.

Kevin squirmed away, but Dobbs was able to catch him and sink his teeth into Kevin's cheek in the skin underneath his right eye. It was the spot where Kevin had no feeling from the beating he received. They had broken his orbital socket and destroyed the nerve there. He saw his blood in Dobbs' mouth.

As hard as he could, he smashed Dobbs in the temple with the rock, and Dobbs, stunned, lost hold of Kevin's trigger finger. Kevin was able to point the pistol into Dobbs' chest. He squeezed off two shots.

Dobbs stopped biting him, and his body shuddered with each blast. Kevin smelled the gunpowder. He could hear the whistle of Dobbs' last breath as it passed through the hole in his chest.

He was pinned underneath Dobbs and could feel the front of the windbreaker soaked through with blood. As hard as he tried, he couldn't get out from underneath Dobbs' body, which was beginning to get stiff and cold. When he thought that they might find him stuck underneath Dobbs, pistol in hand, with two holes in Dobbs' chest, he panicked. The adrenalin rush gave him the desperate strength to claw out from underneath, and he stumbled back into the woods behind the house.

He touched his face and looked at the blood on his hand. Kevin was doubled over. He couldn't get enough air into his lungs. He tripped on some branches and fell forward on his face as he tried to run through the forest back to his Explorer. He got up onto his knees and forced himself to take long, even breaths, and that helped him to stop hyperventilating. He still couldn't stand straight, but he could walk slowly as he bent over, grabbing at the brush to steady himself.

It was light out now. The struggle with Dobbs sapped his strength, and it seemed like it took hours for Kevin to reach his SUV. He leaned over the steering wheel inside the cab, and he looked into the rear-view mirror at his face. The bite could have been worse. Dobbs didn't get too much of a chance to chow down before Kevin plugged him.

He waited for a school bus to pass before he entered the road again. He looked at his arms and hands as they held the steering wheel. They were scratched and bloody.

Kevin leaned over the steering wheel to steady himself as he drove slowly. It was only a short way back to his house.

Sue's car was not there. She probably took Charlie to school. Erica must be on the school bus.

Inside the mud room off the garage, he stripped off his clothes. He reached into the breast pocket of the blood-soaked windbreaker and retrieved the pistol.

"I've got to get rid of this," he said out loud to himself.

Naked, he returned to the garage. There was a vise attached to his workbench. He walked over to it. With all his strength, he tightened the vise around the pistol, and he walked to the wall where he hung his saws and found the hacksaw. He was too weak to saw the pistol. He needed the blowtorch to melt it.

The automatic garage door opened on the side that Sue kept her car, and she pulled in.

"Oh my God, Kevin. What happened?" She tried to touch him above the elbow and lead him back into the house.

"I have to get rid of this." He still held the hacksaw, and he tried to line the saw up, but he couldn't. He dropped the saw on the concrete floor.

"You have to get in the house, Kevin, you're hurt."

He relented, and he let her lead him back up the stairs into the house.

"I didn't see you this morning. Something made me worried, and I came back to the house. I knew it. I have to call into work and tell them I got the flu or something." She took out her cell phone. They stood in the mud room on top of the bloody clothes as she lied to her boss that she was ill with the flu and couldn't get out of bed.

Kevin watched her. He was so overcome with what had just happened, he couldn't make out her words. He waited for Sue to tell him what to do next. He felt immobilized.

He watched her ball the clothes and shoes up into a bundle and take them through the sliding glass door out onto the deck, and she threw them into the barbecue pit. He was shaking, and he wrapped his hands around his body. Sue returned and rummaged under the kitchen sink and grabbed a can of lighter fluid. She returned to the back deck and doused the clothes and sneakers with the lighter fluid and lit them. It made him think that she had seen him do this when he had taken care of Primo and Lurch and that was why she knew what to do now.

Sue took him by the elbow to the bathroom.

"It was Dobbs," Kevin told her as she cleaned the wound underneath his right eye and closed it with butterfly Band-Aids. "All along. He got his for what he did."

"Shh." She filled a bath for him and helped him in. "I'll be right back. I want to check on the barbecue."

Kevin leaned back in the bath and felt something missing in his mouth. "Oh my God."

"Susan! Sue!" He ran downstairs looking for her, dripping water on the floor. He nearly slipped on the tile in the kitchen. She was on the back deck inspecting the flames. He banged on the glass sliding door.

"What is it?"

"My bridge. It must have fallen out in the fight. Oh my God, Sue, they'll find it. They'll send me to jail forever, and I'll never see you and the kids again." He wailed his arms and sobbed, and when she opened the sliding door, the synthetic burning smell of his sneakers and clothing filled the house.

Chapter Forty-One
Sue Knowles

Sue reached for her keys on the counter. "Where do you think it fell?"

"Right by Dobbs' mailbox where we were fighting."

She went through the door back into the garage and got into her car.

* * *

Sue passed the private road that led to Dobbs' house. She found a driveway and turned around, and this time she entered the road. She remembered the house. They had been there for the end-of-season Little League party.

There was yellow police tape around the mailbox extending into the thicket.

"Okay, where is everybody?" She parked the car on the road and walked to the area where the leaves and the grass were disturbed. It was sticky with blood in spots.

With the heel of her wedge she moved the leaves and grass. "Please, please, let me find it." She kept looking over her shoulder. When she looked down, she saw the glint of the wire from the apparatus. She bent down and picked it up, and put her hand that she held it in into the pocket of her raincoat.

Just as she did that, a white Ford Taurus pulled in the driveway.

"Oh God," she whispered to herself. The driver was Sheriff Crawford and the passenger was Celeste Santiago.

Celeste Santiago walked directly to her. Sue's hand was clasped tightly around the bridge inside her pocket. "What are you doing here?"

"My son lost his retainer. We were here yesterday to leave something in the Dobbs' mailbox and this morning when I took my son to school I asked him where his retainer was. He said he was playing with it and he might have dropped it out the window when we were here yesterday. It's the second retainer he's lost, and they cost five hundred dollars."

Crawford had come over too, and he and Celeste were staring at Sue.

"Sue, did you know that Mr. Dobbs was murdered here this morning?" Crawford asked her.

"Oh my God! No, I didn't know that."

"Didn't you think something when you saw all the police tape?" Celeste was watching her, trying to decide if she was lying or not.

"I'm sorry, I'm sorry." She brought her hand to her mouth and began to sob. "I didn't know. We just couldn't afford to get him another retainer, and his teeth are so crooked. I have to go. I'm late for work."

* * *

When she pulled into the garage, Kevin was in there in his goggles, using the blowtorch to melt the pistol. He turned to her, and she held up the crushed bridge. Sue was pale and she looked like she was about to cry again.

He turned off the blowtorch and took the bridge from Sue. "It's too damaged to repair it."

She began to cry.

"Are you okay?"

"I'm fine. It just hit me. What happened to Dobbs and everything else. It's one thing to hear about it, but it's another to go there where it all happened."

"I had to do it." He looked into her eyes.

"I know," she said. "It was awful. Celeste Santiago and the sheriff showed up. There was blood on the grass. I was so afraid. I think that Celeste Santiago suspects something."

"She doesn't know anything."

"I must really love you," Sue said to him.

Sue saw that Kevin didn't know how to respond. He went back to the blowtorch and turned it on.

Sue went into the house. She took the wine bottle out of the cupboard and with shaking hands poured herself a large juice glass full of it.

Chapter Forty-Two
Matt Prey

Matt was late for Dylan's game. He was in the sand-covered playground behind the brick schoolhouse, overlooking the baseball fields below. Matt tried to find Dylan in a sea of fifteen teams playing games simultaneously. "Holy crap." He couldn't remember the color of Dylan's uniform.

For a moment, Prey's attention was distracted by the group of boys who played on the shiny aluminum slide. They formed a human train down the incline. One boy pushed his sneaker into the face of the boy in front of him. The boy who got his face mashed by his friend's sneaker thought it was hilarious. They giggled together and landed in a heap in the sand. Matt smiled.

He turned back to the field, and he spotted Vera sitting alone with Taylor in her spot between third and left field.

He made his way across the field to where they were sitting. He saw the boys on the two teams lining up and slapping each other's hands. He was pissed off at himself for missing Dylan's game. Fucking work prevented him from seeing his son's game again.

There was something missing with Dobbs gone. While the games were going on, Dobbs was always exhorting the boys, and after the games Matt remembered Dobbs' voice. *"Good game, way to play, way to hustle."*

It was the deposition of a stupid car accident case. The idiot lawyer from the insurance company made him miss the train because the moron went on and on in the deposition asking every question under the sun. It should have been done in an hour; instead, it went the whole day.

Bankman, that prick, didn't give a shit. Bankman wasn't satisfied with the millions he had; he wanted more money. Bankman wanted him to have a more prominent role in the firm. It was a bunch of bullshit. Bankman was never going to give him a piece of the action. He tried not to think about it and to just enjoy the beautiful day.

At least the weather made everyone in a good, friendly mood. Winter was finally behind them. There were leaves and grass, and it was warm out.

"Oh, honey, you missed it. Dylan just hit a beautiful double." Vera stood as he approached.

Dylan came from the group. Matt gave him a high five. "Mommy told me. Sorry. I got stuck at work."

"Daddy's here." Taylor hugged his leg, and she giggled as Matt bent down and tickled her in her armpits.

"I parked on the other side."

They lingered on the field.

"Do you want to have some wine later?" Vera smiled.

They could put the kids to bed early. It had been a while.

People were leaving the field, folding chairs in tow. Dylan saw some kids on the team, and he walked over to them, and Taylor found some other little girl that she recognized.

"Maybe now things will calm down a little."

"Will you go and get the wine?"

"I just want our neighbors to stop hating us."

"Do you want to go have pizza?"

"I want to get out of my suit. I'll see you at home."

They walked in opposite directions. He had to go up the hill to the parking lot behind the elementary school.

Of course, he didn't wish that Dobbs got murdered, but now that he had, things were quieter. It had been a couple of weeks since it happened. The novelty of it wore off, and nobody talked about it anymore. Kevin Knowles had not been around at all. People said he was all torn about it since he and Dobbs were so close. At first, when

Dobbs was killed, the league was going to cancel the whole season, but then Matt heard that Dobbs' wife said that Dobbs would have wanted the season to continue. Petey Dwyer's dad took over the coaching, and Dylan got to play, which was better than when Dobbs and Kevin ran the show and Dylan rode the bench.

With his large girth, Matt struggled up the hill. By the time he reached the top where the playground was, he was out of breath, sweating, and his features were flushed from the climb. He bent over and rested his hands on his knees to catch his breath. This was ridiculous. He had to lose some weight. When he was able to stand straight, he saw that the boys he had seen playing on the slide were gone. Down below, the fields began to clear as other games ended.

Chapter Forty-Three
Kevin Knowles

Kevin waited inside his Explorer in the parking lot behind the school. When he saw Matt Prey, Kevin got out of his car and followed him.

Kevin had thought that with the trial over and Dobbs gone, things would get back to normal, but that didn't happen.

He was afraid to leave the house. He sat in the loveseat overlooking his backyard and thought of what Matt Prey knew or didn't know. Did Prey know that he had targeted Ray Santos? Did he know that he was the one who murdered Dobbs? Thoughts like these took hold of him. What if Matt Prey went to Celeste Santiago and spilled the beans? He had to find out what Prey knew. It weighed on him. Kevin walked up to Matt just as Matt reached his vehicle, and he blocked Matt's path.

Prey looked at him curiously. "Hey, Kevin, what's up?"

Kevin saw that he had startled him. He still had the bandage on his face where Dobbs had bit him. Human bites took a long time to heal. "I need you to take a drive with me."

"For what?"

Kevin opened his jacket to make sure that Matt saw the Glock in the holster of his waistband. Matt's eyes went to it, and they grew wide with fear.

"What about?"

"I need to talk to you privately." He moved closer to Matt.

"Why can't we talk here?" The parking lot was nearly empty.

"No." Kevin was trying to maintain his composure. "My car is over there. I want you to get in and take a ride with me."

"What're you doing?" Matt's voice rose an octave. "Are you kidnapping me? My wife's expecting me. She'll know something's wrong."

"Listen to me." Kevin tried to make his voice sound calm and even. "I'm not going to hurt you. I just want to talk to you." The truth was that, at that moment, Kevin didn't know what he was going to do to Matt.

Matt stood his ground. "I'm not leaving."

"I'm telling you to get in my car." He looked around and saw that he and Kevin were the only ones left in the parking lot. "If you're smart, and you want to get home to your wife and kids in one piece, you'll get into my car." The thought crossed his mind that if Prey went missing, it wasn't good that he could be identified as the last person seen talking to Prey. He would cross that bridge if he had to.

"If I don't, what're you going to do?"

"How 'bout I bash your face in with the butt of my weapon?" He rested his hand on the butt of the pistol. He studied Matt, and wondered if Matt had seen the tape of the beating he received at the hands of Primo and Lurch that Nooney recorded.

* * *

Matt's heavy, labored breathing filled the cab as they drove in silence around the town. Kevin opened the car's windows. Azaleas in shades of white, pink, and red were beginning to bloom on the yards of the houses they passed. Tulips were bursting through the earth. The beauty of it all almost made Kevin forget why he was in the Explorer with Matt.

"What do you want from me?" Matt broke the silence.

"I'm not sure." Kevin hesitated. How should he put this so Matt understood where he was coming from? "I want to make sure that you know everything." It didn't come out the way Kevin thought. He screwed up the words. He was so overwhelmed and frantic that he could be prosecuted again and could go to jail that he couldn't find the right words.

"Everything? What are you talking about?"

"Like I said, I want to make sure you know everything." Again, he was frustrated that it didn't come out the way he wanted. That was not what he wanted to say.

"What does it matter to you that I know everything?"

"Because I want you to have the whole story before . . ." That wasn't what he wanted to say either.

"Before what, Kevin? What're you going to do to me?"

"I told you, I'm not sure." He banged on the steering wheel with his hand. "Stop asking me, or you'll be fucking sorry."

"If you kill me, it's not like you're killing some crackhead. I have a wife. I have kids. I'm a lawyer. This is not something that's going to be swept under the carpet like some misdemeanor murder."

What did he mean by *killing some crackhead*? Was he talking about Nooney? Did he know that he killed Nooney?

"I see how you are with your kids. You're a good father." Kevin tried to change the subject. He didn't want to let Matt know that he hit a nerve.

"They'll find out. You won't get away with it."

Kevin saw that Prey was still defiant. He would change that. Before he was done with Prey, he would be a slobbering fool soiling himself from fear. "I want to show you something." He pointed underneath the bandage, where Sue had fixed his face after Dobbs tried to bite his eye out. The wound was in the shape of a half moon.

"Look at this part of my face by my cheek; the bandage is because I'm always banging into things and injuring myself, because I don't have any feeling there after the attack." With his left hand, he held the steering wheel, and with the right hand, he lifted the bandage and showed Matt.

He turned to see Matt's reaction to see if Matt knew what he was talking about. "See, when I smile, it doesn't move. I can't feel a fucking thing there. Not hot. Not cold. All on the account of those punks that jumped me. In the freezing winter my face could be frozen, and I don't know it. So, when you say to me, *They will find out,* frankly, I couldn't give a fuck. All I want from you is to tell me what I want to know."

"What are you talking about? What is it that you want from me? I don't know anything. I work for somebody. That was why I was working on this case. I'm just trying to get by."

Now he saw that Prey was afraid. Somehow seeing another's fear emboldened him, but it also made him angry. "That's the problem." He shook his fist at Prey, who moved as far away as he could from him. His arm was up, ready to block the blow. "The only thing that matters to you is your little fucking lawyering mumbo jumbo bullshit. You only see what you want to see!"

They passed over the causeway that ran across the reservoir. The brown shore had craters like the moon.

Kevin felt himself coming apart. He couldn't control how angry he felt at Prey right at this moment. He knew there was no reason for it, but he couldn't help himself. He was depraved. "Now you know what it felt like to be in the trunk of that car. Taken to my ruin. I want you to know. Do you feel me?"

"Yes, I know." Kevin could tell Matt was trying to appease him and say whatever he thought he wanted him to say.

They came to a cul-de-sac in the woods. The colors began to fade as dusk settled in.

It was too much for Kevin—the stress of the trial, and then for it to end in a mistrial, followed by Dobbs' death. He wanted to know if Matt Prey knew that he had planned Ray Santos' murder. Because if it got out that he had targeted Ray, that it was not just a mishap, that there was a motive, then they would go after him again. He had to make sure that never happened. What about Primo and Lurch? Did Prey know that Kevin had executed them? And Nooney? If he knew about Primo and Lurch, did he know that he was part of an operation with McBride and Ryan to rip off drug dealers?

Kevin parked. "Good. Get out!"

"What are you going to do?"

"Get out."

Kevin walked around to the passenger door. He pointed the Glock at Matt, and when Matt ducked down, Kevin opened the door and pulled Matt out to the ground.

"Please don't kill me."

"Do you feel completely without hope?"

"I do." Matt tried to say again what he thought Kevin wanted to hear. Kevin could tell he still hoped that he could talk his way out of this.

"I want my hope back." Kevin let the weapon fall down at his side.

"How can I do that?"

"Get up and interlock your fingers behind your head and walk."

They walked into the forest under some big pines that cast shadows as the sun faded.

"Oh my God." Prey could see this was hopeless. He stopped and turned away from Kevin. Kevin knew he didn't want to see him pull the trigger.

"He won't help you. You need hope to find God." He put a bullet in the chamber. "What happens if you breathe a word of this?"

Fear had taken his ability to talk. He shook like he was cold.

"Think of your wife, Vera. Do you see her face? Think of your kids, Taylor and Dylan. Now, close your eyes; make their faces go away. Do it! Do you feel how much love you have for your family?"

As he held the gun on Prey, he felt he could read his mind. That he had broken Prey's mind down so that he could see it going a mile a minute trying to figure how to say the right thing.

"Okay, let's go." He had Prey walk in front of him back to the Explorer. "That was close." He whistled. "You don't know how close you came to getting one between the eyes. It still could happen if you say one fucking word about this to anyone."

Matt sat in the passenger seat, still shaking. He was like a zombie.

He pulled into the parking lot by the baseball fields, alongside Prey's car.

"Next game is Tuesday. If I feel up to it, I might make it. Maybe I'll see you there." He watched Matt walk haltingly to his car.

He wasn't sure what he had just done. Had it gotten that bad? Was he losing his grip?

Chapter Forty-Four
Matt Prey

Thankfully, when Matt got home, Vera and the kids weren't there. He was so sick, he barely made it to the toilet. He knelt over it to heave, and after he was done, he was too weak to stand.

For some odd reason he crawled into the shower with his clothes on, and he closed his eyes. When he opened them again, Vera was standing there with a look of disbelief on her face.

"I think I got food poisoning."

"But why did you go into the shower with your clothes on?"

"I didn't realize."

"Should we take you to the hospital? What the hell happened, Mattie?" Only Vera called him that. There was no reason why, she just did, and nobody else ever had. "You said you wanted to go home and change, and I tried to call you on the cell to let you know we stopped for pizza 'cause I wanted to see if you wanted anything, but you didn't pick up. Oh my God, are you okay?" She helped him from the shower and had him sit on the toilet bowl. He still had his tie on.

"I'll be fine. I had a tuna fish sandwich for lunch that must have been bad. I got real sick." He couldn't tell Vera the truth.

"You look terrible."

"Please, just get me to bed. I'm too weak." He did take his belt and socks off. Vera had to help him out of his dress pants from his suit, and she deposited them in a wet puddle on the tiled floor of the bathroom. He didn't remember going in the shower with his clothes on. Matt looked in the mirror.

Who was that? He didn't recognize himself. His face was gray, and his lips were blue. He really did look like shit, like he'd been through the ringer.

Vera wrapped a towel around him, but he still shivered.

Taylor came in the bathroom. "What's wrong with Daddy? Why is he all wet?"

"Daddy's not feeling so good." She helped him up from the toilet and put an arm around him as she led him to the bedroom.

Dylan was in the hall. "Is Dad okay?"

When she got him into the bed, he said, "I need some water." His mouth was parched.

When she left him alone in the bed, he was overcome, and tears welled up in his eyes at the ordeal Kevin had put him through.

Kevin could have blown his brains out. They were right on the cusp of things going real bad. He could have been murdered by that lunatic.

"I don't want to be fucking here anymore," he told Vera when she returned with the glass of water.

"I thought you said things were getting better here." She put the water on the bed stand.

His face was turned away from her. He desperately did not want to tell her what happened with Kevin. He was afraid that she would know. She could read his mind. They had been married that long.

"I just need some rest."

He didn't know if he'd ever be the same. He kept hearing Kevin cock the pistol and the bullet enter the chamber, designated for him.

Chapter Forty-Five
Sam Free

Sam liked to go to the post office and collect his mail. He liked opening the box on the wall not knowing what he'd find once the little door swung open. Most of the time it was flyers and junk mail. When things were quiet like now, and he didn't have any work, he checked the box every day. At least he had money in the bank, thanks to Bankman and the lawsuit that made Millie Santos a rich woman. Today, inside his postal box, there was a cardboard envelope that held a disc.

"Huh?" He pondered the cardboard package. There was a long line of people waiting. Of course, there was only one clerk. The other one was on break. In the post office they didn't give a shit if the line was around the block when they took their break.

He studied the package on the way back to his apartment. There was no return address, but it was postmarked from the post office on Fordham.

When he plugged it into his hard drive, the footage that appeared on his PC's screen was from a camera outside a building. There was nothing familiar to him about the location. It could have been any apartment building in the Bronx, Queens, Brooklyn, maybe even Staten Island? It caught a tall man completely covered and disguised entering the building. The quality of the video was pretty good, but he still couldn't make out anything about the tall man who wore a long coat and a black wool ski mask that covered his face. The rest of the tall guy was covered by a long coat.

In the next frame, there was a shot of an elevator door open, and in the shot was the back of two men.

Sam paused the video on the two men. It was a view from the rear. One of them was dark and big and he had a big thick neck with folds of flesh. The other man he couldn't make out because only a silhouette of him was caught in the frame.

In the next image, the tall man in the ski mask and long coat was in the picture, and he was holding something in his hand. There was a fleeting glimpse of the thin man with a wide-eyed look of fear on his face, as if he had just seen an apparition. There was a huge explosion and everything went dark. Sam played it again and again, and paused it over and over. Finally, after watching it many times, he could discern that the tall man in the long coat was holding a sawed-off shotgun.

What was familiar about the image of the man with the rolls of fat on his neck? Where did he know that man from?

He took out his cell phone and found the email of the tape that Frank Cortez had sent him of Kevin's beating. There it was. There was the image of the back of the man's neck. The one who was hitting Kevin with the two-by-four, and when it broke, he stabbed away at Kevin writhing on the floor, rolling, doing everything he could to squirm away from the sharp edge of the broken two-by-four that the heavyset man tried to stab him with. It was the same guy in both videos. Maybe bull neck was getting what he had coming? What goes around comes around. Who had sent him the video of the shooting?

Loco popped into his head. That always bothered him. How did Millie know Kevin's street name and why was he thinking about that now? What did it have to do with him getting this video in the mail? Sure, Ray Santos, her husband, was a snitch for Dobbs. And Dobbs was dead. They said he was most likely killed by someone he had locked up. An old vendetta from an aggrieved perp. Sam didn't think so.

Loco. He remembered seeing it on Millie's screen of her phone. It was so quick, he couldn't be sure that that's what the text message said. But he was almost positive.

That name, it kept popping up.

After thirty years of his life in this line of work, he learned that when he had a gut feeling, he should go with it. What was it about Millie? She wasn't as shaken up about her husband being murdered as he would have expected. Maybe it was the millions she got for being his grieving widow? It was also the way she talked about Ray that made him think she didn't care that he got killed. Was he getting closer to figuring this all out?

* * *

South of Fordham, on Webster, because it was such a flat and wide street, there was a good view uptown of the gray fortress, the building where South Bronx Realty was located.

Sam and the minivan blended right in the parking spot. He watched and waited for Millie to show her face. He didn't even know if she was at work today. As usual, the area was mobbed with people going in and out of the stores that lined both sides of the block.

He wasn't the cop he used to be. Back in the day, he could remain on surveillance for days at a time in his van. That was especially true in those days that he partnered with Frank. One of them would sleep while the other watched. Now that he worked alone, and he was older, he did it in shifts.

Over three days, he tried to break it up into stints of a couple of hours at different times of the day.

On this first day, he did the afternoon. At five, he followed Millie when she caught an Uber that took her to her apartment building on Southern Boulevard, across from the Bronx Zoo.

Millie was probably living like a mouse. She was lying low and not doing anything with the millions she got in the lawsuit, but she would. He guessed that soon Millie would be gone. She certainly wasn't going to stay with Lapidus in that shit hole.

He hoped that if he tailed her, he'd get lucky before she eventually disappeared with her loot.

In the video, the tall, thin, completely covered shooter had to be Kevin. Sure, you couldn't prove it, but he was tall, like Kevin, and it looked like Kevin's stride when he walked.

No. It wouldn't surprise him that Kevin had capped these two. Was Kevin evening the score against everybody that he felt had betrayed him? First it was Nooney, then Ray and Dobbs. He didn't have any proof. The tall figure in the video could have been anyone.

He got to know Kevin real well from all those years working together on Narcotics, and when he worked with Kevin in the Sheriff's Office before the shit hit the fan and Sam was locked up. The Kevin he knew would seek vengeance on everybody he felt betrayed him. Pushed to the brink, he wasn't sure any cop he knew would not have succumbed and made them pay for what they had done to him.

He would try again to come by South Bronx Real Estate in the morning.

The next morning, it was 10:40 on the dash clock when he saw Millie leave the gray fortress. She had a brown paper shopping bag when she got into the rear of her Uber. It was a Prius that he followed on Mosholu Parkway, around that wide curve, past the Botanical Gardens on one side and the park on the other side with the baseball fields, where the Jamaicans played soccer on the weekends. There were no lights in the park at night. The Uber went straight, right up Allerton, and Millie got out quickly at the El. She disappeared up the steps to the platform. A Downtown 2 subway car was approaching the station, and Sam didn't have time to park and follow her. Instead, he followed the train to White Plains Road. If she wanted to make sure she wasn't being followed, she'd go to the White Plains Road stop and come out one of the two exits. There was one exit by Pelham Parkway and the other further north by White Plains Road. He guessed the north exit, but nobody came out except for an old guy with a gimp who had one of those canes that looked like a claw with toes at the end. He cut across traffic to the other entrance, and there was Kevin's white Explorer waiting. He could barely make out Millie's tiny frame in the front seat.

How stupid was Kevin to use his same white Explorer? Kevin's desperation was causing him to make mistakes. Mistakes were what caused one to get caught.

Kevin must have seen Sam because he pulled off, but there was traffic stopped at the light of Pelham Parkway and White Plains Road. It was always busy at that corner, and Kevin couldn't get away. Sam got out of his minivan and approached Kevin's Explorer and slapped the rear window.

"Let me in, Kevin!" he shouted, because he knew Kevin would not want the attention that Sam, a six-foot-two bald guy who looked like a cop, would attract. "Let me in, Kevin!" He kept shouting until Kevin unlocked the button on the back door, and he was able to open it and slide in the back seat.

On the console, between the two front seats, there was a Glock. Millie's feet swung off the seat. When he hadn't seen her for a while and then he saw her again, like now, Sam was always struck how, at first glance, she appeared like a little girl, until he looked closer and saw her age. She kept her hair in a long braid tucked into the azure bubble parka. On the floor was the brown paper shopping bag, and he was able to glance inside. There were stacks of money there.

"What the fuck do you want, Sam?" Kevin turned to look at him. He held the Glock in his hand.

Sam had saved Kevin's life way back in the day. Would Kevin remember that? And would that prevent Kevin from shooting Sam? He hoped so, but he wasn't sure.

"Congratulations, Millie." He ignored Kevin.

"For what?"

"What are you gonna do with all that loot?"

Traffic eased and Kevin pulled into a side street off Pelham Parkway.

"I dunno why's that any of your business."

"Say, how'd you two meet?"

"What the hell do you care for? You ain't a cop. Why you so curious?" Millie turned to him.

"Curiosity killed the cat," Kevin added.

"I'll bet you know Loco here because Dobbs was his boss and Dobbs had Ray as his CI. Did you decide to keep it all in the family when you hooked Nooney up as Kevin's CI? Except maybe that didn't work out so well?"

"I think you give me way too much credit here. I'm just a home girl from the *boricua.* My husband got killed, and I sued the police department and they gave me a settlement."

"Explain something to me, Millie. What are you doing meeting the man who shot your husband? It looks like you got a shopping bag full of money there. What's up with all of this?"

"No, what's up with you?" Millie turned again, and she was small enough that she could stand on the seat and point at Sam. "What the fuck do you want, man? You got no right bothering us. If I want to meet with Kevin, that's my business. Whether I got money in a bag or not, that's my business."

"That was why you kept calling Ray on his cell in the building that day, so that Kevin, Loco man, could shoot him. You wanted him to keep answering. Loco here might have thought it was a gun he was pulling out in a drug prone location." Sam shook his head in disbelief; these two thought they were fooling everyone, but they weren't fooling anyone.

"I don't understand you, Sam. Why are you bothering us? You have no right." Millie pointed back at Sam in the rear of the car. He would tell them in a minute why he had come here to confront them.

"God knows you earned your settlement money living with Ray all those years."

"You don't know the half of it. Ray was a son of a bitch to me. What the fuck would you do if a couple of million dollars fell on your doorstep?"

There was quiet inside the cab. Sam still wasn't sure what Kevin might do. Kevin had to remember that Sam had saved his life when those dealers in Washington Heights had put a stun gun to his neck and dragged him to the roof of some building. They were going to throw him off, and Sam had bashed one guy's skull in and saved Kevin's ass. It was a long time ago, but you don't easily forget things like that.

Kevin began driving again.

"I think you put a cap in Dobbs and the others because someone dimed you." Sam reached in front and patted Kevin on the chest as he drove north. They were on the Sprain headed to the Taconic.

"You're mistaken, Sam. It wasn't me that had anything to do with Dobbs' death. We coached baseball and basketball together. We were very close. I was broken up for a very long time about his death. I still am. He was my lieutenant."

"Oh bullshit. I knew Dobbs. He was my lieutenant too. Dobbs wasn't a good person. A lot of people disliked him enough to murder him. He fucked a lot of people over in his day."

"Sam, you can say whatever you want. The only reason I don't put a cap in you is because we were cops together. I'm with Millie here. I don't know why you're following us. I could say you attacked me, and I had to shoot you in self-defense. I'm sure Millie here would back me up."

"Or you could give me what I want, which is my piece of this action, for keeping quiet about this scheme," Sam said.

"What?" Millie looked at him like she might look at a crazy person that wasn't making any sense.

"I commiserate with you. Hey, who wouldn't have done it in your situation, but that don't change that I want my tribute. It was justice that you got for yourself. Bronx Justice. Nobody could fault you for that, but just like you got yours, I want mine. I know everything you two did. It was a plan to kill Ray so that you could collect from the city on the lawsuit. So now I'll take my one hundred grand to keep quiet."

"You're fucking delusional, Sam. Get the fuck out of the car. We didn't do nothing that nobody else wouldn't a done. So, fuck off, and besides, you can't prove none of it. Get lost and fuck off."

Sam wasn't surprised that Kevin acted that way. He expected it. He also knew that Kevin wouldn't just leave this alone. He was too worried about being tried again for the murder of Ray Santos. No, he would be hearing from Kevin again. Kevin was looking for closure. Sam figured that Kevin might think that giving money to Sam would make Sam part of it, and that Sam wouldn't be able to rat him out because Sam would get into trouble also for taking the money.

Chapter Forty-Six
Sam Free

The next morning, Sam hurried to the dirt parking lot where he kept the minivan. He and Linda Esposito had been texting all morning. She had a free period at Columbus High School, where she taught Social Studies and American Literature, and Sam was going to meet her for breakfast at the Riverdale Diner.

He still felt guilty about playing around on Iris. What else was he supposed to do? He was lonely for a long time, and it didn't appear that Iris was coming home anytime soon.

Yesterday Iris called him out of the blue and told him she and her mom were thinking about putting Nathan, her dad, in the Hebrew Home, the same place Iris worked. He felt bad for her. She was their only child, and they depended on her to take care of them.

He thought about Poughkeepsie, and after the trial, and what Linda Esposito had done to him on their tryst. He was excited to see her again.

He found the minivan and unlocked it and sat in the driver's seat. Sam felt something was not right. He was about to turn to look in the back seat, and then he felt the muzzle of the Glock pushed into the back of his head.

"I think you knew that after I threw you out of my car, you would be seeing me again."

"So what's up with you, Kevin?"

"I swear to God I almost fell asleep waiting for you."

"You look tired." Sam studied Kevin's face in the back mirror.

"I was thinking about when this all started. It was a long-term buy op. A bodega on Webster."

"I know exactly where it happened. Have you ever seen this?" He handed Kevin his cell with the tape of the beating. "Go on, see it for yourself."

As Kevin pressed play, Sam heard Kevin's screams in the background, and he looked in the rear-view mirror and Kevin's face was white with fear, like he was watching a horror movie. Kevin's screams still went through Sam every time. The tape ended.

"It was me, McBride, and Ryan. It was real fucking cold, and it had just snowed and a lot of the cars on the block had been snowed in by the plows. Nooney had introduced me to these crazy Cuban Marielitos. I should've known better. I was supposed to be player/dealer from New Jersey. The first buy was for an eight, then the second buy was for half a key. It was to set them up for that night when we arranged for me to buy a whole key.

"Except that night, Nooney didn't show up. So, there we are; I got twenty-five thousand dollars on me. I figured, fuck it, let's do the buy. These guys have seen me twice already; if they bring the key, Ryan and McBride will storm in, and we'll take down the whole operation and have plenty of spoils."

"Unbelievable that you guys were up to the same old shit that we used to do when Dobbs was boss."

Kevin ignored Sam and continued. "So, it's so fucking cold that everything is covered with these foot-long icicles. They hang from the canopy of the bodega right there on Webster by 1275."

"I know where it is."

"Let me finish. Don't you want to hear it from the horse's mouth, how this jumped off? Sure, you see the tape. Don't you want to really know what happened?" He handed Sam's phone back to him.

"Well, nothing you've said so far was what I hadn't figured out on my own."

"Can you just let me finish telling you what happened? Is it too much to ask?" He gestured at Sam with the Glock. "So, there's Primo, who is the big dark one, and Lurch. I come in the bodega that night, and Primo came out from the back, and the first thing he says to me is *where's Nooney.* I tell him, *forget Nooney,* I came to buy his product. He tells me I have to go downstairs with him to do the deal. That he's worried it's a lot of weight, and he doesn't want to do the deal up here in the open where somebody could walk by. I'm not going to the basement with these two. He tells me I don't need to be worried, that I have dealt with him before with no problem.

"I got no weapon and no kell to call for help. I remember thinking that I should try to look at their hands. Shaking hands will always tell you what a perp is up to. Funniest thing, Primo's hands were inside his pockets."

He didn't want to hear the story, but Kevin was so focused on telling it, and he held the Glock. He couldn't get a good look at what Kevin was doing back there. It was unnerving.

"So, I do. I follow Primo and Lurch to the basement, down these circular metal steps, and I'm following his fat neck down the stairs. At the bottom of the stairs, he turns with his fingers ringed with brass knuckles, punches me dead in the face, and suddenly my teeth are gone. Where once I had teeth, my gums are mushy and soft."

"Oh shit." Sam grimaced. Poor Kevin.

"I want you to understand what I went through, which is why I done what I done. Those two animals beat me with two-by-fours, and when the wood broke, they used them as spears to try to stab me to death. Don't let anyone tell you that vengeance isn't any good and it's wrong because they're WRONG. It feels good as fuck!"

"Okay. You don't have to shout at me, Kevin. I get it."

Kevin seemed on edge and out of control. Sam heard him reaching for something. Kevin took a plastic bag and emptied it on the front passenger seat. It was a lot of cash. "If money is what you want, there it is. Go on, take it."

Sam thought that Kevin would shoot him now with this money in his car and make it look like a deal gone bad or a disagreement. Why else would he give him cash?

"I won't kill you because you did save my life when those guys tasered me and were going to throw me off the roof, but that doesn't mean that I won't ever kill you if you gave me no choice."

For a moment, Kevin was quiet. Sam wondered how much money was on the seat next to him. He still wasn't sure Kevin wasn't going to put a cap in the back of his head.

"They ripped off my clothes, and they wrapped me in this carpet that smelled like piss and threw me in the trunk of a car. They knew I was a cop. When they were beating me in that basement, I saw Nooney down there. He was videotaping the whole thing. I wasn't supposed to see him. He was supposed to stay hidden. I don't know why he taped it. Doesn't everybody tape everything these days? Nooney dimed me to Ray, who was his godfather. And Ray dimed me to Dobbs, because it was Dobbs who was renting to these drug dealers and getting a part of the action. We didn't know that Dobbs owned that building.

"It's funny the things that go through your mind at times like those. I was breathing in the carbon monoxide because the exhaust from the muffler was seeping from the cracks in the trunk. I remember thinking that they were taking me down to the Hudson to blow my brains out and throw me into the icy water. That way all the forensic evidence would be washed away. Maybe, when the ice melted in the spring, they'd find my bloated corpse. To tell you the truth, I wasn't even sure I was still alive until they tossed me onto the frozen ground in Pelham Bay Park. I remember lying there, pretending to be dead, because if they saw I was alive, they were sure as hell going to kill me. I heard the snow crunch under their boots, then one door close, then the other close, the rusty muffler roared, the tires spun, and the car pulled away. There I was, with the moon high, yellow, and full above me, and I could see the cars on the Hutch and the lights from Number Six at the El. That was what I remember till I woke up in the hospital. I think McBride and Ryan must've found me."

Sam looked in the rear-view mirror and saw Kevin put the Glock in his holster.

"Then Millie helped me and we put this plan together, and the rest is history. You ain't going to tell anybody about this, not because you're afraid or because I gave you some money. You won't tell because you would've done the same thing if you were me."

With that, Kevin pulled back the sliding rear door of the minivan, and Sam watched his tall frame disappear.

He counted the money. There was fifteen thousand dollars. Ridiculous when he wanted a hundred thousand.

Linda Esposito called on his cell. "Where are you?"

"Sorry, I got held up. I'll be there in five minutes."

"Okay."

The Riverdale Diner was only a couple of blocks from his house. Kevin was right. He would've done the same thing.

What about Frank? What was he going to do? Frank would have to accept that it was Dobbs who killed Nooney. He couldn't disprove that Dobbs had killed his godson. He had to accept it. It was difficult for a dead man to prove his innocence. Especially a piece of shit like Dobbs.

Chapter Forty-Seven
Millie Santos

That night it had been as cold as a witch's tit. She had gone to 1275 to look for Ray. She knocked on the super's door on the first floor. No, he didn't know where Ray was.

Millie knew that Ray was probably hooking up with some young girl. He liked those *chicitas.*

In the street someone's car had gotten stuck in the ice and they kept pressing the gas to try to get out. The sound of those spinning tires and the smell of burning rubber filled the air.

Just as she got back into her car, Millie saw them. They were bad guys that sold weight out of the bodega next to 1275. They were putting something in the trunk of their car. It was wrapped up like a body.

She followed them. They drove over to Pelham Bay Park, and they dumped it. It was a naked man. She recognized it was Kevin Knowles, who worked with Dobbs in Narcotics. He had hired her godson Nooney to work as his snitch.

She didn't know what to do. He wasn't going to live very long out there in the cold. She went back to 1275 to look for Ray. Maybe he would know what to do?

Kevin was a goner if she didn't get help for him right away.

At the bodega she saw McBride and Ryan, and she told them that she saw Kevin in the park and she brought them to Kevin. Maybe she could cash in on this good deed if she needed a favor in the future.

They took Kevin to Mount Vernon Hospital, and that night she had a plan.

She visited Kevin at the hospital many times, early morning, before anyone else. He was too beat-up to talk.

She spoke to Kevin about how he could even the score with her *cabron* of a husband, and she could be rich. Of course, Kevin would get a tribute for his actions.

It was a perfect plan. At first Kevin didn't say anything, but as he got stronger and stronger, Millie could see that he was on board.

When he got out of the hospital, they would meet for breakfast and discuss it. Kevin had the idea about the cell phone, and how a cell phone could look like a burner.

Slowly, their plan took shape.

Chapter Forty-Eight
Kevin Knowles

Charlie was consumed with the screen of the video game as he sat across from his sister Erica, who rested her head against her arm on the tabletop. Kevin was spreading syrup on the waffles that had just popped out of the toaster. Sue had left for work.

"Sit up, Erica. And Charlie, put that video game away."

Erica mumbled and sat up and Charlie put the video game on the table.

Kevin was Mr. Mom. After all the money the city gave Millie in the settlement, the police department decided that Kevin was a liability. He didn't care that they forced him to retire. He was ready to quit being a cop.

"How's that?" he asked them, as he watched them eat.

"Perfect," Charlie told him.

"Great, Dad," Erica grunted. She was always cranky in the morning. He hoped that she wasn't up all-night texting her friends.

He didn't miss the job. Maybe he missed the excitement a little, but he was sitting pretty. He got three-quarters disability from the police department, and with the one hundred and fifty grand of tribute money he got from Millie, he had no worries.

He looked out onto his backyard through his sliding glass doors. He was digging out a large section of his backyard to make a garden. He waited for the kids to get their bookbags.

"Do you have your lunch money?"

"It's right here." Charlie showed him the money he took from his jacket pocket.

"What about you, Erica?"

"I got it, Dad. Can you take me to the bus, please?" She rolled her eyes as she walked into the garage and took the front passenger seat of the Explorer.

Erica took the bus, and he took Charlie to school. His kids were as different as night and day. Erica was the tough one, and Charlie was the one kids on the bus picked on.

He dropped Erica with the group of girls waiting at the end of his street by the mailboxes. The parents waved as he drove Charlie over to the elementary school.

Kevin's face had completely healed from Dobbs' bite. At least now he could leave the house without being so fearful.

He stopped over at Ralph's to get a cup of coffee before he headed home. He might take a run over by the reservoir today. Now that he had time on his hands, he thought he might start training for the New York Marathon in November. Things were much better than they were, but he still woke up in the middle of the night in a panic. After Sue helped him with Dobbs, he and Sue had started to notice each other in a way that had not happened since they were first married.

He went to the counter and ordered the coffee to go, and turned toward the room. He saw Sheriff Crawford sitting by himself at one of the tables. He motioned for Kevin to come over.

"How you been, Kevin? I know it was very hard for you when Dobbs was killed."

"It was a shock. I'm still in shock. I take it one day at a time, but it's hard."

"I know that you two were very close."

"I miss him."

"He was a good guy. He gave his whole heart to the community."

"Did they arrest anyone yet?"

"No. They think it was probably someone who he had arrested in the past. He put them in jail, and they came back to even the score.

State Police took over the investigation. I haven't heard that they have any leads."

"How's Debbie, his wife, doing? And little Brian?"

"As best they can under the circumstances."

Kevin saw the way Crawford looked at him, like there was something he needed to get off his mind.

"Listen to me, Kevin. I understand they forced you out of the department. You just say the word, and I would take you back in the Sheriff's Office in a minute. You were an asset to the office when you worked there before, and you'd be an asset to have back anytime."

"Thanks. I'll think about it, Sheriff."

"Just say the word, Kevin."